MW01135593

SHATTERED SHIELD

CAMDEN MAYS

Copyright © 2019 Camden Mays

All rights reserved.
ISBN: 9781793114907

Cover designed by Book Design Templates

This book is a work of fiction. Names, characters, places, and incidents either are products of the author's imagination or are used fictitiously. Any resemblance to actual persons, living or dead, events, or locales is entirely coincidental.

DEDICATION

For my late loved ones; mother, father, and brother.

The cost of freedom is always high, but Americans have always paid it. And one path we shall never choose, and that is the path of surrender, or submission.

— John F. Kennedy

CONTENTS

ACKNOWLEDGMENTS   I

CHAPTER 1   1

CHAPTER 2   7

CHAPTER 3   19

CHAPTER 4   31

CHAPTER 5   41

CHAPTER 6   51

CHAPTER 7   61

CHAPTER 8   73

CHAPTER 9   87

CHAPTER 10   97

CHAPTER 11   109

CHAPTER 12   117

CHAPTER 13   127

CHAPTER 14   137

CHAPTER 15   145

CHAPTER 16   153

CHAPTER 17   161

CHAPTER 18   169

CHAPTER 19   177

CHAPTER 20   187

CHAPTER 21   193

CHAPTER 22   205

CHAPTER 23   213

CHAPTER 24   219

CHAPTER 25   227

CHAPTER 26   239

CHAPTER 27   247

CHAPTER 28   255

CHAPTER 29   263

CHAPTER 30   273

CHAPTER 31   283

CHAPTER 32   289

CHAPTER 33   299

ABOUT THE AUTHOR   311

ACKNOWLEDGMENTS

With deepest gratitude, I would like to thank my family and friends for their support. Most of all, my wife Debbie, whose love inspires me every day.

CHAPTER 1

The Sonoran Desert, U.S. and Mexican Border

The heat of the day gave way to the cool of the night, typical of the arid desert climate of El Chango, Mexico. A small clan of hopeful migrants crossed the border without incident along the worn and littered path that gave evidence of other sojourners who had made the passage. Wearing a black cowboy hat and western shirt, the middle-aged guide led them across the shallow river bed, up the other side of the riverbank working to avoid sensors set by the US Border Patrol. The guide recognized the spot and motioned for the others to rest. They huddled quietly around bushes in a large sandy ditch.

They were now in the portion of southern Arizona's Sonoran Desert that belonged to the Tohono O'odham Nation. A Native American tribe that sits on an estimated 2.7 million acres including over sixty miles of the Mexican border. While the tribal leaders had worked with U.S. Customs and Border Protection (CBP) to stem the tide of an estimated ten thousand crossings each year, it was a difficult political landscape to navigate.

The people of the land were becoming increasingly frustrated with the Border Patrol's tactics and insensitivity to their culture and way of life. The use of helicopters and drones had affected the wildlife and impacted the hunters' ability to catch their game. Due to the rising tensions and frequent conflicts, the Border Patrol had curtailed the use of aviation surveillance as part of a compromise with the indigenous people. The less monitored area created an opportunity for migrants.

A truck, driven by a Native American, was scheduled to arrive in just a few minutes to transport the immigrants to a small town in southern Arizona. Their destination was Our Lady of Guadalupe Mission about twenty miles to the north. That would be the end of the tour they had purchased.

They situated themselves to rest, waiting for their transportation. A young mother nursed her infant, and a senior man took to whittling a stick. The teenagers in the group were excited and couldn't sit still. Others stretched out, and some even lay down to sleep. A man with the hooded sweat-jacket put some distance between himself and the group and sat on a large rock. The hood covered his dark face as he sat on the ground with his legs crossed. He clenched the straps to a gym bag in his lap and never spoke a word, making no effort to blend in with the group.

The guide's young nephew served as his assistant and had found a higher vantage point to watch the sandy improvised road for traffic. It was not long before the guide strolled up next to his nephew and pointed down the road.

The guide asked if he had seen the signal.

"No."

Just then, the headlights could be seen through the darkness, bouncing up and down as the vehicle responded to the bumps and dips in the road.

"Ahí está," the guide told the crowd, anxious to complete his part of the mission.

"Your transportation is here." He practiced his English on the hooded man.

"Look!" the assistant shouted. The high beams of another vehicle turned in from the west. The rendezvous area was nearly half a mile from the border, and the trucks were approaching fast.

"Border Patrol!" He screamed.

The clan quickly began to race back the way they came. The middle-aged guide led some back down the path toward the border fence. The senior man went in a different direction. The assistant started to flee but noticed the young nursing mother had stumbled with her baby.

He returned to assist her. It would cost him dearly; he had lost valuable time trying to get the mother and baby up from the ground. They did not even get halfway back to the fence before two officers jumped from one of the trucks and seized the three.

Meanwhile, the hooded man ran, carrying his bag, back down the ravine opposite of the direction of the others. He had hoped the patrol would follow the larger group. He was right, with one exception.

A young, Hispanic CBP officer had spotted him through the darkness and set out to track him. He let his partner out of the truck to help pursue the larger group, while he drove in the direction of the lone target.

The truck stopped just short of the edge of the ravine. The officer jumped out and slid down the embankment. He held his flashlight with one hand and a gun with the other, running in the direction of his prey.

"Stop!" He repeatedly shouted in Spanish.

He thought he had lost him when he picked up the tracks left in the soft, moist sand. His flashlight followed the trail, eventually leading to the black gym bag the illegal immigrant had discarded.

The officer looked around, holstered his weapon, and knelt over the bag. His eyes widened as he opened the bag. Just as he reached for the bag's contents, a dirty hand covered his mouth, and the dark, cold steel ten-inch blade of a Kizlyar Falcon tactical knife circled across his neck, dispersing a warm gush of blood.

The CBP officer fell to his knees, grabbing at his throat while gurgling blood. He turned, collapsing, reaching for his now empty holster. He looked up at the man who had just cut him, taking a good look at his face, and then choked one last time.

The hooded man tossed the officer's pistol into the bag

and zipped it closed. He then turned and wiped the blade clean on the officer's uniform. He rolled the officer over to take his wallet looking for his ID. He wanted to know the name of the man he had killed.

He flicked through the photos of his wife and baby. He wiped the wallet with his jacket and dropped it on top of the body that was still oozing blood. The pictures and cards dislodged and lay scattered around the dead CBP officer.

While the other Border Patrol officers were scattered pursuing the immigrants, the hooded man, ran further down the ravine to make his escape. After nearly half a mile, he slowed his pace to catch his breath. A little further up he saw a beam from a tactical flashlight and heard a voice from the edge of the ravine.

"Stop right there!"

The command came first in Spanish, then repeated in English.

The Native American police officer with The Tohono O'odham Nation had just pulled over his battered pickup truck to answer nature's call when he saw the hooded man trekking down the ravine.

Officer Sanchez had seen the Border Patrol vehicles from afar and stayed clear. He was one of the tribe's sixty-eight police officers. They were understaffed and underpaid for a thankless job. The police department had only six to eight officers per shift to cover over four thousand square miles.

Attempting law enforcement in an area roughly the size of Connecticut, with drugs, crime, and illegal border crossings was futile. *If you can't beat 'em, join 'em,* Sanchez had reasoned.

"Wait. It's OK. I'm the one that was supposed to pick you all up," Sanchez hollered out.

"Someone must have tripped some sensors. Come on I'll get you to the Mission."

The hooded man said nothing but turned and followed Sanchez up the embankment of the ravine just as the police officer's radio squelched.

"Sanchez, what's your twenty?"

Sanchez stopped mid-climb.

"Patrolling west of two."

"Border Patrol is reporting an incident south of San Rafael, near the river beds."

"Copy that."

Before he turned around, the hooded man's black tactical knife pierced through his lower back. Officer Sanchez laid there paralyzed but alive as his assailant took his gun and radio.

He struggled to fight back as the evil man removed his police jacket and swapped it with the hooded jacket. His mind was reaching to grab his attacker, but his body was not responding.

The attacker stood over Sanchez and looked at him, satisfied that his victim looked enough of the part of an immigrant to buy him some time. He gave a deep cut to the officer's inner thigh slicing the artery and leaving him to bleed to death.

The terrorist threw his bag in the pickup and drove away to meet his connection at the Church Mission.

Abu al-Himyari was in the wind.

CHAPTER 2

McLean Virginia

Cole Cameron turned on the television and flipped the channels to land on his favorite news station. He peered across the large kitchen island where he mixed his protein drink. His body containing the sweat of his earlier run. A news alert flashed, the heading along the bottom read, *Illegal immigrant kills Border Patrol Officer.*

The news helicopter provided aerial shots of the scene where the murder occurred and earlier clips of the immigrants taken into custody. Presumptively, the report indicated, there was drug cartel involvement in the slaying.

A fairly non-descriptive sketch of the hooded suspect flashed on the screen followed by images of the officer's family, causing Cole to pause the blender that was mixing his shake. The report continued with political guests discussing the issue of the porous U.S. and Mexican border. Cole quickly grew weary of the political debate and clicked the remote control to end the garble.

As he finished off his drink, he wondered what waited for him today. What assignments would fill his task sheet? What calls had to be made? Which reports required additional attention? And why did his old colleague Grant Ramsey reach out to him?

He bounced upstairs, stripping off his shirt and shorts, he walked to the shower, leaving a trail of sweaty clothes along the way. Cole lathered and rinsed his hair, and thought about his last argument with his ex-wife, Grace.

They had been apart for over a year now, and as they finalized the divorce, the last remaining issue was the house. He had offered her half of the appraised value, but she insisted on selling it to maximize the market value.

Over the last few years, he had led a torn life. He struggled between his career commitments and the impasse in his marriage. They both had drained his happiness and energy. He was sad but relieved when they had finally decided to divorce. *Something had to give.*

Stepping out of the shower, he gazed at the clock to get a bearing on his available time. He quickly dressed and headed downstairs stopping by the study on his way out.

He opened the email Grace had forwarded from the Realtor about a showing for the house.

He grunted and closed it without a reply.

***

Counterterrorism Center - Langley

In no time, Cole was swiping his badge and punching his security code at Langley. He was anxious to get to his desk at the Counterterrorism Center (CTC) to organize himself before his scheduled briefing with McCune. Some familiar faces but only a few with smiles greeted him on the way to his desk. Some he knew by name, but many he didn't.

In the post-9/11 era, the CIA overhauled its antiquated organizational structure to include ten mission centers to better address national security problems by integrating all of the capabilities and resources of the Agency. CTC was one of those centers and was tasked with preventing and disrupting security threats. It provided both operational and analytic functions.

It felt strange to be working among so many people, but to have so little knowledge of them. It was a stark contrast to the way he managed his consulting firm. Even when the firm grew to nearly a hundred employees, he knew most of the employees and their families.

After settling in and sorting through some emails including the National Intelligence Daily (NID), Cole made his way down the hall to Nancy McCune's office.

McCune was promoted to the head of CTC nearly three years earlier after serving as an EU Associate Deputy Director. The Director of the CIA, Henry Kingman and the Deputy Director of Operations, Kurt Friedlander were both big fans of her work at the European Mission Center. They sought to make her the Deputy Director there, but McCune had requested assignment to CTC in the U.S. to be close to family, not to mention the political benefits of being in DC.

Some staff and officers at CTC felt that she was too political for their liking, expecting her to be groomed for the Director of Operations when Friedlander moved on. But to Cole, she was just another bottleneck in the bureaucratic process.

He thought of her office as one giant red tape dispenser. She had command of staff and operational teams focused on various terrorist groups. So far, she had relegated Cole to less than significant roles. As an Operations Staff Officer, he felt as if he had to prove himself all over again with a new commander but lacked the opportunity.

To Cole, McCune was somewhat competent but seemed to have a chip on her shoulder. She was in her late fifties and was perhaps bitter that it had taken her so long to get ahead.

He had little regard for her callous leadership style. He was sure that her overbearing and perfectionist behavior served to protect her self-interest and would eventually leave a bloody trail of career carnage. His career would most likely be one of those casualties. Cole recalled the vigor with which she had cleaned house when she arrived.

An operation battered with faulty intelligence and poor execution had been the demise of her predecessor. McCune was determined to avoid those mistakes or at the very least do a better job covering them up.

Her door was open; he could see the Associate Deputy Director shuffling through papers as she stood behind her desk. He knocked anyway.

"Ma'am."

McCune lifted her head and flipped her auburn, shoulder-length hair back and with a glance said, "Come in Officer Cameron." She continued moving files and papers.

Cole stood in front of the desk, waiting for her to suggest that he be seated. He hated the formality McCune required. Her predecessor was a likable man who had always used first names. Cole was uncomfortable, waiting for her to sort through and meticulously organize everything on the desk.

Eventually, McCune placed the last file in a drawer and whipped her cell phone out and made a few taps on it. She then turned back to the computer on her desk and tapped on the keys.

"I'm sending you an email and some data files that you'll need to sort through and provide assessment reports," she said, hardly making any eye contact at all.

"Yes, Ma'am." Cole forced out, thinking, *does she think I'm in preschool here?*

Cole stood there waiting for additional information, but McCune was not the kind to rely on verbal communication. It was difficult for him to adjust to her management style. He remained standing.

McCune opened a file folder and began her familiar commentary.

"Now, as to the matter of this AIJB Intelligence Report," she said taking a deep sigh. "Your threat analysis was redacted and submitted to the Department of Defense and Homeland Security. Your assessment seemed to be a reach and contradicts previously published reports."

"With all due respect, Ma'am, my assessment was based on current intel as I cited in the report. We know that Hasni's network is looking for indirect state sponsorship. I'm convinced that his close ties to ISIS as well as his amped-up rhetoric, the threat escalation is warranted as well as the additional resource commitment I recommended in the report."

Cole knew he should stop there, but he couldn't.

"Ma'am, I've been on this group since my first day at CTC. When Hasni emerged as the leader, his network across the globe nearly tripled in size. And that's the ones we have on our radar. His influence should not be underestimated."

Cole was surprised when uncharacteristically, McCune rose up from her chair and leaned forward, forcing him to look at her green eyes.

"We can't go off half-cocked after every leader that is 'down on America.' If we did two-thirds of the world would be blown up by now." She paused to compose herself.

"Your email is waiting for you. It's a 'flash' priority. It will require you to move a little more quickly and even work a little later than you're accustomed to in the corporate world."

Cole cringed and fancied telling her to shove it while walking out. *What the hell did she know about running a business?* He argued to himself. He knew she wasn't a fan of his, but he didn't know why.

Instead, of the dramatical exit he fantasied about, he took her last words as his dismissal.

He nodded and then turned to leave her office.

"Oh, Officer Cameron."

McCune stood and walked around to the side of her desk near the window.

"You know Grant Ramsey, right?"

McCune's question startled him. She had never shown the slightest interest in his personal life. He tried to gain composure, as he turned back toward her.

"Yes, Ma'am. We went through some training together. Grant and I worked together on a couple of assignments but after his dismissal," Cole caught himself talking too much.

McCune was now standing, with her backside leaning against the edge of a table near the window. She folded her arms.

"Have you heard from him lately?"

What the hell is going on? He wanted to shout, but instead answered, "As a matter of fact, I did, last Friday afternoon he called me and asked if we could meet for coffee to catch up."

After a brief pause, he stepped toward the door.

"Will there be anything else?"

"No, that's all for now." She gestured as if to shoo him off while returning to her desk.

Cole moved quickly down the hall to his desk and opened his secure email from McCune. It was another typical assignment for him as he worked to synthesize analytical and operational information on terrorist groups.

Cole wanted to get a handle on the background information available to him. Various sources were used to collect intelligence of this sort, such as the FBI, Homeland Security, or INS and CIA's field operatives. A system of analysts would filter the information he received.

Cole's responsibilities usually entailed working with a team of expert analysts to fit the different pieces together to identify potential threats. Field agents were called upon to acquire additional information as needed.

Cole was a capable field agent, but over the last two years, following Grant Ramsey's dismissal, McCune had tied him to analytical work, and he rarely was let off leash. For the most part, he had to be content with working from the office.

He scrolled through the computer screen, viewing the scanned copies of documents such as shipping manifests, material data sheets, and transcripts. Some of the documentation still needed translating from Arabic to English. Cole was busy; pecking the keyboard, clicking the mouse, sending selected items to his laser printer. He felt like he was solving a giant jigsaw puzzle, but with only a fraction of the pieces.

After capturing an overview, Cole reached over grabbing the papers ejected from the printer. He placed them in his shoulder satchel with the legal pad, stood up and straightened his jacket. A glance at the clock told him the day was moving along too fast. He needed to pick up the pace.

He walked away from his desk, and down the hall, to meet Amy Wiggins, a communications expert, who served as a logistics coordinator. He enjoyed working with Amy. She had a great demeanor and got things done.

Cole could see the top of her blond head over the cubicle wall as he approached her desk. He smiled, as he considered her a scent of fresh air in the otherwise stale environment. Most everyone seemed conservative and wore dark tones around the office, but not Amy. Her constant changes in hairstyle and sense of fashion matched her energetic and individualistic personality.

Out of the corner of her eye, she saw Cole approaching and responded to his smile with one of her own.

"Hello, Amy."

"Hey, Cole. When are you going to give me a real challenge?" she asked with a grin.

"Just the usual, I'm afraid."

Cole pulled file folders from his satchel. Amy sat back down in her chair and closed a couple of the windows on her computer screen. She moved the mouse over and popped open a new window.

"We need a copy of the chain of custody for this shipment of hydrogen cyanide that's shown on this shipping manifest."

He rested his left hand on the back of her chair while holding a copy of the shipping manifest in the other.

"When we're done here, I'm running a couple of data sheets over to Gagnon for chemical analysis."

Cole thought aloud. "Someone around must think I can read Arabic; there are still four or five documents that need translating."

"You don't?" Amy asked, turning to look at Cole's face.

"Don't what?"

"Speak Arabic."

"Yeah whatever, neither do you."

Cole had finally recognized her humor. It was timely. He felt the tension ease. Amy was one of his favorites at work.

She reminded him of the kind of people he had enjoyed working within the private sector.

"I thought I showed you how to use the translation software? Amy said with a raised eyebrow signaling her disapproval.

"Twice actually," replied Cole, "I prefer the human touch, you know. I think you techies are just too trusting of all of this artificial intelligence stuff."

Amy just shook her head at her colleague's resistance to adapt. She sorted various documents and images on the computer and sent them to a language analyst. Cole leaned on her desk and sorted through some of his notes.

"So how are you and Richard doing?"

"You mean Robert," Amy replied, rolling her eyes in disgust at Cole's forgetfulness. He didn't forget. He just enjoyed eliciting a reaction. She continued working on the computer, denying him the satisfaction of his mischievous efforts.

"He's at a business conference in Chicago. And to answer your question, we're doing great…" Amy hesitated "…this month."

Cole continued scribbling notes and working with Amy to wade through the documentation. She had begun a background search on a corporation listed as the shipper on one of the manifests. He grew impatient, as he watched the stream of data flow across her screen.

"May I?" Cole asked pointing to the phone stationed at her desk.

Amy nodded.

He picked up the receiver and dialed an extension, looking over the cubicles, as he waited for an answer. Cole could see Amy looking in his direction, as he dialed another analyst' extension. Getting no response, he let out a deep sigh.

"You know we Millennial's don't answer the phone, right?" Amy jabbed, as she continued working through her tasks.

"Let me know when you get that chain of custody."

Cole waved as he left her cubicle. Just as he turned down the hall, he looked over the cubicles to the glass wall of McCune's office. McCune was standing and talking to an attractive brunette, in her early thirties, that Cole did not recognize.

I hope she can handle McCune, Cole sympathized. He saw their meeting interrupted by Raymond Hernandez, an assistant director with Homeland Security. *What a pair. McCune and Hernandez*, Cole mumbled. *I feel safer already*.

The day marched along at the usual rapid-fire pace. He had promised Grace he would get with the Realtor to set up a time for another open house, but finding any personal time today would prove difficult. The thought remained as a slight distraction throughout the day, but Cole had grown accustomed to pushing aside his own concerns and focusing on the task at hand.

He and Amy worked together to prepare another Intelligence Report on the Arden Islamic Jihad Brotherhood (AIJB), a group with ties to ISIS and new radical leadership. Cole was becoming the in-house expert on the extreme Islamic terrorist group that was gaining influence and power. The intelligence gathered suggested they were looking for alliances to sponsor potential nuclear or chemical attacks.

A competent field team leader, Darryl Capps, had gathered intel. Cole smiled when he saw his friend's name on the report. He and Cole had served on a few operations together and seemed to hit it off well.

Darryl Capps had taken Cole Cameron under his wings to teach him the ropes and sharpen his field game. Cole was learning new skills from Capps, especially when it came to self-defense and weapons.

Over the last few years, Capps worked with Cole to improve his marksmanship with his standard issue Glock 22 and the Colt M4A1 assault carbine. Every now and again during their get together at the shooting range, Capps would surprise him by pulling out a different exotic firearm. Since Capps was one of those elite officers for the Military Special

Projects (MSP) and Special Operations Group (SOG) he had virtually any weapon available at his request.

MIT, the Intelligence branch of Turkey, had captured an AIJB member in a plot against some political figures in their country. Capps worked with MIT in Turkey to interrogate the terrorist. The operation had yielded some valuable intel that raised red flags at CTC.

The information Capps had obtained had warranted elevating the AIJB up the CIA watch list, but McCune demanded additional analysis.

He and Amy spent that afternoon sorting through documents and reviewing transcripts. Amy was in the middle of making a point when Cole recognized the brunette he had seen earlier in McCune's office.

The brunette walked with confidence down the hall, dressed in a neat black pantsuit and white shirt. She passed right by their workstation. She noticed Cole's glance, both of them. She smiled at him as she walked past him. Cole cracked a sheepish smile and tried to follow Amy's point.

"Are you blushing Officer Cameron?"

Amy had caught him.

"What are you talking about?"

Cole tried to play it off.

"Special Agent Hannah Jacobs, with the FBI. She's thirty-four and single, just like me. Single that is. Oh, make that divorced, part of the interagency *'Can't we all just get along'* program sponsored by our ever-efficient federal government."

"Well aren't you a wealth of useless information." Cole chuckled.

"OK, back to these tasks."

It was late when they marked the final task off the list. While most of their findings were inconclusive, the report nevertheless reinforced what Cole had already reported. The AIJB was gaining influence and working to acquire large-scale destructive capabilities. And they had some human intelligence data (HUMINT) that suggested the AIJB were holding hostages in Al Mukalla, Yemen. But nothing concrete and the AIJB had made no public demands, and the identity of the hostages was unknown.

More information was needed, and Cole recommended a covert operation in Yemen. The report was packaged and submitted to McCune for review.

After completing their project, Cole and Amy left the CTC office together. Cole thanked Amy for her help. She searched through her purse for her keys as they left the lobby.

"Hey Cole, do you want to get something to eat?"

"Some other time maybe," Cole replied. "I've got to get home tonight. Don't you ever get tired?"

"I'm exhausted." Amy said, collapsing her shoulders, "but I've got to eat."

"Have Richard pick you up something," Cole suggested as left the lobby, still within shouting distance.

"It's Robert!" she shouted back, "And he's in Chicago!"

CHAPTER 3

McLean Virginia

Cole took a seat with his bottled water at a small round table outside the coffee shop, positioning himself with a view of the entrance. The warmth of the sun reminded him of the weather he grew up with in Southern California, but never fully appreciated until he left there.

But this was McLean, Virginia with colder winters and humid summers. *My God, how he hated the humidity.* But the moisture in the air was not a concern on this pleasant day that hinted of springtime. The temperature was approaching a comfortable seventy degrees. He took his suit jacket off and neatly laid it over the back of the chair next to him. *Ah, just right.*

As Cole perused his surroundings, he wondered why he always found himself meeting at a coffee shop. *I don't even like coffee*, he thought. A quick drink of the bottled water he had bought and a glance at his watch let him know that he should see Grant approaching the entrance soon.

Cole wasn't sure why Ramsey was so insistent on meeting with him. It had been nearly two years since they had seen each other.

As he sat at the open table, Cole could feel the sun heating his white dress shirt. A glance to his right revealed two college-age women sipping lattes and chattering about nothing. At the table in front of him were a couple of middle-aged men, smartly dressed, with a laptop on the table in front of them.

Unable to see the screen, Cole was intrigued by their intense expressions. He had half a mind to get up, walk over to the trashcan stationed just beyond them, merely to get a glimpse to satisfy his curiosity.

One more table down sat an attractive young woman around thirtyish, reading a book with her cup of coffee. The sun seemed to reflect off her light brown hair that went just past her shoulders. Her navy-blue skirt moved slightly higher up her thigh as she crossed her legs. Her white blouse was unbuttoned low enough to cause Cole to be self-conscious.

Don't stare, he had to remind himself. *Where the hell is Grant?* Cole thought as he moved his gaze from the young woman back to the entrance.

Cole saw some of his brother Jack in Grant, who had come to the Agency after serving in the Marine Corps and with Naval Intelligence. They had only worked together on a few operations before Grant was dismissed by the CIA nearly two years ago. His thoughts drifted to his younger brother, Jack.

Growing up together in Southern California, the Cameron brothers were inseparable. From little league to playing running back for the Torrance Tartar's football team, Jack seemed to follow in Cole's footsteps.

After graduating high school, Cole was excited to be accepted as one of the twelve hundred incoming cadets at the United States Air Force Academy in Colorado and expected his younger brother to be right behind him in two years.

Instead, Jack joined the Marines and never missed an opportunity to heckle Cole that *'if he'd had any balls, he'd join a real fighting unit.'*

Cole landed a role as an Intelligence Officer while Jack was more comfortable being the *'tip of the spear'* as he called it.

The brothers' paths also diverted when it came to family. Cole had married his high school sweetheart, Grace, while at the academy and Jack made no effort to settle down. Just a few months into their marriage, Grace presented Cole with the surprising news that they were expecting. Soon after daughter Jessica was born, Cole's worldview was changed forever.

After graduating from the USAFA Cole Cameron went to the Officer Training School (OTS) at Maxwell Air Force Base in Montgomery Alabama to complete his required ten-week officer training while Grace and baby Jessica remained in Colorado waiting for Cole's assignment. The OTS was designed to develop the necessary skills of teamwork, discipline, leadership and military management.

Following OTS, Cole was assigned to the 10th Intelligence Squadron in Langley Virginia, which teamed with the 30th Intelligence Squadron of Air Combat Command (ACC). There with the 10th, Cole learned how to conduct information operations and harmonize and synthesize intel from multiple sources and correlate them in near real-time to combat command elements. It was there where he acquired the skills the Agency sought to utilize.

Another patron bumped into his table to squeeze by the crowded outdoor seating and brought Cole back to his purpose. Just as he lifted his eyes, he saw Grant Ramsey meandered his lanky six-foot-four-inch frame through the door of the coffee shop, looking around the indoor seating area, then squinting through the glass walls and waving to Cole.

He gestured with his hand his intentions to get a cup and then head over.

The coffee shop reminded Cole of his ex-wife's annoying obsession. *Grace could roll the window down and smell her way to her favorite coffee shop.* Cole thought.

According to Grant Ramsey, his dismissal from the CIA was due to faulty intelligence and indecisive leadership. There was a blown mission that resulted in civilian casualties.

He believed that he became the scapegoat for McCune's mistake. But Cole knew Ramsey's story was just one side of it but also, he couldn't completely discount what he had asserted. He considered that the Agency may have unjustly put the pinch on Grant.

In a different way, Cole Cameron also felt pinched in the Agency. He was as a career switcher, caught in the middle of the two dominant groups in the Agency's operations group. There was the old guard of seasoned officers, most of them in their fifties or older, who knew how to navigate through the bureaucracy while cleverly ensuring their interests. There was also the younger, up and coming group of highly recruited professionals, bent on making rapid career ascent at any cost.

Cole had often felt patronized by both groups. Although not a novice, he lacked the experience of the old guard and the highly specialized expertise of the younger career climbers.

What a crock! Cole thought, as his mind wandered trying to find something of significance to validate his decision to join the Agency. He was a man weary of hacking through the jungle of red tape only to have the policymakers of the upper floor impede progress with poor management.

He saw Ramsey approaching. Grant had his own set of problems. He was living in New York and came down to DC on rare occasions to see his kids. Cole took a deep cleansing breath, hoping to remove the toxins of his negative thoughts.

As Grant made his way to the table, Cole stood up.

"Grant, good to see you. Man, how long has it been?" Cole offered with a grin, looking up at the four-inch taller Grant.

"Too long Cole, how are you?"

They shook hands and took their seats. From Cole's position, he saw around Grant and noticed the young woman two tables down looking at them. She smiled at him as he glanced at her.

They exchanged pleasantries, and then Ramsey asked, "Have you thought about getting out?"

Cole looked inquisitively at Grant as if to ask for the appropriate reference.

"The Agency" Grant replied, intuitively.

Cole wasn't sure where to begin.

"You know Grant, when we lost my brother Jack, I thought I was doing the right thing. I really believed that I could make a difference. My ex, Grace thought I was suffering through some kind of early mid-life crisis."

"Yeah but, you know that forty is the new thirty."

"Yeah at forty-four, I keep telling my body that," Cole chuckled.

"Well, shit what do you expect, you gave up a nice gig with that consulting firm and moved your family across the country."

Grant was right about that. He thought.

"Yeah, that just pushed us over the edge we were already headed that way."

Cole stopped just long enough to take a drink of water.

"How about you, Grant? How's life as Chief of Security with a big conglomerate like Vistacom?"

"You wouldn't believe the technology and sophistication used in corporate espionage. Still, it's not much of a thrill ride, but hell, I'm making a lot more money."

The two laughed. Grant started to say something else when Cole beat him to the punch.

"So, Grant why did you want to meet me?"

"Cole, we're always looking for good talent, and I know you were kind of on the bubble after McCune took over. So I wanted to check in."

Cole's expression must have given him away. They were not friends, and Grant's line seemed inauthentic.

"OK, OK, the real reason I wanted to meet with you is that I needed to talk to someone outside the office. Someone with your kind of experience."

"What do you mean?"

"You know your environmental background with the company you owned in the private sector."

"Is everything OK?"

"I'm not really sure. That's why I wanted to meet in person rather than talk over the phone. I think I have stumbled onto something and I'm not sure who to trust."

Cole motioned for him to continue.

"I'm pretty sure that I'm under some surveillance and

we're upgrading our communication systems as we speak. This all happened when our firm wanted to investigate…" Grant paused to sip his coffee and avoid being overheard, while the two businessmen got up to leave.

Cole thought about his conversation with McCune. He caught himself feeling paranoid.

"Maybe you should contact McCune. What if this has something to do with your past operations?"

"I don't think so. Besides, McCune and I didn't exactly part on the best of terms. As far as I know, McCune could be the one having me tailed."

Ramsey seemingly relaxed, taking another sip of coffee.

"Look, I don't know how serious this is. I just know that once I started digging, weird things started happening."

"What do you mean weird?"

"Someone is screwing with me, Cole. Our firm wanted to look into a company that we targeted for acquisition. It's an environmental company named, The Roslin Environmental Group. Do they sound familiar at all?"

"Yes, vaguely." Cole scratched his brow trying to jog his memory.

"I believe I met one of Roslin's officers at a conference in San Francisco several years ago. If I remember right, they offered services similar to my firm's but had a primary focus on research and development. Back then they had a few defense contracts with a specialty in biohazards. That part was outside our wheelhouse."

Grant nodded.

"Well, they've grown since then and expanded their services. We were performing your typical risk assessments and background checks, and I was personally performing your not-so-typical investigation if you know what I mean?"

"Yeah." Cole nodded, knowing Grant's reputation as a 'cowboy' who would bend the rules to get his mission done.

"Everything went haywire after we decoded some suspicious data within Roslin's system about their VX project. Hell, I thought the production of VX was outlawed years ago."

"That's a nasty nerve gas," Cole inserted as if Grant needed an explanation.

"Production was banned except for some research purposes, and even then, it is limited to something like twenty pounds a year I think."

"Shit, that's not much."

"Well, it only takes 10mg of contact to be lethal. But this stuff is highly regulated and monitored."

"I get it, but I'm talking about sensitive data related to government contracts being transmitted to untraceable systems," Grant asserted.

"They must have caught our sniffing because everything was wiped out before we could track it down. Anyway, since then I've had to watch my back. Our IT guys also blocked some hacks on our systems, they don't think we were compromised, but I've got that weird feeling you get. I think maybe I've been trailed a couple of times."

"Maybe someone on your team…"

"I'm not sure. But that's why I'm here. I don't know who to trust."

"Grant, you should go to McCune, just to be safe, or at least the FBI!"

"Shit, I don't trust her, Cole! And if I go to the FBI, they'll want to know how I came across this information, which could implicate me legally."

His frustration was becoming more apparent. "I can't afford to get slammed with bogus charges on this."

"Bogus?" Cole raised his eyebrow at Grant.

"Cole, I'm heading out west to find out more about this VX issue."

"You mean, possible issue." Cole corrected.

Grant moved back in his chair, relaxing his shoulders.

"I'm flying out to Los Angeles next week, to Roslin's headquarters, then over to Tucson to their Research and Development Center. I have an asset there that I brought into play before all of this went down."

Cole chuckled internally at the term *'asset.'* Grant was still using spy lingo.

"I think she can provide some additional intel. I was hoping I could leverage your background and have you look it over," Ramsey continued. "Look, just give me some consultation on this. Just until I know what I'm dealing with."

Cole sighed. "Grant, you're asking the wrong guy for help here. I'm seriously considering throwing in the towel and crawling back to California."

"No. I'm asking the right guy," Ramsey argued, "Cole, you know how the system works, whether it's the CIA or FBI, it doesn't matter. You know the bureaucracy will throw out enough hurdles to make it impossible to get to the bottom of this. You said yourself that the system has castrated you. Well, here's a chance to grow your balls back. I'm not part of that system anymore. I can find out what's going on at Roslin and if I find anything concrete, I'll go to the FBI. But I need your help first."

"Just to look things over?" Cole asked for reassurance.

Grant nodded then asked, "Do you still run through the park near your house?"

"Yeah, now that the weather is getting better." He lifted both arms as if to say *'why?'.*

"A couple of years ago, I used a spot behind the concession stand near the main complex as a dead drop." *More spook-speak*, Cole thought.

"Really?" Cole asked in disbelief. He was surprised that this old-school practice happened in his neighborhood.

"Yep, she was a smoking hot Russian girl, too. Anyway, there's a white plastic pipe behind the concession stand. It's a phony venting tube with a removable cap. That's the dead drop."

"Do you really think that's necessary?" Cole asked with a slight tilt of his head.

"I know someone is trying to track me, so, I think so."

"What about the other person who knows about this drop site?"

"She's no longer in the country and has been out for some time."

"What about a mark?" Cole asked.

"I'll place a diagonal slash mark with a thick red marker on the east wall of the main complex that houses the restrooms." Grant continued.

"That should be just outside the Men's room?" Cole asked verifying his bearings.

"Right. But it will need to be checked on a regular basis because there's a crew that cleans up any graffiti about once a week."

"Well, let's hope we never have to use it," Cole said.

Grant picked up his cup, forgetting he had finished off his coffee. He put it back down. Looking at Cole, he breathed a deep sigh. "Thanks, Cole. I won't forget this."

"Well, I may be looking for a job when this is all over, so I'll hold you to it."

They stood up together, and Cole reached over to pick up his suit jacket lying on the back of the chair. He glanced toward the young woman that had caught his eye, two tables down. She was gone. He wondered how she could have left without his noticing.

The two said their goodbyes and headed to the parking lot. Cole cracked a smile, as he watched the tall Grant Ramsey squat down to fit his head inside his rental car. Cole was leaving later than he had expected and dreaded being caught in rush hour traffic.

Cole felt the heat on the leather-upholstered seat as he started his car. The music playlist he had been listening to, seemed louder now. Turning the volume down, he moved into the traffic, as he tried to sort out his conversation with Grant. Part of him believed that Grant was overplaying it, and he seemed paranoid. But Grant Ramsey was a seasoned pro and not easily shaken.

As Cole drove home, he tossed thoughts around in his head, *who would be tailing Grant? Maybe Grant is...*

His cell phone rang, interrupting his thoughts, "This is

Cole."

"Hi Cole," Grace's uneasy voice came through the audio system.

"Hey, Grace."

"Cole, have you reviewed the list of things the Realtor sent?"

"Not yet, I've been busy."

"Cole, this is the last piece of the settlement. Then I won't have to call you anymore. You dragging your feet on this is not helping anyone, including Jessica."

"I know, I know. I'm sorry, I just need some time to get all of the touch-ups and stuff done."

"And you need to call Jessica when you get a chance."

"Let me guess. She needs more money," Cole smirked.

"No. She just had a few questions for you. I think there is something wrong with her computer. OK. I've got to go, please look at those emails and remember, don't forget to call Jess."

"Alright. Be careful out there."

"What is that supposed to mean?"

"Nothing, just be careful is all."

"Bye Cole!"

Cole saw the call disconnect on screen and rubbed his brow thinking about his disjointed communication with Grace. Then he scrolled through his contacts, and he smiled as he thought of his daughter, Jessica.

She had her Mom's beauty and her Dad's stubbornness, he thought. She had insisted on going to college in Southern California at UCLA where Grace's father was an alumnus. At least her Mom was close. But the distance for Cole was hard to take. But she seemed at home there. He pushed the speed dial on his cell phone.

Later, after arriving home, and helping himself to a plate of leftovers, Cole sat at the kitchen island. He scrolled through the emails on his phone while eating. The bright LED motion sensor light lit up his back patio.

Cole got up and walked outside just in time to see his next-door neighbor's cat leaving a deposit in his landscaping straw. "Get!" he yelled at the cat. "Damn it, Strawman!" he gritted through his teeth, remembering the nickname Jessica had given the cat.

Back in his study, he did a quick Internet search of the Roslin Environmental Group and clicked his way to their corporate website. Cole scrolled through the web pages, curious to find out more information about their services. He scanned through the list of officers, looking to see if he could recognize anyone.

He pointed at one photo and tapped on the screen, *Hey, I know you.* Nothing else stood out to him except the company's substantial growth over the last few years.

He could sense a little envy of their success rising to the surface of his mind. Often, he pondered how far he could have taken his firm, had he stayed there. He had battled this underlying regret for some time now. *How could I have been so naïve?* He questioned himself. This career move had cost him more than money.

Cole had worked hard and enjoyed the accomplishments he had achieved. Now, he felt like *a glorified paper-pushing babysitter catering to wounded egos and an assortment of organizational dysfunctions* — the description he had recounted to Grace on several occasions. He no longer had control. Instead, he felt *like a pinball bounced around from assignment to assignment at the hand of some cruel kid constantly tilting the machine.*

Cole Cameron resigned from the Air Force after five years of service choosing to serve the remainder of his eight-year commitment as a reserve. Grace never really got military life and did not understand Cole's career aspirations, but the primary reason for moving back to California was his father's illness.

Cole and Jack's father, Jim Cameron, started and ran an environmental firm in Southern California and his father's business required leadership to survive.

Cole took over his father's environmental firm and turned the company around preserving his father's legacy and providing a very comfortable living for his family.

Cole sat at the desk, gazing at the flat screen of the computer, but not seeing it. His thoughts continued to drift, reflecting on how his life had changed over the last few years.

He never felt that he and Grace had an inspiring marriage, it was near passionless. Instead, the relationship was a purely functional one that was tolerable with the goal of raising their daughter. Now, Jessica was away at college and his business was no longer his, but belonged to a group of former friends, he now considered strangers.

The things that were dearest to him were all gone. Cole convinced himself that his unconscious quest for some sort of self-actualization had cost him dearly.

CHAPTER 4

McLean Virginia

He could feel his heart pounding in his chest. His shirt soaked with sweat. His eyes stung, as his body's salty moisture dropped from his short dark brown hair, down his forehead, and into his eyes. He tried to wipe his eyes with his shoulder. *How much longer?* He asked himself as he tried to ignore the pain shooting up his left knee. His mind picked up on that train of thought. *How much longer? How much longer could he take this job? How much longer could he put selling the house off? How much longer?* Cole's thoughts dissipated as he concentrated on an uphill climb.

Just as he reached the top of the hill, he could see from his vantage point, the closed concession stand and the public building that Grant had described. He circled the main complex to get to the east side. Without breaking stride, he glanced to see if there was a mark on the wall.

Cole had to laugh at himself as he continued his early morning run, making his way back home. He grunted his disapproval as he passed the For-Sale sign with the smiling Realtor's face plastered on it.

That weekend he and Darryl Capps met up at the range, for training with shooting drills. Their trainer was a 'no-nonsense' professional nicknamed 'Boggy,' or otherwise known as Brian Olsen, a former Navy Seal. After a series of dry drills, they were pinging hard targets set forty yards away with their handguns.

Boggy was meticulous in his tutoring, working with trigger

finger movement and muzzle management. Later they moved to dynamic drills, also known as shoot and run drills with assault rifles and the Glock 22. Moving from one spot to another, and switching from right-handed shooting to left-handed shooting, rapidly ejecting and inserting fresh magazine loads.

Finally, they worked as a team through timed scenario-based exercises for room clearance and hostage situations. Cole was amazed at his big friend who stood over six foot five inches and weighed a good two hundred and forty pounds. Darryl Capps' speed and agility were God-given advantages, but his accuracy and tactical skills were the results of years of training and fervor discipline.

After they completed their training, Cole and Capps grabbed a beer at the nearby sports bar and caught up. Capps would need to head back to the Gulf in a few days, and Cole was unsure when he would see him again.

"You're getting good at this Cole!" Capps offered a rare compliment.

"Thanks, man."

"No, I meant the drinking. You had two this time."

"Oh, that's low, man."

"Seriously, you've got to get McCune to take the leash off. I don't know how you do it in that office all day."

"Yeah, you'd think they'd give me hazard pay for dealing with the political landmines," Cole chuckled. "Hey, have you heard from Grant Ramsey?"

"Not since he rode off into the sunset two years ago why?"

"Well, he asked to meet me, so we grabbed a coffee a few days ago. He's now in the private sector working as the chief security officer for a fairly large firm."

"H'mm. I'm surprised," Capps said as he took another swig of his bottle of German beer.

"Really?"

"Yeah, you know with what happened at Ash Shihr, he looked to anyone and everyone but himself to blame. It was your intel that put us there," Capps said pointing his finger at Cole.

"That's bullshit!" Cole said jerking his head for emphasis. "My intel was solid, and my recommendation was to gather additional HUMINT before any other action."

"Hey, I know," Capps said raising both hands in surrender. "Look, Ramsey is cocky and undisciplined. That's what got him nailed. He tried to blame McCune, but at the end of the day, it was on him. Hell, as I said, I'm surprised he met with you."

"Well, maybe money can buy happiness. Ramsey seems to be doing quite well in his new gig."

"And he didn't say anything to you about the mission that canned him?"

"No...just asked me to look over some environmental data for his firm," Cole said as he finished off the last drop of his bottle of light beer.

"H'mm. Watch your back, Cole."

McLean Virginia

It had been nearly two weeks since his meeting with Ramsey. Cole had developed a new course for his morning runs that included circling the main complex and checking for the mark that Grant would leave. Inside, he hoped he would never see it. The Agency had him busy enough; he didn't need any additional distractions.

As he circled the east side of the building, he almost stumbled when he recognized the red mark. He composed himself and continued running. I need to come back when it's dark, he thought, resisting the temptation to go directly to the dead drop.

That day Cole worked through his task list, one item after

another. Bouncing around from station to station, getting the information he needed and analyzing processed documents. Each completed task created just enough pause for Cole to think about the dead drop and what it might contain. Cole forced himself to breathe deeply, refocus and tackle the next task. Twenty-three tasks later and he called it a day.

Since it was already dark, Cole decided to drive to the park on the way home. He cautiously watched his mirrors. *Whose captain spy now, Grant?* Cole joked to himself.

He pulled into the parking lot near the main complex. Except for the closed concession stand, the area was well-lit. He sat in his car for a few minutes waiting for some teenagers smoking by the dead drop to leave. Finally, they made their way through the park. But now an elderly couple, walking their dog, passed in front of the car. A young female jogger, listening to music with earbuds, was running in the opposite direction.

As she ran out of sight, Cole climbed out of his car carrying an empty water bottle. He was attempting to be inconspicuous by having something to throw in the trashcan next to the vent pipe.

Inconspicuous. Cole snorted. *Here I am at a park in my suit, walking past two trashcans to get to this one.* He could feel his nerves getting to him as he tossed the bottle in the trashcan.

He glanced to both sides as he opened the lid, pulling out a large white envelope. He quickly shielded it inside his coat and replaced the cap, returning to his car. Once inside the car, he turned on his inside lights and opened the envelope. Inside was a note from Grant and a thumb drive.

The unsigned note read:

Hey Buddy, my girl came through. She says they've had suspicious visitors touring their R & D facility. They showed particular interest in their VX project. When she raised questions, she was told they were potential investors with security clearance and not to concern herself. They reassigned to a different area. She downloaded some files for me on the thumb drive maybe you can figure out some of this data on VX. Hope to have something for you in a couple of days so keep running. I think I'm still being followed. Use caution.'

Cole stuffed the thumb drive and note in his case and drove home. He immediately went directly to his study and shredded the note. The machine crunched the document.

Cole laid there in his bed in silence. He was pissed. He was pissed at Grace, pissed that he had to sell the house, but he was more pissed at himself. He had relinquished control of his life to the unforgiving system of the Agency. He had allowed it to drive in the final nails on his failing marriage, and for what? He shot up out of bed and headed to the study.

He pulled out the thumb drive Grant had left for him. He hesitated to stick it in the USB port of his desktop computer, concerned he was crossing the line both legally and ethically.

He glanced toward the doorway; half expecting Grace to magically pop in from two thousand miles away, then inserted the drive into the computer.

Just a handful of files populated the screen — the information mostly related to Roslin's research processes on the nerve gas, VX. He had majored in Military and Strategic studies as an undergraduate at the academy but completed an Environmental Management Certificate program at UCI when he returned to California to take over his father's business.

His education gave him just enough chemistry background to see that nothing glaring stood out in these documents.

"You're chasing ghosts, Grant."

He pulled out a small envelope from his desk drawer and wrote on it: *'Nothing here.'* He then withdrew the thumb drive and placed it in the envelope.

He looked at the clock, 1:47 AM eastern time. He tapped his cell phone and dialed his daughter as he walked to the kitchen.

"Hi sweetie, it's Dad." He continued, "No everything's OK. I just couldn't sleep. I wanted to call and say I miss you."

They chatted for a couple of minutes, and the patio light switched on again.

"Damn cat!" Cole said.

"Dad, you OK?"

"Yeah, it's just that damn cat from next door in our straw again."

"Ahh…Mr. Strawman, he's so cute. I miss him," Jess said.

"Yeah, well Mr. Strawman needs to find a new place. Anyway, I'm looking forward to you coming home for a few days at spring break."

"I know, I can't wait. Brittany and I have a lot of things planned," Jess said referring to her best friend who was a stable fixture at the Cole house. Cole considered her his adopted daughter.

"Yeah, well make sure you find some time for me," Cole said.

"Don't worry; we will Dad."

The call ended, and Cole headed to bed upstairs. He smiled thinking of all of the fond memories of his daughter, still sleep evaded him.

***

Counterterrorism Center - Langley

The next morning at CTC, Cole Cameron was again working with Amy preparing a jacket of intel with additional information on a suspected hostage situation with the AIJB. If the sources on the ground near Al Mukalla, Yemen were credible, then a cell group had three captives. The question was who and why?

As Amy combed through communication pieces with Cole, he shifted gears on her.

"Amy, have you ever come across intel related to the Roslin Environmental Group?" Cole's voice was softer than usual.

Amy swiveled her chair around to look more directly at Cole.

"I didn't see them referenced anywhere in the jacket here." Her hazel eyes looked over her black small-framed glasses.

"No, this is related to another matter."

Amy paused, "No Cole, I can't say that I have." She abruptly turned back to her computer. Cole watched her for a few seconds. Amy's response seemed uncharacteristic like her warmth had vanished. Just then it reappeared.

"You better focus on this jacket or McCune will have your ass," she whispered with a laugh.

Amy got them back on track.

"Look, this number that we tagged as a suspect with the cell group in Al Mukalla has been pinged. NSA is running the decryption. I mean usually, the burner phones are used and then discarded. Which is what we thought had happened with this one. It's been silent for over two weeks but just was used last night."

"Maybe we got lucky, and they got sloppy."

"Or they're throwing us off our scent with a rabbit chase."

"Either way, nice work. Let me know when you hear back from the NSA," Cole said as he walked away.

✳✳✳

Al Mukalla, Yemen

The devoted Muslims completed their Maghreb prayer and slowly exited the Mosque. A young man rolled up his prayer mat and glanced over his shoulder to see who was still left. Satisfied with the familiar faces, he walked out of the Mosque down the narrow street in Al Mukalla, Yemen unaware that a veiled woman, was carefully trailing him.

Finally, after several minutes of walking the young man entered a house on the outskirts of Al Mukalla. The woman, Pearl Fahimi, sent a text to her handler giving the location of a suspected terrorist, Abdul Mahib.

Inside the small house, Mahib followed the instructions of his leader, Aakif Muhamad Hasni. An elderly couple and a young female sat quietly on the floor, their hands zip-tied in front of them.

Mahib was proud to be recognized by his leader, and trusted with the responsibility of these hostages and knew he played an essential role in Hasni's plans. His two friends in the room no longer saw him as an equal, but now with his elevated position and status, he was seen as a leader in their network.

Mahib picked up the flip phone and dialed a number. As the line rang, he looked across the room at his captives hoping that soon he would have the opportunity to take their lives. They only deserved death in his mind, but for now, they served the will of Allah.

"Sameer," Mahib said hearing the phone answered on the other end.

"Yes," came the nervous reply.

"Have you completed the task you were assigned?"

"Yes. It is complete. Everything as you instructed. Please, let me speak to my family."

"No. You were told not to mention them. You will see them again soon. But we have one last request. We have a guest arriving on Sunday, make sure to welcome him."

"Yes, but please. I don't understand."

"Sameer, please make sure our friend feels welcomed."

Mahib ended the call and looked at the bound young woman and said, "Even as an infidel, your brother, is serving the will of Allah."

✳✳✳

Counterterrorism Center - Langley

Amy made a rare appearance to Cole's desk. "I've got

something you're gonna want to see," she said motioning for him to follow her.

They met in a crowded Ops room with screens filling one wall, and another wall painted whiteboard wall had Arabic scribblings.

"Bridgette gathered some HUMINT suggesting this house…" Amy tapped the keyboard and a satellite image of the outskirts of Al Mukalla, Yemen appeared on the screens zooming into Mahib house, "…is where the hostages we've heard about are. Still don't know who, but it just so happens that the call that we got the ping on earlier was generated from here as well."

"How confident are we on the HUMINT source?" asked Cole.

"Very confident, sir. It's Pearl and you know she's proven to be reliable on multiple occasions," Bridgette said.

"Let's get mission specs drafted for a SOG team and brief McCune, see if we can't get in there and do some good."

Later Cole and McCune reviewed the details and the proposed mission. The mission laid out three objectives; first, get confirmation on captives, second gather additional intel for the whereabouts of Hasni, and third, disrupt any planned activity. Cole pushed hard to lead the group, but McCune insisted he remain at CTC and that Darryl Capps and a language analyst by the name of Amir join up with a Seal Team CENTCOM would assign. Cole's frustration was apparent; this was his project, his intel, he wanted to be in front leading. Later Capps and Amir were called in and briefed.

❋❋❋

McLean Virginia

It was nearly midnight, and Cole stopped by the park on

his way home. This time he waited to open the envelope at home. He went directly to the study and opened the envelope from Grant. This time there was just a note and a key.

The note read:

Now I know I'm being followed. Getting harder to shake them. I'm going to try to find out who it is, but they are definitely professionals. Can't risk email or phone yet. I'm going back to Tucson; my asset may have more information.

He began speculating on Grant's situation. Perhaps he had stumbled across other corporate espionage activities. Maybe someone else is trying to learn about Roslin or just countering his efforts. His concern for Grant was growing. But he had more pressing matters with the growing AIJB threat.

Cole plopped onto the couch and stared out the window. Silence had become his new roommate, and since Jess had moved off to college, he felt as if he was sleepwalking through life. The days came and went in such a blur that he had trouble distinguishing them. With each sunset, the pain of loneliness grew. In his chest, he felt the heaviness of depression. He lacked energy and focus.

The stillness of the house that weekend brought Cole to an emotional halt. It was in complete contrast to his typical weekday. The solitude that he so often craved was now unbearable. The weekend progressed at such a slow pace that Cole found himself mindlessly flicking the remote control, hoping to find something of interest. He had thought the weekend would be an opportunity for reflection. Instead, it was a prison. He was the inmate serving a two-day sentence of loneliness.

On Sunday morning, he sat lifeless at the computer in his study. From the window, he could see dark clouds rolling in. The encroaching darkness coincided with the dimness of his heart. He felt drained, empty and numb. The sound of thunder roared, jarring him out of his semi-comatose state. The rain began to peck on the roof matching the sound of his keyboard as he typed his resignation letter.

CHAPTER 5

Al Mukalla in Yemen

Darryl Capps was the last to climb aboard the helicopter at the extraction point near the coastal city of Al Mukalla in Yemen. The big athletic built, African-American, leaned back and looked across at Abdul Mahib, lying in a fetal position, blindfolded and gagged with his hands and feet secured with tie strips. He then took a panoramic view to make eye contact with the six other men that had served as his team, five Navy Seal team members, and Amir Abdullah, a fellow CIA officer. He nodded to each of them, *Job well done!*

Amir, the language analyst from Langley, was sweating profusely. His nervousness was apparent to all. Capps' reached across and slapped his knee.

"You did great." He said. "Everyone has got to lose their virginity sometime. Now you'll have a story to tell all the pencil pushers at Langley." Capps' humor allowed Amir to release a little tension with his laugh.

The helicopter flew just a few feet above the ocean in the Gulf of Aden until arriving at the USS Ronald Regan. Waiting to welcome the team on the landing deck was the ship's security officer, two Marines and another CIA contact, known only as "Phillips."

Phillips was a master interrogator. He had the latitude to use unconventional methods to extract information and had a reputation for getting results. Rumors had it that he had acquired the nickname, 'Phillips' because he had once used a screwdriver as a blunt instrument during an interrogation.

The two Marines released the tie strip around Abdul's ankles and escorted him to secluded quarters on the ship. An additional Marine guarded the door to the quarters and saluted the naval officers. Capps, Amir, and Phillips followed them into the tight quarters. The naval officers reminded Capps that they were guest aboard the ship and that the prisoner was their responsibility for the next four hours until they reached the transport rendezvous.

They were at an impasse. Capps knew that the three dead hostages they found signaled danger and that time was of the essence. He also knew that once they transported the prisoner, it would significantly diminish the likelihood of obtaining information. The naval security officer refused to leave the prisoner alone with Capps' team.

Capps left the room and used a secure satellite phone to call Special Operations Command (SOCOM) who in turn, called the U.S. Armed Forces Central Command (CENTCOM). He returned to the room that served as a testosterone magnet. The thick tension remained for several minutes. No one in the room spoke a word until all heard the abrupt command of "Attention!" as the captain of the ship entered.

His gruff voice matched his personality, "Well gentlemen, it looks like we got ourselves a hell of a conundrum here," he said as he scanned the room.

"A word Mr. Capps." He commanded or requested it was hard to distinguish. They walked outside the room and down the hall out of the hearing range of the Marine positioned at the door.

"We're going to leave this prisoner in your custody. You do what you need to do to get what you need of him. But you better not kill him and whatever happens, never happened aboard this ship. Is that understood?" the captain concluded, with his face just inches from Capps.

"Understood, sir."

They returned to the quarters where the Captain relieved

his personnel. "Officer Burke, let's leave these gentlemen to attend to the needs of our guest." As the Marines and the naval officer left the room, the captain looked around at the three, marveling at the mix.

Amir was overtly anxious and fidgety, Phillips had an eerie coldness to him, and Capps emitted a take-charge attitude.

"Damn, you sure are an odd group. Are you sure you're all on the same side?" The door closed behind him.

The captain's observation added to Amir's anxiety. He stepped toward the door, "Maybe I should leave?" He suggested to Capps.

"No, we need you here to interpret."

Abdul, mouth still gagged, was now breathing heavy, bracing himself for the pain that he was destined to feel. With eyes still covered, he could only hear the movement of the men in the room. He listened to the sound of a zipper opening, as Phillips made his preparations, removing selected tools from his bag, like a mechanic preparing to work on an engine. He heard the sound of metal instruments clinking on the hard table from behind him.

Abdul shook in terror and began mumbling with his muzzled mouth. Capps removed his gag and blindfold while motioning for Amir.

"Ask him if he has something to say," Capps instructed.

Amir didn't have to ask. "He's just praying," he replied.

"Ask him anyway. Tell him he can avoid much pain if he cooperates now." Capps demanded.

Amir obliged Capps' request, but the offer was not accepted. Abdul began cursing and citing verses of the Koran. He spat on Amir, calling him a dog and a traitor to Islam. Amir wiped the spit from his face and trembled as Capps placed the gag back in Abdul's mouth and nodded to Phillips to proceed.

Phillips showed no emotion as he leaned over Abdul, stabbing him in the shoulder with a syringe. He pressed down on the needle fully injecting its contents into Abdul. Capps noticed Amir's faintish expression.

"This will just help him be more lucid," he assured.

Phillips wasted no time, reaching for a set of snipes lying on the table.

Capps interrupted him. "Let's give the drug a few minutes to set in."

Phillips stopped and said nothing. He folded his arms and paced around Abdul.

Amir moved in front of Phillips and leaned over Abdul. Speaking into his ear, Amir repeatedly asked Abdul to talk. Abdul's reply remained steadfast. It was a shake of his head "no." Amir pleaded more urgently, and Abdul matched it with more violent shaking of his head and screaming through his gag.

Amir felt a hand pull at his arm, dragging him away from Abdul. It was Capps; he led him to a corner of the room, stood in front of him and put his hand on Amir's shoulders.

"You saw the three dead bodies, right? You know Abdul has valuable information that we need immediately." Amir turned his head looking at Abdul.

"What if he has nothing, you will have tortured him in vain," Amir argued.

"He does know something. I need you to help me get it out of him." Capps patted Amir on the shoulder and gave a nod to Phillips, as he moved with deliberation. He picked up the snipes and lifted the pinky finger of Abdul's left hand. Abdul began shaking and gasping for air.

Amir began shouting at him in Arabic, "Tell us what you know!"

Abdul screamed curses through the cloth gagging him and shook his head in protest. Phillips gave one last glance, looking for approval. Capps consented with a nod.

Abdul screamed with a horrifying pitch over the sound of his bone-crushing, and faint thud as the finger fell to the floor. Amir yelled in Abdul's ear, his face red from anger and shame.

"You fool, tell them what you know. It will only get worse."

Abdul's shirt was soaked with sweat, his pants were now

wet with his blood and urine, as Phillips sealed the wound to stop the bleeding.

Several minutes passed, and Capps removed Abdul's gag. He cursed looking at Amir. The two were engaged in a heated argument about the Islamic faith.

"The Koran strictly forbids the actions your group is engaged in," Amir argued.

"And your actions?" Abdul slurred in Arabic. "You have been deceived and will suffer the wrath of Allah with the rest of these dogs."

Amir grabbed his shirt and shook him.

"You are the fool that is deceived, now tell us about the hostages!"

Abdul laughed, "the hostages?"

Amir felt Capps tug again.

"Go up on deck and get some fresh air. We'll call you if we need you."

Amir stumbled from the room and made his way to the deck of the ship. The night wind blew in his face and against his sweat-soaked shirt. The sudden chill caused Amir to tremble; he rested himself on a rail and looked down at the white splashing of water produced by the ship's speed.

Down in the quarters below, Capps and Phillips proceeded with haste. Another finger, another injection, and more violent screams of anguish brought Abdul to the verge of complete shock. Capps slowed down the process and pulled out a photo of Abdul's family.

Phillips held Abdul's head back by his hair, forcing him to look at the photo. Capps gestured with his hand, grabbed the snipes, and clasped the handles together so that Abdul could hear the sound of the steel. He pointed at his family, indicating one by one, which ones he planned to eliminate.

Finally, Abdul shook his head 'yes.'

As Amir returned to the room, he quickly turned his head, attempting to hold back the urge of his stomach to regurgitate. The scene sickened him. Two fingers and a tooth now lay in a pool of blood and Abdul was beaten, bleeding and barely conscious.

He looked in disgust at Phillips, who spoke his first words as he wiped the blood off his tools.

"He has something to say to you." His statement was almost arrogant.

Amir stood in front of Abdul, who could barely bring himself physically to speak. Abdul uttered several lines of Arabic to Amir. He repeated the last line twice, then laughed as he spat up more blood. Amir was stunned and looked at his watch.

"What is it?" Capps demanded.

"I think we're too late."

✳✳✳

CIA Headquarters - Langley

The echo of her heels tapping the hard floor of CIA headquarters alarmed the lightly staffed office that Sunday morning. Shanelle Glover didn't even knock as she ran directly into the office of the Director of the CIA. Henry Kingman was on the phone, remarking about the unfortunate turn in the weather.

"I know Frank; I was hoping I could give you a chance to redeem yourself from our last golf tournament." He chuckled as he listened to the response. His serenity was interrupted by Shanelle's intrusion.

"Excuse me, sir, we have a critical situation!"

* * *

Tucson, AZ

An hour earlier that morning in Tucson, workers were beginning to make their way into the Roslin Environmental Group's Research and Development Center. The usually full parking lot had cars sparingly scattered with a few dozen huddled close to the main entrance. Most employees coming in on this Sunday morning were maintenance workers, security and a handful of technicians working on a high priority project that was falling behind schedule.

Yasser Nassif stepped out of an old Toyota pickup. His long dark hair waved in the desert breeze along with the hood of his loose-fitting windbreaker. He glanced to his right noticing a white van with a crew of workers. He took a deep breath of the desert air, feeling a sense of accomplishment as months of training had prepared him for this day. The arrival of one of Hasni's most trusted leaders, Abu al-Himyari had provided much-needed inspiration. *Hasni will be very proud*, he thought almost audibly.

Nassif followed a female lab technician through the central doorway into the large granite lobby. He approached the security station where two armed guards greeted him.

"I'm here to see Sameer Bashar." He announced. The guards checked their computer screen.

"Let me call him, looks like he just got in."

While one guard placed the call, the other asked for identification. The young man obliged the guard, showing his Arizona Driver's license. The guard copied down the information and noticed Nassif's student ID as he placed the license back in his wallet.

"Great school. My sister just graduated from there." The guard said.

"Mr. Bashar said that he will be with you shortly," interjected the guard with the phone as he noticed sweat on the brow of Nassif. "Is everything OK?"

"Yes, everything is fine," assured the young man.

"Well, he'll be coming out of that secured entrance to your left."

"Thank You," Nassif replied, as he moved toward the highly secured entrance labeled *Authorized Personnel Only*. He stood waiting for just a few minutes. The guard, still within speaking distance, asked, "So what are you studying at the University?" before he could answer a frayed Sameer Bashar arrived.

"Who are you?" He whispered. "What do you know about my family?"

His nervousness captured the attention of the guards. One spoke up. "Is everything all right, Mr. Bashar?"

Bashar nodded. "Yes, so sorry. A family matter."

"What is the code, today?" the young man whispered.

"What?" Bashar asked in disbelief. "I've already done everything they have asked."

"You must tell me the code."

Bashar hesitated.

"If I don't give them the code now, they will kill your family. Now, what is the code?"

"It's C74BY8!" Bashar whispered back, his voice trembling in fear.

"What about my family? How will I know they are safe?"

The young man raised his hand to signal for Bashar to wait a moment and punched the code on his cell phone sending a text message to another party.

A cell phone vibrated in the white van. The driver looked at the text message appearing with the code C74BY8.

The young student dropped his phone and stripped off his jacket revealing a powerful package of explosives strapped entirely around his body. He grabbed the detonator attached to the package with what looked like a curling phone cord.

Screams of terror broke out in the lobby as the few people there fell to the floor. Two employees ran out the front entrance. Momentarily immobilized by fear, the guards then instinctively drew their weapons yelling at the man to remain still as they tried to position themselves.

The young man reached with his free hand to grab Bashar, using him as a shield, he back peddled toward the secure entrance to the east wing.

"No one move!" he shouted as he positioned himself.

"What are you doing?" cried Bashar.

"You have served Allah well," Nassif said calmly.

"My family?"

"You will see them in heaven," as he prayed.

"Oh my God!" Shouted the guard.

"Praise Allah!" Nassif concluded.

He closed his eyes and pressed the button on the detonator sending a violent earth-shaking blast rippling through the facility. As windows on cars shattered, pieces of metal and chunks of concrete hurled through the air becoming lethal projectiles. An enormous billowing cloud of gray smoke towered above the building.

Alarms sounded, bells rang, and water erupted from the sprinkler system throughout. The entire east wing entrance collapsed. A young woman crawled along the ground, bleeding from her shoulder and head. An older man, walked around in circles in a state of shock, his hair and face covered with gray ash from the blast. The few unfortunate souls that remained were now in total shock and horror. Some collected their senses trying to help the injured few they found.

Three men in the white van quickly donned environmental suits equipped with air packs. They posed as first responders and rushed into the previously secure east wing research area housing the nerve agents. They could see the severity of the damage. A maintenance worker trapped in the rubble was calling out for help before choking on the toxins. A young female worker in a lab coat staggered toward the three men but soon collapsed to the ground grabbing her throat as she succumbed to the smoke and toxic air.

The three protected men made their way to a vaulted chamber and entered the code, releasing the locks of the door.

Inside the chamber, they surveyed the mini vacuum canisters and refrigerated units until they saw the label "VX" and then reached two shelves below to a group of canisters labeled "Y44." They had found their prize.

They removed the canisters, placing them into large hard cases packed with dry ice. They left just as quickly and efficiently as they had entered. As they were exiting the research area a young man, lying on the ground with his leg severed, pulled at the suit of one of the crewmembers, pleading for assistance. The crewmember jerked free and continued on his way.

They hurried to the van, removing their air packs and pulling their suits down, tying them off at the waist. In no time, they were driving out of the parking lot. Just as they turned right, they saw approaching police cars and other response vehicles with lights flashing and sirens blasting. They sped past, never noticing the van, its passengers, or its dangerous cargo.

***

CIA Headquarters - Langley

Director Henry Kingman had just picked up the phone when the news reporter on the flat screen behind him began to report on the devastating blast. Shanelle dropped her files and stared at images from the blast scene in disbelief as the camera revealed graphic images of death and destruction.

"Get Kurt Friedlander from Operations and Nancy McCune from CTC. I'm going to want some damn answers. And have McCune get all available CTC personnel at the Mission Center immediately." Kingman ordered.

CHAPTER 6

McLean Virginia

The laser printer next to his desk spewed out his resignation letter. Cole snatched it and sighed as he recognized the finality of his decision. He was not accustomed to feeling defeated, but this job had done just that. It had left him feeling less of a man, somehow incomplete — a rude and cruel exchange for the sacrifices he had made. His cell phone rang interrupting his thoughts.

"Cole." It was Amy. "Have you seen the news?"

"Ugh…No. I've been…"

"Well, you should turn on your TV. I'm sending an encrypted text, but we need you to come in, it's urgent."

"Be there in thirty minutes."

"Pack some clothes; you may need them."

"I've got a go bag ready. I'm on my way."

Cole laid the letter on his desk and hurried through his closet pulling out his go bag he kept prepared for such a call. He scrolled through Amy's text and flicked on the television to catch the news as he continued packing. He grabbed a couple of nutrition bars, not knowing when he would have the opportunity to eat again.

The news revealed the scene of an explosion on the screen. He turned the volume up to hear more clearly. *Where is this?* Then as if answering his question directly, the newscaster repeated the location. *Roslin Research and Development Center.*

What the hell! Cole thought. He dialed the cell number of Grant Ramsey but just got his voicemail. "Grant, it's Cole. We need to talk. Call me." Cole looked at his watch, knowing that time was getting away. He had to get to CTC fast. Glancing over to his study as he came to the bottom of the stairs, he could see the desk. He stood for a second contemplating, then took the letter and placed it in his case and was on the road.

✱✱✱

Counterterrorism Center - Langley

A territorial tug of war was on display for all to see in the Mission Center large conference room. The packed large room had representatives from various agencies. But the key players were Raymond Hernandez from the Department of Homeland Security, Charles Thompson with the FBI and CIA Director, Henry Kingman. They were barking at each other like junkyard dogs defending their territory.

Kingman stood behind a table near the front of the room in his maroon golf shirt and khakis, with his thinning gray hair. In spite of his casual appearance on this Sunday morning, he still commanded the respect of those around him. Charles Thompson likewise conveyed an air of authority, and unlike Kingman, he was dressed in business attire, absent the tie.

Each stood tall and carried themselves well. The same was not accurate for Raymond Hernandez, whose silver-framed glasses matched his graying hair. It wasn't his small stature or that his clothes seemed a size too big for him it was that everyone could see he tried too hard to impress.

Amy had overheard their bantering as she prepared the situation room for the briefing. Accusations flung about lack of intel getting to the FBI, but soon the banter stopped when they were connected via satellite to the situation room at the White House.

The President appeared on the screen, flanked by several advisors and the Director of Homeland Security, Sarah

LeJune. The President issued a directive for the FBI to lead an investigation of the bombsite. But he also issued an order for deployment of an interagency AIJB mission team to work independently from the FBI investigation with the primary objective to ensure that no further attacks materialized from the terrorist group.

The team would leverage the capabilities of the CTC mission center and be untethered by typical red tape. It was clear the President was leaning on the experience of Kingman.

"Now Henry, you and Charlie work it out, but put your best damn people on it and get me some damn results!"

The call ended, and Kingman took charge.

"McCune," Kingman began, "Who's your lead on the AIJB?"

"That would be Cole Cameron, sir."

"What's his background?"

"Air Force Academy grad and served with 10th Intelligence Squadron about five years before returning to the private sector in California where he owned an environmental consulting firm before he joined us after losing his brother to an IED in Kabul."

"Alright, I want him leading this team," Kingman ordered

McCune nodded but squirmed just enough to catch Kingman's attention.

"Is there a problem, Nancy?"

"Well sir, while Cole has served on few missions in the field, I think we may want to look for a more seasoned resource, and I'm just…"

Shanelle handed some papers to Kingman, and he interrupted McCune.

"We don't have time for this shit. It's Cole's reports that have been screaming for threat escalation. You're his commanding officer, so you act as liaison from CTC. He leads the mission team unless there is something else that I need to know about?"

"No sir, Cole will lead the team and I will liaison from here."

Kingman continued across the room, "Charles who's running point for the FBI?"

"We have Special Agent Hannah Jacobs, who has been dedicated resource to CTC as part of our interagency efforts." Thompson paused, knowing it was not the time to bring up the lack of cooperation, and instead continued. "She is on her way in now."

"Mr. Hernandez, what will DHS contribute to this interagency team?" Kingman reluctantly asked.

"I will personally be involved with the mission team." Several heads turned at that reply.

"With all due respect, the team will benefit more from an experienced field member than an administrative officer." Kingman rebutted and even got a nod of agreement from Thompson.

"That decision was cleared by Director Le June," Hernandez responded with a nasal tone that did not complement his assertive stance holding up his phone with the text for all to see.

"Very well," Kingman said. "Let's review the operational objectives before we brief the team."

✳✳✳

McLean Virginia

The honk of a car horn behind him shook Cole out of his temporary hypnosis. He had lost track of time at the intersection near the coffee shop where he'd last seen Grant. As the rain grew heavier, Cole could feel his body responding to the stress of mixed emotions.

He was concerned for Grant, dealing with his divorce settlement, but he somehow felt alive again. Blood was finally flowing through what had felt like his corpse. This assignment could help him discover once and for all whether he should submit that letter in his case.

✳✳✳

Counterterrorism Center - Langley

Amy greeted Cole as he stepped off the elevator with his jacket still wet from the outside rain.

"Cole," she whispered, "Roslin?"

Cole shrugged his shoulders to signify his uncertainty. He and Amy were in casual clothes. Cole had on dark jeans and a heather colored quarter zip pullover athletic performance type shirt.

"I've got to grab some files," Amy said leaving him to walk the rest of the way alone. "McCune wants to see you in her office before you go to the briefing."

Cole shook his head and smiled. Then one quick look through the glass walls turned his mood somber as he saw McCune preparing for the briefing.

"Ma'am." Cole greeted McCune entering her office.

"Officer Cameron," McCune began. "You'll be taking the lead on an interagency AIJB mission team with the objective of ensuring there are no additional attacks. You will get the details in the briefing, but I just wanted to let you know that we'll be counting on you."

"I appreciate your confidence," Cole said with doubt to McCune's motive. McCune began walking to the door but stopped as Cole continued. "I need you to know something. A couple of weeks ago, I spoke with Grant regarding Roslin Environmental."

McCune closed her door and motioned for Cole to continue and then folded her arms.

"He wanted to know if I knew anything about the company from my private sector experience. Anyway, he said he was doing some basic research for his company and was following leads that had him concerned."

"How would this relate to the AIJB bombing?" McCune asked unfolding her arms.

"Oh, I'm not sure it does, but he indicated there was suspicious behavior regarding Roslin's VX project," Cole said.

"VX?" McCune questioned.

"Yes, Ma'am."

"We will need to question Grant Ramsey if you hear from him have him contact us immediately. In the meantime, let's keep this information between us."

"Certainly."

The two left for the conference room. As Cole followed her, he noticed that even on Sunday, she wore her business suit. Her auburn hair bounced as she walked down the hall. Cole glanced over at Amy who looked worried.

Just before entering the situation room he noticed Hannah Jacobs coming through the CTC entrance. As they entered the room, McCune whispered to Cole reminding him of the need for flawless execution on this operation. *I should pull this resignation letter out and hand it to her now.* Cole thought.

Cole saw the facial expressions of those in the room conveying the gravity of the situation.

"We're still waiting for a couple of others. Everyone, please take a seat." Kingman directed. Amy pointed to a chair next to her.

"Thanks," Cole replied taking the available seat.

Cole surveyed the room to see the group of people gathered. He paused when he came to Hannah, who had found a seat next to her director, Charles Thompson and another young man in his mid-twenties. She flung back her dark hair as she situated herself. She noticed his gaze and smiled back at him. Cole nodded a *'hello.'*

"I see your friend is here with us," Amy teased having caught their mild exchange. Cole turned and looked at Amy shaking his head in disbelief at her knack for observation.

Soon Kingman gathered everyone's attention and began to walk through the intel they had gained about the attack.

The lecture style room with tiered seating was near its capacity, and everyone seemed to have something to contribute. Still, the meeting moved at a quick pace. It was as if someone had just unloaded a dump truck of intel that needed to be synthesized. Cole and Amy each scribbled down notes as they followed the information flow.

He felt a sense of accomplishment as he recognized that much of the data about the AIJB had come from his and Amy's previous efforts. The familiarity with much of the details allowed Cole's mind to contribute commentary at various points. He tried to understand the AIJB's targeting of Roslin. More features waved across the screen, as Kingman shared intel that Capps and Amir had gathered in Yemen.

"We are running the identity of the three dead hostages in Yemen that were held by the terrorists. Capps' interrogation of Abdul Mahib uncovered the AIJB's plan of the bombing attack in the U.S. Unfortunately, Mahib did not know the specific target and intentionally released the information minutes after the bombing occurred at Roslin. We're not sure why they choose Roslin."

Photos and bio-sketches of known AIJB members panned across the giant screen as Kingman continued his report. Then a large image of Hasni swiped across the screen.

"Aakif Muhamad Hasni, the elusive AIJB leader," Cole explained to those in the room.

"That's right," the Director said. "We need to get everything we can on his network."

Thompson added, "The FBI has field agents arriving at Roslin as we speak. They are also handling the investigation of the blast."

"It doesn't make sense..." A senior CIA officer spoke up as if he was reading Cole's thoughts. "...A bombing on a Sunday morning, in a place with just a few people, as opposed to a crowded public facility."

"We believe the bombing may have been an attempt to create an environmental fall out of some kind. Crews are responding now to evaluate the environmental impact of the blast. But our concern is whether or not this is an isolated incident for the AIJB. Therefore, the President has issued a directive for the deployment of an interagency mission team that some of you will be assigned to." Kingman continued, "McCune will have liaison command of this joint operation code-named Titan Shield, and I want to stress that speed and efficiency are critical on this."

McCune picked up from there and continued to lay out the operational objectives and plan to leverage the mission center capabilities for the interagency team. She began to introduce the team members with each one acknowledging themselves to the rest of the group as she went along.

"Officer Cole Cameron will take the lead on Titan Shield; the team will also have Officer Amy Wiggins and Officer Amir Abdullah of the CIA. Abdullah is still in the field but is scheduled to leave tomorrow. He should be available by Wednesday afternoon." *Great. Amy is incredible, and Amir is an excellent language analyst.* Cole thought as he sized up his team.

Then Thompson contributed, "From the FBI's perspective, we will be investigating the blast scene. Also, while we have had several of the suspects you saw listed under light surveillance, we will now be putting on a full court press for all the suspects we have identified."

Thompson turned and pointed to the table where Jacobs and her colleague were seated. "For the interagency mission team, we will have Special Agent Hannah Jacobs and Agent Jason Albright." *Ah, the young guy next to Hannah.* Cole gathered. "Jacobs has worked with your agency on a couple of recent projects and knows her way around here, and Albright is one of our best chemical and biological experts," Thompson concluded and nodded to Raymond Hernandez.

Hernandez stood and projected his voice, "And I will personally be accompanying the team for observation and to ensure all Homeland Security objectives are satisfied." As if his standing gave more authority to his words. Cole nodded to each indicating his appreciation for their support. The nod wasn't as warmly received as he had hoped.

"Thank you, Officer Hernandez," Kingman said in a dismissive tone. "Folks we've been going at this for several hours now, let's clear the room and let the mission team get to work."

The room began to disperse, and the mission team members began to gather around Cole. Hernandez strolled up as if he was in charge.

"Let's take five before we pick this up," and walked out to chase down McCune before Cole could even reply.

"You sure you're our leader?" Hannah asked as she and Jason Albright followed the others. *This is just what I need, everyone working his or her own agenda,* Cole thought.

"Well, I'm here Cole. What do you want to do?" Amy offered.

"Let's take five. That might be the last reasonable thing we ever hear from Hernandez."

Amy laughed and patted him on the shoulder. *It's going to be a long ass day,* he thought.

CHAPTER 7

Counterterrorism Center – Langley

Cole was back in the lecture room getting better acquainted with Jason Albright. The young chemical engineer impressed Cole with his background. Albright seemed equally interested in Cole's diverse experience, but Cole kept the attention on Albright.

He could tell from the way Jason carried himself that he was relatively new to the FBI. He seemed to follow Hannah Jacobs' lead and lacked the confidence she displayed. During their conversation, he continually pushed his glasses up the rim of his nose, whether they had slipped down or not. Cole tried to put him at ease by asking more personal questions.

"So, Jason, why did you decide to join the FBI?" Cole asked, just as Hannah Jacobs entered the room with Amy. Before Albright could answer, Cole's cell phone rang. He looked at the caller ID. It was Grace. It might be the last chance he would get for a while to chat, so he excused himself and looked for some privacy. He walked to the edge of the room where he could see through the glass into the hall where Hernandez was ranting about something to McCune.

"Hi Grace," Cole tried to sound routine to disguise his stress from the team.

"Cole, I need to talk to you about the offer on the house."

"I can't do that right now, Grace, I'm at work, and we're just starting a meeting." He felt like the group was monitoring his conversation as he moved further toward the corner of the room for more privacy.

"Cole this is important."

"Grace, I just can't. You can do whatever you want."

"Cole, no I can't, it needs both of our signatures."

Grace, I'll look at it later. I have to go now."

There was only a click and then silence. Cole rejoined the team.

Hannah looked toward the door watching for Hernandez.

"Just for the record, because this is a domestic threat, I believe the FBI should be taking this."

Albright looked at Hannah then at Cole, Amy squirmed a little in her seat next to Cole.

"I can appreciate that Special Agent Jacobs…"

"Hannah, please," Hannah suggested lifting her eyebrows with the request.

"Sure, Hannah. Look I've been here long enough to know that if we let it, the bureaucratic turf war will bog this thing down and hinder the operation. I'm not interested in who gets credit; I'm only interested in making sure the AIJB doesn't obtain the capabilities for another attack."

Amy jumped in. "You guys should know that Cole has done a lot of work on the AIJB and he has been pushing to have their threat rating raised for some time."

Hannah nodded, and Albright just smiled, relieved that the tension seemed released. But that moment of ease quickly turned again as Hernandez marched into the room, with his suit jacket open, he put his hand on his hip.

"Alright, I think the first thing we need to do is…"

"Whoa, Whoa." Cole firmly asserted. "Were you in the earlier meeting?"

Hernandez stuttered.

"I'd like to get us started if you don't mind, now if you will please take a seat and allow me to do my job, I would appreciate it," Cole pointed to an empty chair.

Hernandez stood for a moment and fumed about his rank and his opinion about why he should be taking the lead on this operation.

"Well you're in good company," Cole interrupted.

"Hannah here thinks the FBI should lead. You think the DHS should lead and the person I think should lead this is still over in the Gulf of Aden."

Hannah almost laughed and had to force her mouth shut. Albright seemed nervous, and Amy just sat tapping her pen on her notepad.

Cole paused and calmly made his point.

"Thank you all for expressing your concerns, now you have two choices, either you sit here as a team member of Titan Shield or get out now and send in your replacement. The choice is yours to make, but make it now, because we do not have time for this shit."

He paused again and added, "The Olympian gods are knocking at the door, and we've got to stay one step ahead of them." He hoped his Greek mythological reference would calm down the little Napoleon.

"The Titan Shield and Olympian gods, I get it." Albright laughed. "Let's hope we don't have a repeat of Titanomachy!" Young Albright waited for a reaction from the group and seeing none was offered; he clarified, "you know, the battle where the Olympians defeat the Titans?"

The group looked at each other as the pun missed its mark and then they all looked at Hernandez. He said nothing but pulled the chair out and sat down just as Cole knew he would. Cole suspected Hernandez was in desperate need for some recognized achievement within his department to continue his career advancement.

Cole knew he would not pass up this opportunity even if he had to play by someone else's rules. As Hernandez adjusted in his seat, Hannah looked over to Cole with a partial smile and nod as if to say '*alright, then.*'

He skillfully led the facilitation of the team's discussion of assignments and critical objectives and was pleased with the progress they were making. Amy secured an available Ops room that would serve as an AIJB Task Force war room. It was a little on the small size but would allow them to get started.

"How soon before your FBI team in Tucson can gain access to Roslin's R & D facility?" Cole asked.

"My understanding is that while the first responders are completing their work, a team will be working on getting the bomb's signature. They'll most likely retrieve any security footage that might help them in the investigation," Hannah replied.

"See if they can do an inventory on Roslin's VX supply."

"Why VX?" Hannah asked.

Albright found his opportunity to participate. "VX is a nerve agent that is relatively easy to manufacture and requires readily available precursor chemicals. Because of its high lethality rating, like sarin, it's a likely agent for a chemical attack if the group has access."

"And Roslin was working on a VX project, so we know it was there," Cole offered.

"Yeah, but why VX? There are all sorts of chemicals there at Roslin. Look, all we know is a suicide bomber walked into the facility outside Tucson and killed nine people wounding a dozen more," Hernandez questioned.

Hannah seemed confused. "We are all sharing information here, right?" she asked. "What's your concern about VX as opposed to anything else?"

"Some intercepted communications mention VX," Cole said. "It could be nothing, but I feel strongly that it's worth checking into."

"OK, I'll make sure the field team in Tucson gets the information," Hannah replied.

"In the meantime, I suggest we head to Los Angeles to Roslin's headquarters; we need to meet with their security and executive officers. They may have some internal information that can help us determine if this was a strategic attack or a fluke. Amy, make sure we have secure communications and bring field laptops for retrieving and decrypting data," Amy nodded.

"Why don't we just have the FBI team or JTTF out of LA handle it?"

"Remember all we're doing is looking for AIJB. We're not investigating Roslin. Stopping the AIJB is our objective. To me, it starts with understanding why they targeted Roslin."

The group chewed on it.

"McCune will be here with more analysts that we're adding to the team. I don't know about you guys, but I would like to roll up my sleeves and get in the thick of it."

They all nodded.

"Jason, I think we'd like to have atropine and diazepam on hand as a precaution in case of contact with VX."

"Absolutely!" Albright agreed.

"What's atropine?" Amy asked with some concern.

"It's the antidote for VX," Albright answered.

"Wonderful," Hernandez moaned.

"Raymond it might be a good idea to check with Customs and Border Protection to see if there are any middle-eastern detainees from border crossings," Cole continued down the list.

"Well, I am constantly kept abreast of issues with CBP through my daily reports. There's nothing out of the ordinary there," Hernandez insisted.

"Just the same, if you wouldn't mind shaking the trees a little to see what falls out. If the AIJB wanted to penetrate our borders and they have some connection with Roslin, the Arizona-Mexican border would seem like a logical place. Just see if any red flags have been raised along the southern border."

Hernandez reluctantly nodded acceptance of the task and jotted down a few notes.

"Hey, I'm feeling like the girl at the prom that nobody wants to dance with," Hannah joked.

Before Cole could respond, Amy smirked, "I doubt that."

Cole tilted his head to give Amy a look and then back to Hannah, "Since your Director offered full resources, can you get us a private FBI jet to Los Angeles?"

"Right on!" Albright showed his youthful enthusiasm.

"You expect a lot from a first date, don't you?" Hannah

jabbed.

"Only from the Prom Queen," Cole tossed back immediately regretting his words knowing that he was probably violating some PC policy.

✳✳✳

Los Angeles, CA

The red sun was setting over Los Angeles as the team disembarked from the small jet on the Santa Monica airport runway. The Prom Queen had delivered the goods. They were able to avoid the larger airports of LAX or John Wayne airport.

Cole stuck his head through the door appreciating the native palm trees and red sunset sky. He stood at the door and took a deep breath to take in the setting.

"Looking for air you can chew?" Hernandez mumbled as he tried to squeeze past him in the doorway.

They were arriving later than Cole had hoped. The procurement processes of red tape and Hernandez had cost them valuable time having to return home and pack for the trip. But eventually they were airborne, and the flight over had given them some time to review intelligence reports, confirm the meeting with Roslin executives, and become better acquainted.

Cole stepped off the plane with pretty much the same opinion of the team members that he had before the trip. He chuckled as the small-framed Hernandez struggled to come off the plane with his over-packed luggage.

An FBI field agent was waiting for them with an oversized SUV. The team loaded their gear and drove to a hotel near the airport. Hernandez sat in the very back seat, perched like a dog excited for a trip. Cole riding in the passenger seat in front gazed out the window looking for signs of changes to the LA scene, Amy slouched behind him.

"Miss your old stomping grounds?"

"No. Actually, I thought this is nothing like the place I grew up; everything has changed. And my last four years here we had moved the firm to Ventura County and lived up in Thousand Oaks."

Cole thought of Grace. He had wanted to wait for more privacy but didn't feel as if he could afford to wait any longer. He texted her from his cell phone.

Grace, I'm in LA on a job. I was hoping maybe to meet with you while I'm here. I'm probably only here for a couple of days. Please call me on my cell.

In the hotel lobby at the Marriott, Hernandez was securing the assistance of a bellhop while the rest of the team made their way to the elevator. They all looked exhausted except Albright; the wiry young chemist had slept half of the ride.

"So, what are we doing tonight?" He asked in a chipper tone.

"We?" Hannah questioned rhetorically. "This part of 'we' is getting some dinner and then sleep."

"The hotel restaurant looks pretty good. You guys want to meet down there about 8:30?" Amy asked as the elevator ascended.

Everyone agreed except Cole.

"I'll skip this one tonight. I'm sorry, I need to take care of a couple of things. We start at 7:30 tomorrow morning."

It was quiet as the door to the elevator opened.

"Room 715, this is me, see you in the morning, Cole," Amy said dragging her luggage in the room.

Hannah pushed her room key into the slot to room 716 across the hall. She turned to Cole and offered a smile. It was a smile that seemed to ignite something in him. Every time he saw it was like the striking of a small match, producing a tiny fire of passion that burned for a few brief seconds.

Albright ducked into room 720 and Hernandez had 722. Cole's was further down the hall, 727. Inside the room, Cole made another attempt to call Grace and then another message for Grant. He was getting nowhere.

He threw off his shirt and was debating on room service or going out when he heard a knock at the door. He peered through the spyglass expecting to see Hernandez with more paperwork to complete. But it was Amy.

He threw his shirt back on and opened the door; aware she was still wearing her same clothes from earlier but had freshened up.

"Hey Amy," Cole said awkwardly while holding the door open.

"I just wanted to make sure everything is alright. You sure you don't want to join us for dinner?"

Amy seemed genuinely concerned, and since she was the closest thing to a friend Cole had, he divulged his final settlement and that he was hoping to get Grace to let him keep the house instead of selling it.

"She wants me to sign the offer on the house. Something just doesn't feel right. Maybe things are changing you know." He shared he was hoping to see her while he was here in LA.

"Well, if you don't hear from her tonight, come on down and join us for dinner. I'll get an extra seat just in case."

"Thanks, Amy."

Just then the ding of the elevator was heard as the bellhop pushed the cart loaded with luggage down the hallway toward Hernandez' room. Amy and Cole looked at each other and laughed before slipping back into their rooms.

Cole left one more message for Grace, telling her where he was staying and then jumped in the shower. Later, he dressed in black slacks and a dark striped shirt. He pulled out his sports coat laid it across the bed and waited for a call.

Meanwhile, in room 716, Hannah was prepping in the mirror when Amy came over. She had texted asking if she could borrow her hair iron. Hannah let her in while she was finishing up. The girls shared the mirror doing their make-up and enjoying a few laughs.

The mirror reflected a softer more feminine side of Hannah as she wore a black dress cut moderately low in front and higher up the leg than she would typically wear on the job. The stone hanging from her silver necklace gave an occasional glitter as it reflected the lights to the mirror.

"So, do you have a thing for Cole?" Hannah asked catching Amy by surprise.

"What? No. I've got a boyfriend, thank you very much. It's not like that. He's just one of the few guys I care about."

"And he's divorced?" Hannah asked.

"Yeah, I think they're finalizing the settlement. I guess his ex is out here. I think she moved out here about a year ago. His daughter is here too, a sophomore at UCLA. But Cole is really a great guy. I hope it works out for him."

"I'm sure you do," Hannah said, applying her lipstick.

"Yeah right, I've seen the way you look at him," Amy said pointing at Hannah with her eyeliner.

"Well, he is handsome, but I never mix work and pleasure."

"Then I guess the black dress is for Hernandez?" Amy joked as she left Hannah's room.

Cole sat on the edge of the bed looking for a return call from Grace or Grant. He looked at the clock on the nightstand. 8:45. His stomach demanded attention. *What the hell.* He thought as he decided to join the group for dinner.

Cole adjusted his coat sleeve as he walked from the lobby into the hotel's restaurant. The tables were neatly arranged with elegant candles and centerpieces. Maroon napkins with silver rings accented the white table clothes. The warm lighting and pleasant aroma were inviting.

Cole felt somewhat embarrassed for arriving so late, having earlier rejecting the offer. He surveyed the dining tables and noticed the group with an empty seat between Hannah and Amy.

"Hey, here comes the boss," Albright said causing Amy to turn around and smile.

"Great you're here. Join us."

"I apologize for being so late," Cole offered. "I was hoping for some other plans to work out tonight, but they never materialized. Thank you for saving me a seat. Have you ordered?"

"Yes, we just did," Hannah replied as she sipped a glass of red wine.

Cole caught the waiter's attention and placed his order.

The group enjoyed their conversation, each sharing funny stories about their early days on the job. The laughter and wine served Cole well making his heart seem lighter. It was the most social enjoyment he had experienced in some time. It was as if he had stumbled onto an oasis in the desert.

Cole was especially growing fond of Titan Shield's youngest member, Jason Albright. He loved Albright's humor and youthful energy. Hernandez remained an enigma, and Amy just grew sweeter. But it was Hannah, who like the wine he drank, intoxicated him.

As the server removed the dinner plates, Hannah turned her seat toward Cole. She crossed her legs that were now next to his, revealing her smooth thighs. He turned toward her, and the two seemed to have locked in on each other, shutting out the conversation of the rest of the group.

She shared her story with him. How she had grown up in a small town, joined the FBI after obtaining a degree in Criminology and how the job had impacted her life.

"OK, enough about me, what's your story?" she asked.

Cole felt like he was on a date. Her attractiveness mesmerized him. His sheepish grin revealed the haunting spell she had cast on him. Just as he started to share particles of his life with her, he felt a tug on the arm of his sports coat.

"Is that Grace?" Amy asked, pointing through the entrance of the restaurant to the hotel's main lobby. She had recognized her from the photos on his desk.

Cole excused himself and Hannah produced a reluctant smile, then gazed out the window into the night-lights. Cole hurried to catch Grace. She looked as if she was about to leave. It had been so long since he had seen her. She was wearing a white skirt and a bright pink top that accentuated her blond hair and hazel eyes.

"Grace," Cole chirped.

Grace forced a smile as he approached to hug her, but it felt awkward to him.

"I was just leaving you a note because they had tried your room, but you weren't in."

"Yeah, we were just having dinner," Cole pointed with his head. Grace looked at the table. The entire group was looking at the two of them.

"Why don't we go up to my room?"

"I'm not sure that's a good idea," Grace said nervously.

"What? Come on let's go." Cole took Grace by the arm, and she quickly pulled away.

"Cole, I came here to get you to sign this power of attorney paperwork so I can handle the sale of the house since you're not responding to my emails." They stepped toward the sitting area of the lobby to give some distance from the desk clerk, but both remained standing.

"I know, Grace, but I thought we could talk about things. I've been thinking. You know things are changing at work. I can feel it. Perhaps there is way," Cole stopped himself.

"Look, I came here to give you this." She said extending the envelope with the POA document. "Cole, it's what we agreed to, and you owe me that. Please just sign the paperwork and send them back so we can both move on. I can't do this anymore."

He sat on a couch in the lobby holding the envelope.

"I don't know what you want from me," Cole said shaking his head in frustration.

"I came here to get closure, Cole. That's why I came here."

"The house is the last thing I have. I love that house. Why are you insisting on selling it? I'll give you half the market value. I mean, when Jess visits…"

"Jess loves it here in California; you're going to have a hard time getting her to want to stay very long in that house."

"What?"

Grace looked toward the table of Cole's colleagues.

"We're not getting any younger, Cole. We've got to move

on with our lives!"

Cole just put his head down not knowing how to reason with the woman. After a pause, Grace took her purse and straightened her skirt.

"Try to see Jessica while you're here."

She had evaporated, like a fog that lifted, leaving a clear view. It was now black and white, in plain sight, leaving an unavoidable reality. Cole recognized the finality in Grace's voice. She was determined to make him move on from the house he had built like they had moved on from each other.

CHAPTER 8

Los Angeles, CA

Cole struggled to pull himself out of bed as the alarm clock annoyingly pierced the silence of the room, jarring his weary senses a second time. The first was resolved with the snooze button. Traveling east to west was usually easy for the early rising Cole, but the previous night had been a restless one in which his thoughts raced around in his head like race cars repetitively circling the track.

At this point, he had just enough time to get a short workout in and clean up before meeting with the team. He willed his body into submission, donning black shorts and a gray tee shirt, for a quick trip to the fitness room.

The wall-mounted television in the fitness room of the Marriott hotel was dialed into a local news station, reporting on the weather and various other regional issues. To Cole's liking, another exerciser adjusted the channel to a national news broadcaster that was reporting on the bombing in Tucson.

Cole paused in between sets on the weight machine to listen to the scattered details. He recognized the images shown. The FBI was working to identify the 'post-blast' crime scene. Their efforts would help determine the bomb's signature, confirming what Cole already knew; it was the work of the AIJB.

Once the newscast shifted to other stories, Cole found his mind sorting scattered thoughts. As he progressed through his lifting routine, his random thoughts moved in rhythm with his pushing and breathing. *Where is Grant? How can I keep this up? This job? Hannah?* He dwelled on that thought remembering their dinner from the previous evening.

With each repetition on the machine, his exertion provided a release of stress. *Finished,* he said to himself, as the sound of the weight's plates clanked for the last time.

As Cole exited the elevator on the seventh floor, he had a brief exchange with Hernandez who was going for breakfast, already dressed in a dark blue pinstripe suit.

"Half an hour?" Cole said, gently reminding Hernandez of the team's scheduled rendezvous in the lobby

"I'll be ready. I have to have a solid breakfast for the medication I take." Hernandez explained and then diverted Cole's concern. "It's your Boy Wonder that you need to be concerned about."

Cole proceeded to Albright's room and knocked on the door. After a few loud knocks, Albright appeared in his boxers and a tee shirt, apparently awakened by Cole's banging. His hair was pointed in all directions as he held the door open with some difficulty. His eyes were squinting from the brightness of the lights in the hallway. His room was still dark with the curtains drawn.

"Jason, you have to get ready, man. We start in half an hour."

"Sorry, man. Just a little wiped out. Hannah dragged me out last night, and then Hernandez snored so loud I heard him through that stupid shared door. I mean, I had to stuff towels and everything." Albright recognized Cole was growing impatient, "No worries, I'll be ready."

As the door closed, Cole looked at room 716 down the hall. Hannah going out last night surprised him. He returned to his room and before long was ready to meet the team in the lobby. His cell phone rang in the elevator on the way down. The caller ID was blocked, Cole answered anyway.

"This is Cole." But there was no reply. *Maybe it's the elevator.* He thought.

"Hello," He tried again, just as he exited into the lobby,

only to hear a click from the other end. His curious expression must have seemed odd to the team that already gathered with one exception, young Jason Albright.

"Good morning, guys," Cole warmly began as he looked for eye contact with the group standing in the lobby. Hernandez hardly looked up as he worked with his cell phone. Hannah didn't even smile or respond, and eye contact was impossible for Cole. She hid her eyes behind her large dark sunglasses. *Was she hiding red, bloodshot eyes from her late night or was she putting up a guard against him?* Cole reasoned that it could be a little of both. Amy was the only one to offer an actual verbal response.

"We'll give Jason a couple of minutes," Cole suggested.

"I'll get him," the defunct Hannah finally spoke, feeling responsible for his delay. She walked a few feet away and texted him on her cell phone.

"He's coming now."

Hernandez never lifted his head from his cell phone but growled in disapproval. Cole stepped toward the desk clerk, handed him a large express delivery envelope, and asked if he could make sure it was picked up by the carrier.

"Any word from Tucson on the post-blast investigation?" Cole asked Hannah, testing her emotional state more than anything else.

"No, I'll be sure to let you know something as soon as I do," Hannah responded in a slightly curt fashion.

OK, now I know something's wrong with her. Cole thought.

Albright stumbled from the elevator with his shirt still untucked. The group's response to Albright was almost comical to Cole; Hannah shook her head, Amy raised her eyebrows, and Hernandez heaved a sigh of disgust. Cole on the other hand, laughed with "Gee-whiz" as they left the hotel.

The FBI had left Hannah with the keys to the SUV. She looked at Cole as they approached the vehicle, still wearing her sunglasses in the dark parking garage.

"Since you know the area, do you want to drive?"

Cole was taking the keys when the compliance conscientious Hernandez reminded the group that only an employee of the FBI could drive the vehicle.

"Oh, darn," Cole muttered sarcastically handing the keys back to Hannah.

"Sh...."

Hannah held back her frustration as she grabbed the keys. But Cole took delight in her disgruntlement and found her even more irresistible, smiling at her as he climbed into the SUV on the passenger side to navigate.

The team maneuvered through the maze of freeways at a languid pace because of the morning traffic. But it gave them time to discuss the agenda for their meeting with the Roslin executives. Everyone was contributing to the ideas except Hannah, whose rough morning continued as the stop and go traffic exasperated her.

"What the hell is he thinking?" she shouted as a car darted in the available space between her and the vehicle in front of her.

Cole chuckled at her torment, knowing she was reaping her rewards from a late night. She noticed he was taking pleasure in seeing this side of her, so she adjusted herself and fought to appear composed.

"So, you want me to take the lead on the questioning?"

"That's right," Cole confirmed. "We need to convince them to let Amy look through their communication systems for any leads, and give Jason and I access to their project files associated with VX."

"What is your fixation on VX?" Hernandez asked from the back seat throwing his hands in the air. Cole ignored him.

"What if they refuse to give us access? I don't think we have enough information to obtain warrants," Hannah ascertained.

"I think they'll want to cooperate with us. I know I would if I were in Roslin's shoes."

Hernandez snorted from the back seat. "Let's hope their legal representation is as open-minded as you are."

"Well if not, that's where you come in. You'll be able to use your artfully tuned skills as an attorney to negotiate for us. Right?"

Before Hernandez could respond, the team's secure cell rang. He answered, pushing the keys to encrypt the call. It was McCune, wanting a status check and reporting on additional intel coming from the field operations, as well as the bomb's signature at Roslin.

"And how reliable is that?" The group heard Cole ask. "I see. Yes, I'll let you know of any developments and the results of our meeting with the Roslin executives."

Cole finally disseminated some of the information he had received.

"Well, the preliminary work on the bomb's signature shows hints of ISIS, but we're not ruling out anything. Some of the people at Langley want Titan Shield ditched. But they also know that the AIJB has close ties with ISIS, so we're still considering this an AIJB attack. Capps is trying to gather additional human intel to confirm Mahib's confession of AIJB's responsibility in the attack."

The group sat quietly, digesting the information. "Oh, you need to head east here on the 210 Freeway," Cole motioned just in time for Hannah to change lanes.

"So, are we on the right track here with Roslin?" Hannah asked, what the whole group was wondering.

"I think we should hand the Roslin investigation off and head back to DC," Hernandez asserted. Not waiting for a response, he dialed his cell phone.

"What are you doing?" Cole turned completely around in his seat to ask.

"I'm calling to make arrangements for us to go a different direction on this."

Hannah adjusted her rear-view mirror to see Hernandez more clearly as Cole asserted, "You will do no such thing. We are here, and we will look into Roslin before heading back."

"This is a waste of time," Hernandez argued.

"Look, I've got a feeling on this. We take today, tomorrow

at the most and we're out of here," Cole continued.

"We're already here," Amy agreed.

"Yeah, I'm in. Let's see where this goes," Hannah contributed to the growing consensus. "I'd hate to think we came all this way for nothing."

"Well, I wouldn't call last night 'nothing,'" Albright said, surprising the group. Hannah abruptly adjusted the mirror giving Albright a stern look.

Amy's mouth dropped open. She leaned forward in the seat and whispered to Hannah "You and Jason?"

"Not even!" Hannah said with an incredulous tone, loud enough for all to hear.

Albright, knowing he had been misinterpreted quickly tried to remedy the situation.

"No, No. That's not what I meant. You should have seen Hannah at the club all the guys were hitting on her…"

"Jason!" Hannah shouted. "Shut up!"

Cole chuckled again. *This just keeps getting better.* He thought as he noticed he was being harpooned by Hannah's glare of disgust. Cole refocused on Hernandez.

"Raymond, work with me on this, alright?"

Hernandez reluctantly consented to the group's wishes, but immediately went to tapping on his cell phone, sending emails. Cole was sure that the correspondence was the Homeland Security Officer's political jostling to build a case against him. His behavior did not escape Hannah's observation either, as she repositioned the mirror watching his suspicious expressions.

The atmosphere at Roslin's headquarters was one of grief and anxiety. The entrance of the contemporary facility was designed to psychologically convey a warm welcome, but the employees' sense of loss was all that was noticed. The team saw people offering condolences to one another and grief counselors were available to the ailing workforce.

Cole could only imagine how painful the previous day's experience had been for them. Even though Roslin had over twelve hundred employees, they were still small enough to be virtually crippled by the exposure of the previous day.

Cole knew that the emotional state of the executives was worn down from the events. Many had been up through the night. Several were in Tucson. The CEO, COO, and the Chief Legal Counsel had agreed to meet the team. The Chief of Security would be joining them on the phone from Tucson.

While they were escorted to the executive conference room, Cole had the chance to see Hannah's eyes for the first time that day as she removed her sunglasses. If her eyes had been red, they were clear now.

They entered the conference room with the executives huddled over paperwork, except for the one that was later identified as the Chief Operations Officer, who was helping himself to a cup of coffee. They exchanged business cards and handshakes as the team offered condolences. As the COO, Steve Bremen handed Cole his card; he looked at him inquisitively.

"Have we met somewhere before?"

"Yes, I believe we have. A few years back at a conference in San Francisco," Cole replied.

"That's right. I remember. You have a consulting firm up in Ventura County, right?"

"Good memory. But I'm no longer there, of course," Cole said pointing to the business card he had just handed Bremen. "And look at you guys, you've had exceptional growth since then."

"Well, we've managed to work in some key areas that helped us along the way. But after yesterday's events, well…"

"We're really sorry," Cole responded just as the intercom buzzed with a secretary announcing that Chief of Security, William Garrison was now on the line for the meeting.

"How are things going over there, Bill?" the CEO, Ralph Garland asked, speaking into the bat-shaped speakerphone in the middle of the conference table.

"We'll get to the bottom of it Mr. Garland," Garrison responded.

"Has the FBI given you any details of their findings?"

"No, they continue to be very tight-lipped around here."

"Well, maybe our guest today can provide us with some insight," Garland said looking to the group at the table.

Hannah began, "I know this is a difficult time for you and your company and we're grateful that you're taking the time now to meet with us."

"Well, I must say we were expecting the FBI, but not Homeland Security and especially not the CIA," Garland replied, as the group took seats around the table.

"Yes, we are a bit surprised by the assortment of the entourage," The Chief Legal Counsel offered in his baritone voice.

"Officer Wiggins and I are simply consultants, working with expertise regarding a certain terrorist group that we believe may be responsible for yesterday's attack. We're here to assist Special Agent Jacobs anyway we can," Cole said to minimize their concerns.

Hannah sat up straight and took the lead, asking a series of non-threatening questions to put the executives at ease. They assured Hannah and the team they were willing to cooperate.

Building on their cooperation, Hannah proceeded to make more demanding requests.

"We would like to have Officer Wiggins perform an analysis of your communication systems to look for anything that might have slipped through. Officer Cameron and Agent Albright will need to see some of your operational reports on various nerve agents, especially VX."

"Why VX? I don't understand. Do you think that someone in our company was involved with this?" Garland asked in disbelief.

"We're not sure at this time, but we can't rule anything out. Since this bombing took place on a Sunday, with relatively low causalities, we want to examine other possible motives," Hannah replied.

"We have reason to believe that the suspected terrorist group had an interest in VX," Cole added.

"I don't know if I like where this is going," the baritone

voice of the Chief Legal Counsel was a pitch higher this time. Cole couldn't remember his name.

"Mr. Garland," Hannah said ignoring the Chief Legal Counsel, "I assure you, that we will exercise the utmost discretion…"

Hernandez interrupted "We came without warrants expecting your full cooperation, but that can change." Cole and Hannah both looked at Hernandez as if to say *'enough.'* He took their hint and cooled down giving enough time for the corporate attorney to launch into a legal debate. Cole sensed the objectives slipping away.

"Mr. Garland," Hannah broke through, "we can only imagine the stress and pain that you and your colleagues must be feeling. Sir, we do not," Hannah said looking at Hernandez to make her point, "want to add to your stress. We simply want to determine and hold accountable the people responsible for this horrible incident."

The room was silent. Hernandez drew his breath to speak but caught Cole's stare, and Hannah continued her plea.

"And we need your company's cooperation to do that. The families of the victims, your employees, and investors will want to know you fully cooperated with the government in this investigation. We can discuss potential NDAs. Mr. Hernandez can help coordinate any reasonable request."

Hannah's appeal to Garland's motives was genuine, Cole was impressed with her skills and hoped it carried enough weight to win Garland's favor. *If the plea for justice was not enough at least the subtle threat to his company's reputation should convince him.* He thought.

Garland hesitated then agreed.

"Give them whatever they need," he said standing, visibly troubled by the prospects Hannah had presented.

The Chief Security Officer, William Garrison's voice came over the speaker.

"Ralph, that puts us in a very vulnerable situation. I don't like the idea of the CIA or even the FBI messing around with our systems."

"Damn it, Bill! I said give them whatever they need," Garland said, and then paused before continuing to the group.

"You'll have to excuse Mr. Garrison; we've been battling corporate espionage around here. It's been a nightmare." He looked around the room.

"Just the same, Officer Wiggins, if you don't mind, Mr. Garrison will assign one of his associates to accompany you at all times as you work with our communication systems. As for the operational reports, Mr. Bremen will assist you with any reports or documentation you may need. The CEO looked over to Hannah.

"Is that satisfactory?"

"Certainly," She replied. "Thank you, sir."

"If you'll excuse me, I have a plane to catch to get back over to Tucson. Please feel free to use this conference room, and you have my personal cell number on the card I gave you."

Garland left the room with the meeting concluded.

"I'll gather some of the operational reports you indicated and everything I've got on our VX project," Bremen said as he departed and then added, "and, I'll get someone from communications over here to escort Officer Wiggins."

"Thank you." the team replied.

His departure left the team waiting in the room with the Chief Legal Counsel who was determined to watch every move they made. Hannah asked for the directions to the nearest restroom and excused herself.

Amy followed her, taking advantage of the time available. Hernandez said he needed to make a few calls and likewise disappeared, leaving Cole and Albright alone in the room with the gray-haired heavy-set lawyer, who judging from his odor was an obvious smoker.

Cole hoped that he would need frequent smoke breaks leaving them more time alone. The two didn't speak, and the lawyer began tapping his fingers on the table just staring at Cole. *Yeah, the nicotine craving is getting stronger,* he thought to himself. *It won't be long until he needs to step outside.*

Cole was shocked as the Chief Legal Counsel pulled out his cigarettes and was about to light it as he noticed the expression on Cole's face.

"You don't mind, do you?" the overstuffed lawyer had the nerve to ask.

"Actually, I do," Cole firmly replied.

"Oh, that's right, you're the environmental guy," the lawyer said with smug sarcasm.

"Not that kind of environmental guy. Just want to keep my lungs healthy." Cole responded as the women returned to the room. Both Amy and Hannah looked at the two men as if to say *'What's going on here?'* But nothing else was said. The lawyer put the pack back in his coat pocket, swiveled his chair around and scribbled notes.

After waiting for a few minutes, a young Asian man in his late twenties to early thirties arrived and introduced himself. He offered his assistance to Amy with the company's communication systems. One of the company's security officers, assigned by Garrison accompanied them to watch over her shoulder every step of the way.

The two escorted Amy from the conference room to the location that housed the central servers. There she would perform an analysis of correspondence as well as retrieve any pertinent data. It was a long and grueling task, but one Amy was well qualified.

Cole didn't like the fact that Amy was going alone and Hannah easily interpreted his look of concern. "Where's Hernandez?" she asked, in response to his expression.

"He said he had to make some calls," Albright offered. Cole just raised his eyebrows. He wanted to maintain the appearance that this was an FBI investigation and that his role was purely consultative, so he was careful with his words and demeanor. Hannah was aware of Cole's objective and had no problem taking an assertive role.

"Go find Hernandez and tell him to catch up with Amy and assist her with the communication systems," she directed Albright.

"I'll be back in a few," the Chief Legal Counsel had finally given in to his addiction, leaving the room with Albright.

Hannah and Cole were alone in the conference room. There was a brief moment when they gazed into each other's eyes, providing Cole a small taste of what he experienced last night at dinner. Hannah was about to say something, but Cole quickly raised his finger to his mouth. Shh. He motioned. Then he wrote a word on his notepad; *BUGS*.

"Think so?" Hannah whispered with surprise.

"They're way too paranoid," Cole whispered back.

Hannah's look signaled her disbelief, but she played along. Suddenly Cole wished he had let her speak, as he realized her facial expression was softer and more personal than he had seen all day. *What if she just wanted to pick up where we left off last night*, he thought. Regardless, it was too late now; her sober look had returned along with Bremen, and his administrative assistant.

Bremen and his assistant were each carrying a load of notebooks and folders. It was time to go to work. Soon Albright returned as well as the Chief Legal Counselor. The stack of notebooks and files continued to grow throughout the day.

The team broke long enough to grab sandwiches at a nearby deli. Hannah had offered to bring it in, but Cole suggested the break would do them good and give them some privacy.

At the deli, Hannah had her sunglasses back on, but this time for obvious reasons as they sat at an outdoor table. When Hernandez had stepped away to refill his drink, Cole instructed Amy to search the backup servers for visitor logs from the R&D facility. He had remembered Grant's note about the asset's comments on suspicious visitors to the facility.

"You're looking for two men, possibly listed as potential investors." The group looked at Cole curiously.

"I won't even ask," Hannah said, not wanting to open a can of worms just as Hernandez returned to the table.

"Jason and I still have a ton of work ahead. We'll need to stay one more night and try to finish tomorrow by around noon. Amy, will that give you enough time?" Cole asked.

"Oh yeah, I might actually be able to finish up today. If Officer Hernandez could find some creative ways to distract the security lurch assigned to lean over me, it would really help."

"How about Raymond, you think you can create some opportunities for Amy to work more freely?" Cole asked.

"I will not participate in anything illegal," Hernandez said wiping his mouth with a napkin.

"No one's doing anything illegal," Amy said. "How would you like it if some guy was constantly looking over your shoulder while you're working on a computer. It's just annoying."

"Alright, I'll figure something out," Hernandez agreed.

Hannah fielded a call on her cell phone that relayed the information about the bomb's signature. She was visibly ticked. *Here we go again*, Cole thought. But this time her irritation would not be a mystery.

"How the hell did you know four hours before I did, what my own agency discovered?" she said removing her sunglasses to look Cole in the eye.

"They're the CIA, man. We're talking, JFK assignation, Jimmy Hoffa, and the UFOs at Roswell. They know everything," Albright energetically joked defusing the tension.

"Hey, have you ever seen one?

"One of what?" Cole asked.

"You know, aliens."

Albright had the whole group laughing, even Hernandez.

Later that day, Hernandez came through by creating a mild diversion that occupied the security officer's time long enough for Amy to sort through some critical files and download essential information, including the visitor's logs from the Research and Development facility.

Albright and Cole were also making headway through their stacks of research documents. They still needed more time, but they had agreed with the Roslin executives that they would leave by 6:00 PM.

CHAPTER 9

Los Angeles, CA

A s the group was driving back to the hotel creeping along the packed freeways, Cole's cell rang again with an unidentified caller.

"Hello."

Finally, after a brief pause, a soft female voice on the other end responded.

"Is this Cole Cameron?"

"Yes, who's calling please?" Cole asked growing weary of the mystery.

"Mr. Cameron, I live in Tucson, and we have a mutual friend." Cole's body language abruptly changed, causing Hannah to look over to him. *Grant's asset*, He thought.

"Grant Ramsey? How do you know Grant?"

"I don't want to talk over the phone. Grant said I should call you if anything happened."

"Who is this?" Cole asked again.

"We need to meet in person, as soon as possible. I don't know who to trust."

"I'll catch the first available flight tonight that I can get on."

Now the whole group was leaning Cole's direction, trying to follow the conversation. Cole looked at his watch.

"It will probably be between eleven and mid-night before I get in. Can you find a public place, like a bar or something?"

"I know a place," The soft voice replied. "The Owl's Club downtown. I'll be waiting there."

"How will I recognize you?" Cole asked.

"You won't have to. Grant described you to me, I'll recognize you." There was a brief pause as Cole gathered his thoughts. "Mr. Cameron, please come alone."

"I'll be there as soon as I can," he said as they ended their call.

The team was silent waiting for Cole to divulge information. Cole stared out the window at the haze that hovered over the city.

"Guys, I have to fly to Tucson tonight. After you finish up tomorrow, you can take the FBI plane over to catch up with me."

"I don't like this," Hannah said as Amy agreed, "Yeah, neither do I."

"Look, I need you to drop me by the hotel so I can pick up my things. I can take the hotel shuttle over to the airport."

"Jason can drop you off," Hannah suggested. "So, what's going on?"

"I heard you mention a 'Grant Ramsey.' Who's that? Is there something we should know about?" Hernandez inquired.

Cole was thinking of how to articulate his response when the SAT phone rang again. It was McCune wanting an update. The conversation dragged on until they were pulling in front of the hotel.

The team climbed out, and Cole looked at Albright, "Meet you here in twenty minutes." Albright agreed as he took the keys from Hannah. Cole pretended to have something to do in the lobby so he would not have to ride up the elevator with the rest of the group. He wanted to avoid any discussion of Grant. But Hannah seemed to look right through his veneer with her stare as she stepped into the elevator.

Cole quickly packed his bag and headed to the lobby to check out of his room. Albright had texted him earlier to tell him that he was ready. Cole could see the front of the vehicle through the glass doors as he signed out and grabbed his receipt.

He walked to the back of the vehicle, swinging open the back door to load his bags. He noticed other baggage and the two women in the second row of the SUV. After a brief stare, Cole tossed his bags in and slammed the door shut.

"Jason and Hernandez will stay tomorrow to finish up. We're heading out with you," Hannah insisted as Cole climbed in the front passenger seat.

"Yeah Cole, everything I need to do is right here," Amy said pointing to her laptop.

"Besides," Hannah said with a grin, "we lost our FBI plane for tomorrow, and I have a feeling you'll need me sooner than you think."

"Southwest terminal," Cole instructed Albright ignoring the two women.

After a few short minutes, Albright had pushed his way through the LAX traffic and pulled to the curb to unload his grateful passengers.

"See you guys tomorrow afternoon. I'll call you if I come across anything," Albright said.

The three picked up their boarding passes, avoided the long security lines by flashing their badges, and only had time to search for a fast food vendor.

"Does this look alright?" Amy asked, pointing to a fairly crowded sitting area in the terminal. "Let's grab that table," she added.

Hannah made a call from her cell phone before joining Amy and Cole at the table. She plopped down, her body communicating the toll of travel and work they were all feeling.

"I have our rooms reserved at the AC Hotel," she said as she exhaled a sigh.

"The Marriott, again?" Amy asked. "Are you trying to rack up Reward Points or something?"

"Heck yeah. At the rate Cole moves us around I'll earn vacation in no time," she laughed.

Cole felt that Hannah was trying to lighten the air. He knew that she wanted him to tell her about the call and more about Grant. But Cole remained relatively quiet.

It had been an odd day for him as far as Hannah was concerned. Part of the day, she ignored him and conveyed contempt with her body language. At other times, she seemed to warm up. *Women*, he reasoned he would never figure out how to read them. *It's like adjusting a thermostat in a room that was always either too hot or too cold. The elusive consistent comfort zone is impossible to find.*

Amy and Hannah kept each other occupied with conversation, while Cole remained preoccupied with his thoughts. He was anxious to meet the caller, and he tried to push away his thoughts of Grace and their brief encounter the night before.

"So, are you going to meet alone with this mystery caller or what?" Hannah asked breaking up his descent into momentary depression.

"Yes, she seems very upset and doesn't trust anyone. She requested I meet her alone."

"How does Grant Ramsey fit into this?" Amy asked.

"Not sure," Cole said with a shrug. "We better get back to the gate since we don't have assigned seats." They picked up their belongings, returned to the gate, and were herded in like cattle for the short flight.

As they worked their way up the crowded aisle, it became apparent they would get packed in on a full flight. Hannah grabbed a middle seat, leaving Amy continuing up the aisle searching. Cole who had been behind the two suggested Amy come back and sit with Hannah, but she found a window seat she preferred.

Hannah saw Cole hesitate. "You better grab it before it's gone," she suggested.

"Well, I do prize the aisle seat," Cole said tossing his bag in the overhead bin and his satchel under the seat in front. The scent of her fragrance caught him as he sat down. It was a magnetic aroma pulling at him with some invisible power. *This girl is getting to me*, he thought.

"OK, who gets the armrest?" he joked to break his train of

thought.

"Good God, men," Hannah retorted. "What is it about aisle seats and armrests?"

"I'm afraid it's our inferior genetics. We have many built-in territorial issues."

"Must be," Hannah laughed.

In no time they were airborne and the walls that were erected earlier in the day were now down. Hannah's charm was again on display for Cole to see.

"OK, last night I basically told you my life story, but you skipped out before giving me the dirt on you. That's no way to treat a valuable team member."

"Valuable team member? What happened to the FBI plane for the team?"

"Trust me if I hadn't wanted to go tonight it would have been available for me tomorrow. I couldn't see wasting it on Hernandez and Jason," Hannah assured him.

"On a serious note, I was very impressed with the way you handled Roslin. Thank you," Cole complimented.

"You're welcome." She said leaning in closer to him. "Now, enough avoidance, who is Cole Cameron?"

Her brown eyes were irresistible and time swiftly passed as he shared more of his personal life. She appeared genuinely interested.

"So, are you and your wife…Grace, is it? Is the divorce finalized?" her directness caught Cole off guard.

"I guess so," Cole said pausing to take the opportunity to finish off his bottled water then added, "well it's really not much of a guess. I signed a power of attorney for her to negotiate on the house that is the final piece of the settlement."

"Wow. Sorry, I saw the envelope and we sort of overheard your conversation last night," Hannah explained.

"Tell me about Grant," Hannah redirected the conversation having sensed Cole's uneasiness.

Cole was happy to change the subject and felt growing confidence with Hannah, so he spent the remaining flight sharing the details of his conversation at the coffee shop, and even the notes gathered at the dead drop.

He intentionally excluded specific details to protect Grant. At any rate, Hannah now had enough information to know that Grant was on to something at Roslin and had an asset, or informant working with him, the caller Cole was scheduled to meet. He would have to let McCune know the cat was out of the bag regarding Ramsey.

***

Tucson, AZ

They met up with Amy as they disembarked the plane. Cole looked at his watch. It was 10:15 PM, giving him just enough time to check in at the hotel and shower before going to the Owl's Club.

On the way out of the airport, Hannah and Amy had stopped at a restroom together. Amy looked at Hannah through the mirror above the sink, where they stood freshening up.

"You and Cole seemed pretty cozy. I thought you didn't mix business and pleasure."

"Who said it was pleasure and not business," Hannah said as she grabbed the handle on her rolling luggage and walked out.

After checking in at the AC Hotel and taking a quick shower, Cole taxied over to the bar. He entered the Owl's Club in the historic Armory Park neighborhood around 11:15 PM. He surveyed the quaint bar with its swanky western décor, an accurate reflection of Tucson. Only a handful of people were sitting at the bar, most huddled around tables, but the dim lights made it hard to see anyone clearly.

He took a stool at the bar, ordered a light beer and looked around again. To his right, at the end of the bar, was a woman in her thirties. She looked vaguely familiar to him but was apparently not looking for him, as she turned her head to avoid eye contact.

"Let me guess," the bartender said handing Cole his bottle. "A blind date?"

"Something like that."

"Cole Cameron?" the Bartender asked.

"Yes."

The Bartender then nodded to a corner table to Cole's left. He looked for his subject, but the darkness prevented him from a good view. His eyes adjusted to the dark, as he grew closer. There sitting at the table was a slim African-America woman in her early forties.

"Hi, I'm Cole," he said as he extended his hand.

"Do you have some identification?" the woman asked.

"Sure," Cole replied offering his ID to her. "And who might you be?"

"My name is Clarisse Johnson; I'm a Sr. Project Manager with the Roslin R & D group." She sniffled and wiped a tear from her cheek. "I lost some friends in that explosion Mr. Cameron."

"I'm sorry," Cole attempted to console her. "Please call me Cole."

"Very well," she said softly, as she took another drink emptying her glass. Cole saw it and motioned for another round.

"Clarisse, have you seen Grant." Cole didn't know where else to begin but tried to remain sensitive to her emotional state. She slowly raised her eyes to meet his.

"I haven't seen or heard from him since Saturday."

"What did you guys uncover that has you so worried."

Clarisse remained silent, and her eyes were tearing up.

"Look it's OK. Just tell me what you know. I'll get you whatever help you need so that you feel safe."

"I had growing concerns about our VX project. I thought we were researching methods of containment and more efficient antidotes, but we kept producing more quantities of the nerve agent. We produced more than we would ever need and beyond our contract specifications with the government." Her hands were shaking.

"I can't prove it, but I'm certain inventory records, and other documentation were altered to cover these discrepancies."

Cole leaned forward to hear her soft voice more clearly.

"Did you contact the authorities or anyone else within the company?"

"I went to the VP of Research and Development and reported that I had discovered some discrepancies in the reporting. I wanted him to know we violated the stipulations of our government contract. He asserted I was mistaken but assured me he would launch an internal investigation. Within a few days I was reassigned to different projects and later Mr. Alvarez, the VP had an accident."

"An accident?"

"Yes, he was killed in a car accident just a few days ago. It may just be a coincidence, but it really scared me. I know I should have contacted the authorities, but I was concerned for my son. I'm a single mother and…" she broke into a quiet sob.

"It's OK. I understand." Cole waited for her to regain composure.

"Why do you think someone would cover up this production of VX? Who would want to do that?" Cole tried to move the conversation forward.

"I don't know. But this nerve agent is worth millions, just in the quantities we have above our stipulated amounts."

"How did you meet Grant?"

"Well, that's why I'm so frightened now, I mean after the bombing." She hesitated again.

"Why did you give information to Grant?" Cole asked, wanting urgently to get to the bottom of the situation.

"I was going to say earlier, just when I thought I had enough courage to go to the authorities, Mr. Ramsey contacted me. He said he was an undercover agent working to expose Roslin's unlawful activities." Her words took Cole by surprise. *Maybe Grant played this angle to get his information.* He reasoned.

"Did he show identification?" He asked.

"Of course, it was sort of like yours but for the FBI," Clarisse said with a concerned look. "He is with the FBI, right?" Cole just nodded, not wanting to alarm her any more than she already was.

"What all did you share with him."

"I told him about the increased volume of production and the fact that we had visitors who were granted virtually unlimited access to view our procedures and they showed an unusual interest in our VX project. The last time I saw him was Saturday night, right here. I haven't seen or heard from him since."

Cole sensed he was compromised and abruptly turned looking across the room.

"That's when he gave me your information and told me to contact you if I didn't hear from him." She noticed him looking over the room.

"Is everything OK?"

"It's alright. Anyway, tell me more about the visitors."

"The two men came in on two different occasions. I don't remember the date of their first visit, but the second was on Thursday. I believe it was March 6th. I remember because I thought their long visit would cause me to be late to a parent-teacher conference."

"You spoke to the men?"

"Just briefly, I was asked to walk them through our processes, but I did most of the talking. I was told they were risk assessors for our investors, but they just didn't seem like the type. I know that sounds like I'm stereotyping, but with everything else going on, I was just very suspicious," she added.

"Can you describe them?"

"They are both large men; I mean tall and well-built. They were both Caucasian and spoke with what may have been a

Russian accent, but I'm not sure."

Cole asked a few more questions getting details from Clarisse about the VX project, learning more about handling and storage procedures. Then he suggested that she go to the FBI and share the information.

"Well, I've already told Grant everything I know. But I am scheduled to meet with an Agent tomorrow afternoon. Because of the blast, they're interviewing all the R & D employees."

"OK, why don't you give them a call and see if they can see you in the morning."

Cole took the agent's name.

"Call me if you need anything at all. Oh, by the way, have you spoken to anyone else about this?" He asked as they were leaving.

"No, just the VP, Grant and now you," her voice trembled as she recognized the irony of her comments. Alvarez was dead, and Grant had disappeared. She looked at Cole and wondered if he too would vanish.

CHAPTER 10

Tucson, AZ

On the short cab ride back to the AC Hotel, Cole phoned Hannah.

"Sorry, did I wake you?"

"Umm…no just starting to wind down. What's up?"

"I need to get to the blast site now. Did your field office drop off a vehicle for us?"

"No, we were getting a ride tomorrow. But I'll take care of it. Isn't the site still going through chemical clean up?"

"We'll see. It doesn't matter; we need to get over there as soon as possible and have Amy bring the data files she picked up from their headquarters. I'll meet you guys down in the lobby."

Cole sat in a maroon high-back chair in the hotel lobby waiting on Amy and Hannah. He could smell the ammonia in the cleaning fluids used by the cleaning woman mopping the floor as he waited.

As she tossed the mop back and forth, he rolled around in his mind the details of events of the last few days. He still struggled to find a connection between Roslin and the AIJB. *How would they have known about the VX?* He also had difficulty understanding the actions of Grant.

The two women entered the lobby, each now wearing jeans. Hannah stood good two-three inches taller than Amy and tossed her dark brown hair as she carefully walked across the wet marble tiles. Amy dropped her laptop down in the oversized chair next to Cole. Hannah stretched out in the chair across from him.

"The blast has everything tied up around here. I've got a rental car being dropped off," she said crossing her legs. "I guess your meeting was fruitful?" she said, as she slouched further down in the chair.

"Thanks for the car. Yeah, based on what I heard. I have a hunch, but I need to see the site."

Cole recognized their exhaustion as Amy yawned.

"You know, I really can do this one by myself if you guys need some rest," he offered.

Hannah appeared somewhat insulted by his suggestion and sat up straight.

"No way, I'm ready. Besides, you need someone to get you around the FBI field team out there. They've been working long hard hours, and they're not going to like you interfering."

"I'm not going to interfere. If the clean-up crew lets me suit up with the protective equipment, I can get what I need and be out of there in no time."

"What is it you're looking for?" Amy asked with another yawn.

"I'll know it when I see it," Cole said. "Hey, why don't you grab yourself a cup of coffee, the car should be here soon."

Amy nodded and went to get a cup at the counter.

As she watched Amy leave, Hannah softly asked, "So are you going to tell me about your meeting or what? Does she know where Grant is?"

Cole waited for Amy to return and then shared the information he had learned from Clarisse. The attendant from the car rental company came through the door, and Hannah jumped up to take care of the paperwork.

Cole and Amy gathered their belongings and soon the three were traveling east on Interstate 10 to get to Roslin's R & D Center located about twenty-five miles outside the city.

The barricades with flashing amber lights and yellow police tape greeted them as they arrived on the scene. After getting past the initial screening, they were stopped again before gaining access to the command post stationed some three hundred feet from the facility.

The staging area was well organized, with huge light stands projecting bright lights against the building. The sound of big diesel generators filled the night air with constant noise. The air sock at the top of the trailer signaled the wind's direction, letting Cole know they were upwind and safe from any airborne contaminants.

It was just a skeleton crew inside the command post. It had been over forty hours since the initial response, and the bulk of responders were getting a much-needed rest. The field agent left in charge for the evening informed the team that the chemical emergency response crew had not released the east wing of the facilities yet.

He pointed out the area on the blueprints spread across a tall table. Cole moved his hand across the prints, mapping out his course. The east wing and lobby had been affected the most by the blast.

"Is the east wing the side that houses the nerve gas research?" Cole asked, verifying Clarisse's information.

"That's correct," a voice from the other corner of the trailer said. The man approached and extended his hand to the women and Cole.

"This is Jared Baxter," the FBI agent offered.

"Facilities director for Roslin," Baxter completed the introduction.

"Mr. Baxter has been here the entire time. I keep telling him to go home. He helped us get a video feed of the security cameras recordings just before the blast," The agent said.

"Were you able to ID the bomber?" Hannah asked the FBI agent.

"I haven't heard yet. We sent it to your hometown."

"Who's your chemical response crew? Is it a Roslin team or contractors?" Cole asked Baxter.

"We have a contract with a company called Environmental Dynamics, they're working in shifts around the clock to provide clean up and decontamination," Baxter replied.

"So, I guess that's their unit just outside with all the gear. I want to suit up, take a quick look and grab a couple of shots with a digital camera."

"You'll have to sort that out with them. I think you have to be trained or something for that equipment," Baxter said as he ran his hand through his hair.

"Not a problem," Cole said. "In the meantime, Mr. Baxter, would it be possible to get some additional video feed from earlier dates? Ms. Wiggins here has some dates from previous visitors that we wanted to take a look at."

"I don't know," Baxter stuttered, looking suspiciously at the three. "Maybe I should call Mr. Garrison our Chief of Security, that's his area, and he got pretty pissed that I didn't go through him before."

Hannah reassured Baxter.

"Well, we just came from Los Angeles and met with your company's top executives, including Mr. Garrison and the CEO Mr. Garland. They assured us we would have full cooperation. But if you insist on calling him at 1:30 in the morning go ahead."

Baxter conceded.

"Alright, I'll be back in a few," Cole said stepping out of the command post motioning for Amy and Hannah to follow.

"We're looking for two Caucasians, both taller men, visiting at least twice within the last month. One of the dates was March 6th, and they would have a slender African American female escorting them. That should help you filter everything else out."

"This is still going to take a while," Hannah protested.

"Well, I'll try to narrow it down and then upload the files to Langley to cross check on facial recognition for our database," Amy said.

"That's right, upload any video feed you can retrieve from the dates and times that match. We need it before Garrison gets involved." Cole said just as the FBI agent peered out the door of the command post trailer. Cole motioned to Hannah with his eyes.

"Do you have a camera we can use?" she asked, quickly

intercepting the agent.

He then turned and whispered to Amy. "While you're in the system here, see if you can extract and download any previous backup files on their VX project, especially inventory records. I want to see if they match what we have from LA."

Amy nervously replied, "I don't know, Cole."

"Only do it if you're comfortable. But I have a hunch that if we go through the protocol and the FBI waits for Garrison, any valuable information will be scrubbed," Cole said while taking hold of her arm. "Remember our job is to prevent any additional threats, not build a criminal case."

"Alright, be careful in there," she said, while he walked over to the response trailer of the contractor.

A crew worker asked if he could help and Cole requested an environmental suit and air pack. "I can't do that," the worker insisted.

"OK, who do I need to speak to that can make that happen?" Cole asked.

The worker conveyed a message with his two-way radio. After a few short minutes, the bright lights revealed a lone character in a white environmental suit emerging from the rubble. He stomped into the decontamination area and ripped off his air mask and gloves, cursing.

"How the hell am I supposed to get any work done with these interruptions?" he paused, noticing Cole.

"Do I know you?"

Cole remembered the face but could not place the name.

"Cole Cameron."

"Sure, Cole Cameron. I remember you. Man, I got my first certification from your training more than ten years ago. Brian, Brian Smith." He waved at Cole not wanting to extend his sweat-soaked hand.

"Oh, what a small world," Cole said, "I'm with the government now, and I was hoping you would lend me a suit and an air pack and let me take a quick look around."

"Would you be willing to sign a release form?" Smith asked.

"Certainly," Cole replied.

"Alright then, Mark give this man a suit. I'll grab a GX meter to take some airborne readings while we're in there."

Cole donned the suit and air pack. *Just like riding a bike*, he thought, his muscle memory proving true to form from hundreds of experiences in his previous life. Smith changed out his air bottle and was ready to escort Cole into the hot zone.

Before putting the mask on for the final tape up he said, "There's some nasty shit in there, are you sure you don't want to wait another day or two?" Cole had already taped up and gave the whirl sign with his index finger to signal *'let's go.'*

Smith led the way through the debris; around the main lobby that was now a roofless concrete filled pit. Cole could see the east wing entrance completely collapsed, providing easy access into the hot zone.

"Watch your head!" Smith shouted through his mask. Cole ducked under rebar protruding from a concrete slab. He could see the response crew working to neutralize chemical hazards. *What a job*, Cole thought seeing hundreds of vials and containers burned and liquid oozing from some overheated canisters.

Cole's protective boots sloshed through the water-soaked debris on the floor as he looked for the nerve gas vault that he had located on the blueprints in the command post. The crew was not working that far back yet, and the lighting was poor.

"Hold on, let me get a flashlight," Smith said and quickly returned.

Cole took the flashlight looking over the vault. It seemed intact.

"Has anyone gone in here?" Cole shouted through the mask to Smith.

"No. When we did our first assessment, I asked for the code, but the Roslin guys said they would handle the vault. They didn't think anything had been damaged. It looks in good condition to me," Smith said, checking seals on the door.

"I need to get in here," Cole yelled, trying to be heard over the loud generators and equipment behind them.

"Can you have your guy at the trailer give the two-way to FBI Agent Jacobs. I'll see if she can get the code for us."

"Hold on," Smith said as he radioed to the trailer.

Cole checked his air gauge. Smith yelled over, "thirty minutes goes fast when you're having fun!"

A couple of minutes later the two-way had Hannah's voice. "Cole, you there?" she said.

"Hannah, I need the code to the vault with the nerve gas. See if you can get it from Baxter," he muffled through the mask.

Cole leaned against the vault wall; he could feel his perspiration from wearing the suit and carrying the extra weight.

"We'll need almost five minutes of air to get past all the rubble and out of the hot zone," Smith reminded Cole, as they waited on Hannah.

"Have your guy get extra bottles ready just in case," he said, just as Hannah came back over the radio.

"Baxter doesn't have the code. Do you copy?" Hannah relayed.

"I copy. Tell Amy what we're looking for. She may have it with something she uploaded. I'll be out in a few minutes to change out my air bottle. Have her meet us at the decontamination area."

"Got it," Hannah said handing the radio back to Mark.

"Brian, you there?" they heard Mark's call on the radio and Cole handed it over to Smith.

"I'm here. We're coming back out, let's get a couple more bottles ready."

The two made their way out of the hot zone.

"I wish I had a hose line for you; it would save having to carry the pack and go back and forth. But the hoses are all tied up with the working crew," Smith said.

"No problem," Cole gestured now feeling his socks wet from the sweat.

"Man, how is the day crew handling this in the heat of the day?"

"Twenty minutes on and forty minutes off and a shit load of Gatorade," Smith replied.

The two stayed in the decontamination area, just clear of the demolished building entrance, as they waited for Amy. Eventually, they saw her approaching accompanied by Mark, the crew worker from the trailer.

"Did you get it?" Cole asked when she was still shouting distance away. Her face said it all. She had a big mischievous grin like a kid who had just gotten away with sneaking peeks of her Christmas presents.

She handed him the note with the code on it.

"You think it will work?" She asked.

"I sure hope so," Cole said taking the note. "Thanks. Great work," he grunted, feeling the weight of the air pack sliding into its brace strapped on his back. The extra weight of the fresh air tank came courtesy of Mark. Amy smiled, appreciating Cole's recognition and almost skipped her way back to the command post.

Mark watched her leave and mentioned how cute he thought she was.

"Yeah, I wish I had crew workers that cute," Smith said as he raised an eyebrow at the crewmember. Mark responded with a roll of the eyes and said, "That hurts man. I'm out of here," returning to the trailer.

"Let's go see if we can open this thing," Cole said as the two re-entered the hot zone.

They climbed through the obstacle course of rubble again and around drums the crew was using. Cole braced himself while stepping over a chunk of concrete as his eyes caught a bloody shoe with the mangled remains of a foot inside. He tapped Smith on the shoulder speaking through his fresh air mask, "Is that what I think it is?"

"I'm afraid so. The FBI team doesn't want us touching it. They're coming in once we downgrade from fresh air to cartridge respirators. Some spots are worse."

Smith looked at the meter he was using for readings.

"Do you think the keypad will work? There's no power over here."

"I'm guessing the vault was designed to run on a backup independent power source. The keypad should be tied into it," Cole said.

He was breathing heavy by the time they got back to the vault. He entered the code. The sound of a vacuum release was heard as the door slowly opened. Cole gave a *'thumbs up'* to Smith, indicating his victory.

Smith then stuck the wand of the GX meter through the doorway to take an initial reading and motioned Cole in.

"Wait here, I just need to take a quick inventory," Cole yelled through the mask as he took the GX meter with him.

Inside the vault, he did a quick survey of all the contents, wanting to ensure that none of the canisters appeared damaged from the blast. He waved the wand over the containers, shelf after shelf. He then focused on the inventory of VX.

Everything seemed in place but one shelf labeled 'Y44', which had over a dozen empty half-liter canister holders. The empty holders didn't alarm Cole, but he thought the label was suspiciously vague, giving no chemical reference. Cole sat the GX meter down and took digital photos of the entire room, racing against the air running out of his tank.

Smith pounded at the door and held up his air gauge, signaling their need to leave before the air expired. The alarm bell that was meant to indicate five minutes of air remaining began sounding off. One last snapshot and he left the room, entering the code again to seal the vault shut.

"Come on let's get out of here!" yelled Smith. "You'll get my ass fired if something happens to you."

"We don't want that to happen," Cole acknowledged as he followed Smith out with both alarm bells ringing. They hastened their exit going through the decontamination station and removing their gear.

Mark scolded them.

"You guys were cutting it a little close."

"You two sound like an old married couple," Cole joked as he placed the camera in a plastic bag and removed his suit revealing his soaked shirt and pants. As he stepped back into his street shoes, he noticed the women waiting on him outside the command post. The coolness of the desert night suddenly hit Cole's wet clothing, giving him a chill.

Back at the post, Cole cut a small opening in the plastic bag and plugged in the wire to transfer the images to Amy's laptop.

"Alright we're done," Cole said, to an exhausted group. He, however, was energized by the physical activity.

The FBI agent reached for the camera.

"I'm afraid it's contaminated now. Sorry," Cole said taking the bag with him and discarding it into a drum at the decontamination station.

"Cole!" Hannah protested as they got in the rental car. "You could have told me it was going to get wasted."

On the drive back, Cole was trying to shake the chill he felt. Amy noticed it from the back seat.

"Cole you're soaked. Are you going to be alright?" she asked.

"Yeah, I'm fine. I just need to warm up maybe get something to eat."

"Get something to eat?" Hannah objected. "It's almost three in the morning," she said, turning to give him her look of disgust at the thought. "But I do have to say this nightlife suits you well. I mean look at you. You're like a kid at Disney World."

"I agree," Amy said, "I don't think I've ever seen this persistent grin before."

"No, it's more like a goofy smirk," Hannah corrected as the two took turns poking fun at him.

Cole just laughed it off, enjoying the attention of his two female associates. Some of his new-found energy had rubbed off on them as they caught their second wind.

"Look there's Denny's. They're open twenty-four hours,"

Cole said as they drew near the city.

"We are not going into a restaurant with you soaking wet!" Hannah asserted.

"Yeah, the hotel has a list of places that'll deliver, we can get something to share, and you can give us the rundown," Amy advised.

"So, it wasn't the thought of food that disgusted you, it was the thought of being seen in public with me," Cole said, verbalizing his realization.

"Exaaactly," Hannah's response dragged out.

As they reached their floor, Cole suggested they meet in fifteen minutes, giving him enough time to shower.

"Why don't you guys go ahead and order us something. I'll get cleaned up and come over, is that OK?" The usually self-conscience Cole decided to let his guard down.

"Sure. We can use my room. We'll see you in few," Amy said.

Shortly after his shower, Cole knocked at the door. He dressed in jeans and a blue tee shirt, and the girls were both in tee shirts and yoga pants.

As he entered the room with his two female associates, he became aware of how it might look. It made matters worse when the food arrived, and the young delivery guy gave Cole a look of *'you, lucky dog.'*

He must think I'm living out every man's fantasy right now, Cole thought with a mix of embarrassment and machismo. *What the hell, let him believe it*, Cole concluded, choosing the latter sentiment.

"Oh brother," Amy said turning her nose up at the food delivered.

While the food was not very appealing to his appetite, the truth was that Cole was still a starving man. Not famished for food, but the company of friends. His soul's craving was for female companionship.

His participation in this operation had opened his mind to imagine that perhaps happiness was a possibility with the right purpose and the right person. *Focus*, Cole thought, asserting control over his wayward mind.

They talked about the operation and their plans to start the next day around nine o'clock, giving them a few hours of sleep. As time went on and their energy wore down, Amy's eyes closed shut as she succumbed to her fatigue.

Hannah and Cole sat silently and intimately gazed at each other, speaking the language that can only be communicated with the eyes. Cole wondered if she felt as attracted to him as he was to her. He wanted so badly to reach out to her, to quench the yearning that was building inside of him. Instead, he reminded himself again, *Focus* and sighed, "Guess I'd better go."

CHAPTER 11

Tucson, AZ

The sound of the cell phone ringing wrecked the deep sleep Cole was experiencing. He looked at the clock on the nightstand. 6:57 AM. Just a little over three hours of sleep for the staggering Cole. He felt the stiffness in his shoulders from his work the night before. *I'm getting too old for this shit*, he groggily muttered, as he answered his phone with a rough morning voice.

"This is Cole."

"Hey Cole, it's Jason. Hernandez and I are headed over to finish up at Roslin headquarters. Do you need anything from us?"

"Yes," Cole cleared his throat. "I was going to call you later. See if Bremen can get you information on a 'Project Y44'. I'd like to know the chemical components of it."

"Yeah, I got that from Hannah," Albright said.

"You spoke to Hannah?"

"Yeah, I called her first. I just got off the phone with her, and she said you wanted me to call ASAP."

"Oh, she did, huh?" Cole had to chuckle at Hannah's need to share the misery of interrupted sleep.

"Thanks, Jason, see you when you get out here," he said with his voice gaining clarity.

Since he was already up Cole took care of some administrative work that was overdue and reported to McCune the mission status, including the meeting with Clarisse and that he disclosed Ramsey's activity. He could tell

McCune was getting anxious, but also suspected she was holding something back when it came to Grant Ramsey.

It was 9:45 before his co-workers knocked at the door to say they were ready to begin the day. This time all three wore sunglasses.

"We've got to find coffee and quick," Amy said in her zombie-like state.

Cole collected his things, and they drove through the main streets looking for a coffee house. Soon they spotted their target and Hannah quickly whipped the car into a parking space. The two moved like drug addicts anxious for a fix. Cole stayed in the car but changed his mind.

"Amy, grab me a cup of green tea!"

While the women were ordering their coffee, Cole called Clarisse to meet with her again. He wanted to find out more about 'Project Y44.'

"Project Y44?" she repeated his question. "I'm not sure what that has to do with anything. Unless..." She stopped herself. "Cole I've got another call, it's Mr. Garrison, Chief of Security. Can you hold for a second?" Before he could reply she had switched over to the other caller.

Cole wanted to tell her not to let him know that they had met. He hoped she would use discretion.

After a couple of minutes, Clarisse was back on the line.

"Sorry Cole. Mr. Garrison wants to meet with me before I'm scheduled to meet with the FBI. I called them as you suggested, but they can't see me until 1:30 this afternoon. Somehow Mr. Garrison found out about it and wanted to know why I requested an earlier meeting."

"What did you tell him?"

"I told him I had requested an earlier meeting because of some family matters."

"Good, did he seem to believe you?"

"I think so, but he still wants to see me before I go. I'm scheduled to meet him for lunch. Even if I wanted to, I don't know if I can keep information from him. I have to admit I'm intimidated by him." Cole heard her anxiety through his cell phone just as Hannah and Amy re-entered the car.

"Listen, I think you need to go directly to the FBI." Hannah looked over her sunglasses at Cole.

"I have an FBI agent with me right now, Special Agent Hannah Jacobs. Where do you live, we'll come right over?"

Clarisse agreed and gave directions to her house located in a suburb of Tucson. As they drove through the city, the bright sun reflected off the car windshield. The upper-middle-class neighborhood carried the usual array of different vehicles in driveways.

"You're carrying your weapon, right?" Cole asked Hannah. The question seemed to be a strange contrast to their surroundings.

"Yes, always." Hannah calmly replied. "And you?" He shook his head with a positive response.

"Do you think Clarisse is in danger?" Amy asked from the back seat.

"She's certainly frightened, and something is going on here that we can't see yet."

Cole recognized Amy's anxiety, so he tried to calm her down.

"Look, it's probably nothing. This woman has had a lot happen to her in the last few days. It's understandable for her to be shaken."

His words seemed to reassure Amy, but Cole was upset at himself for not trusting his gut. His instincts continued to nudge at him that things were off.

"Here it is," he said recognizing the street address. They pulled into the empty driveway. Hannah did a quick weapon check, and Cole suggested Amy stay in the car.

A housekeeper answered their knock at the door. Her broken English was hard for them to understand. Cole tried his basic Spanish skills that proved equally difficult for comprehension. Clarisse was not home, but he didn't know why. He tried her cell phone, but it went immediately to voice mail.

Then the words clicked for him.

"School and emergency" he translated. "Where is the school?" Cole asked in Spanish. She replied in Spanish with greater speed and more detail than Cole could grasp.

"This has got to be more than a coincidence. Clarisse would have called me."

He tried with the housekeeper again.

"Where is the school?"

"I'll find out," Hannah said quickly dialing on her phone. After going through a couple of transfers, she was finally working with someone who was retrieving the information she needed.

Cole was trying to calm the housekeeper down as his eyes surveyed the photos of the family.

"Got it. Academy of Tucson Middle School on 22nd street," Hannah said as the two rushed back to the car.

"I'm driving," Cole demanded. Hannah tossed the keys to him.

"What's wrong?" Amy asked as they entered the car.

Cole abruptly shifted the car in reverse and peeled out of the driveway. As he was looking over his shoulder, he directed Amy to call the local police and instruct them to pull over any vehicles registered to Johnson's address and to get a description of the car.

Slamming on the brakes, he noticed Hannah, busy on the phone, had not buckled up. It startled her, as Cole reached over across her body grabbing the seat belt and fastening it tight against her. She smiled at his thoughtfulness as the tires squealed again.

"Don't worry about me, I'll be fine back here," Amy said rolling her eyes as she dialed her phone.

"Do you even know where you're going?" Hannah shouted as they sped along.

"22nd Street, right? We just crossed fourth, so I just need to know which way to go on 22nd when we get there."

Hannah pushed the microphone button on her phone:

"Siri, I need directions to Academy of Tucson Avenue Middle School."

Siri replied, "I'm sorry, I didn't get that."

Cole yelled as he jerked his head toward Hannah.

"Are you serious!"

Hannah shouted back, "Cole, just a minute!" She resorted to typing the school into the search bar on the phones map app.

Amy shouted from the back seat. "The police want to know who the hell I think I am to make such a request."

"Give me the phone," Hannah said as she exchanged phones with Amy. "Give him the directions…Hello!"

Cole couldn't keep up with them as they were both talking at the same time.

"Which way? Which way?" he shouted twice waiting for an answer as he came to 22nd street.

"To the right, to the right!"

"It's about a mile and a half up the road."

Hannah had finally spoken to the appropriate person who assured her they would contact her if they found the vehicle registered to Clarisse Johnson.

"She's in a blue Yukon," Hannah said as they each peered through the windows looking for signs of her car. Cole tried her cell phone again, still no answer.

They arrived at the school.

"I'll check with the school office and see if she's been here," said Hannah.

Cole nodded. "We'll keep an eye out for her here." He and Amy stood outside the car as Hannah made her way to the office.

After a short time had passed, Cole saw Hannah returning to the car shaking her head *'no.'*

"She's hasn't been here," she hollered out as her cell phone rang. She stopped to answer the call. Cole could not hear the conversation, but he did not like her body language as he saw her shoulders drop.

She walked back to Cole and Amy, who were now standing side by side.

"They found Clarisse in her Yukon at the intersection of

Kenyon Drive and Pantano Road. She's dead. Witnesses are saying that it looked like an attempted carjacking. They need us over there right away."

Cole's heart sank as he leaned back against the hood of the car. Amy held her hand over her mouth in disbelief and began wiping her eyes under her sunglasses. Cole reached out to console her, and she instinctively fell into his arms.

He looked at Hannah, who had her head down, looking at the ground.

"Tell your people to plow through Roslin. This was not a carjacking. They should start with Garrison." Cole gritted while holding Amy.

Hannah nodded.

"Let me have the keys I'll drive."

She took Cole's hand that was firmly gripping the keys while resting against Amy's back. He didn't realize how tight he was holding them until Hannah gently worked to pry them out.

After she had gently unlocked his grip, she left her fingers intertwined with his a few seconds. They looked into each other's eyes with tenderness until Amy stepped back breaking apart their interlocked fingers and their temporary yet intimate connection.

Hannah pulled the car up to the curb behind a squad car parked on Pantano Road. The silence that they had submitted to on the short drive to the scene was invaded by the noise and sounds of an active crime scene.

Police officers were controlling the growing crowd from the usually quaint neighborhood. Constant chatter was heard over the police radios, and an occasional chirp from a siren signaled a new vehicle needed to get through.

From where they were parked the Yukon Clarisse had been driving was in partial view. The driver's door was wide open. The three sat in the car for a moment, trying to brace themselves for the inevitable.

"Amy, why don't you stay here?"

Amy never said a word, but stepped out and leaned against

the back of the car facing away from the scene.

Cole and Hannah found the officer in charge who had more questions than answers. He continued questioning the two attempting to add up the pieces of his investigation. Cole was growing impatient with the officer, whose slow deliberate method, was adding to his anxiety.

Finally, the officer divulged some information, which he directed primarily to Hannah, "Well, witnesses are saying that two men pulled up next to her while she was stopped here at the traffic light. The passenger opened the victim's car door, there was a brief struggle, and then he shot her twice. One in the chest and one to the head."

Cole glanced over to see Clarisse's limp body still slouched over the center console. As the officer continued sharing other details Cole's glance became a stare. He felt a growing pain in his chest as his eyes teared up. He couldn't help thinking about how he had been with this person just a few hours earlier.

It was the first time he had seen death this tragic and this close. It was his lesson on the frailty of human life, and it would be a lesson he would not forget. He felt enraged that someone could so callously have taken this mother's life. Then he was overwhelmed by a different emotion. It was the haunting sense of guilt, and it would refuse to be quickly evicted from his heart.

"I'm trying to understand why you guys were looking for the victim. I need to know why you had requested a search on the vehicle," the officer continued.

"This was not a carjacking," said Cole.

Hannah stepped between Cole and the officer.

"I've got it, Cole. I'll take it from here. You should check on Amy."

Cole nodded. He joined Amy, standing behind at the back of the car away from the scene. They stood speechless leaning their backs against the trunk of the car that was slowly heating up from the desert sun.

"What's going on here, Cole?" Amy finally spoke for the

first time since they had received the call.

"I don't know. But someone will pay."

As Cole sent those words into the air the new tenant of his heart nudged him. *Maybe I'm responsible for this*, he thought, *I should have done something last night.* Hannah's sudden presence triggered the verbalization of his thoughts.

"This is my fault. I should have taken Clarisse to the FBI last night."

He spun around to look again at the scene for which he felt responsible. He then glanced at the Pantano Road sign next to their car.

"If I came up Pantano Road instead of racing out of there, maybe we could have stopped this." Cole continued on the trail of self-doubt.

"Cameron!" Hannah shouted using his last name for emphasis.

"Stop it. You can't do this. You can't start down this path. You had no way of knowing this would happen."

Cole went to turn away, but she grabbed his arm.

"Look. There are a dozen different routes you could have taken to get here. There's no way you could have known." Now she was pointing her finger at him. "You told her to go *directly* to the FBI. If anything, I should have insisted on seeing her last night."

Hannah paused to catch her breath and find a calmer voice.

"Look I'm screwed up enough as it is, let's not go down this path."

At that point, Cole knew that the burden he carried was his to bear alone. He wanted to harness his mouth to avoid causing Hannah from feeling the weight of guilt he carried.

"Officer Ramirez will need a statement from you. I don't know how much you want to share, but I'm going to call HQ and get one of the FBI agents working at the Roslin site to head over and take over the investigation."

CHAPTER 12

Washington, DC

The wheels of the Cessna Citation greased the runway at Regan International at 12:30 AM. The team looked beat, in addition to the troubling events, the long flight and time zone change took its toll. As the jet taxied to the ramp, Cole suggested a later than usual start at CTC.

He turned to Hannah and said, "Would you like to join me tomorrow morning for a trip out to Reston? I want to check in on Grant Ramsey's ex-wife. See if she has any additional information."

"Sure, what time?" Hannah asked.

"I'll text you a place and time in the morning. I'll see if I can catch his ex on the phone first and make sure she's available."

"Sounds good."

The next morning Cole confirmed a late morning time with Grant's ex-wife, Rachel. He stopped by the park and saw there was nothing new at the dead drop. He met Hannah at a coffee shop near the CTC office. After getting her coffee, she climbed into the Range Rover.

"Wow. Nice car. I must be with the wrong agency."

"Hey, it's nearly four years old and is part of the benefit of having part of my career in the private sector."

The two continued small talk on the drive before shifting to the project at hand. Cole explained that he was hoping to learn more about Grant's situation from Rachel but knew it was a long shot.

He was right. The time at Rachel's was a complete bust. She shared that other FBI agents had already been by to question her, but she agreed to meet with Cole since he had worked with Grant before. According to her, she had not heard from him since Christmas when he had called to speak to his kids, and that was just fine with her.

The only benefit Cole saw from the short trip was alone time with Hannah. He quizzed her about small-town roots and questioned why she did not have the typical southern drawl. Turns out, her mother was an educator at a college and was very strict about proper grammar and pronunciation.

Back at CTC, the team had moved to one of the larger mission rooms to act as their war room for project Titan Shield. Jason Albright continued to coordinate with his FBI counterparts working the Roslin investigation, sifting through chemical sheets and data while Amy Wiggins, the communications specialist, coordinated with the NSA, looking for clues with cyber chatter.

Amir Abdullah had joined the team at CTC and worked closely with Amy parsing threads of communication. Raymond Hernandez of Homeland Security seemed to disappear at long intervals but had briefed the group on border issues.

Cole Cameron and Hannah Jacobs joined the team in the war room, and everyone was working to synthesize all of the information and data coming through.

As the hour grew late, a knock at the glass door revealed a friendly face for Cole. Darryl Capps was back in town and motioned for Cole to walk with him. The two meandered down the hall, and Capps patted Cole on the back.

"Great work setting up the Abul takedown. You were spot on."

"But a little late I'm afraid," Cole sighed.

"Dude, there's no way you could have seen that coming. Hell, no one did."

"Where are you headed?" Cole asked, realizing he was blindly following Capps.

"The cafeteria! Man, I'm starving for some good ol' American food!"

"Sorry, I can't join you, we're knee deep in shit back there and have nothing for the briefing with McCune."

"Bullshit! Man's gotta eat!"

"Nope. Gotta go my friend." Cole said turning to walk away.

"I need to get you back out on the range. Keep your skills sharp. That stuff in there is going to eat you up and then spit you out soft as Jell-O."

"Yeah...yeah," Cole waved his hand as he walked back toward the war room.

"We might have something," Amy said as Cole entered back into the room. She threw up chatter posts on the large screen for all to see.

"You know we've never been able to get a solid lock on Hasni's location."

Amir jumped in and pointed to the Arabic text boxes cascading down the screen.

"So, this is a group chat of numbers pulled from Abdul Mahib's cell phone that we've been surveilling. Seems innocent enough, they are chatting about the best places to get dalma. It is a Middle Eastern dish. It needs to be served fresh and is great with lamb or juicy vegetables."

"OK. I'll keep that in mind on my next trip to the middle east," Cole said growing impatient.

"Well, I know it may be a stretch, but if you look at this message here, the sender uses the Arabic pronoun 'huw(a)' or 'he' in English instead of 'hadha' or 'it.' He is stating that we will plan on having 'him' here in his town next Sunday. What if dalma is code for Hasni?"

"It could just simply be a typo or bad grammar, right?" injected Albright.

"Could be," Amir said with greater excitement. "But Amy and I started to cross reference locations with earlier references to dalma and found that on two other occasions we had HUMINT on the ground suggesting Hasni was at the respective places that correspond with the posts.

"Including Ash Shihr," Amir's voice trailed at the end, and Cole knew why. Ash Shihr was the place of Grant Ramsey's last mission. It ended his career.

"Also," Amy added, "the locations are suspect. Would you really brag about serving dalma in Sayhut?"

She paused then continued, "according to the post, the meal will be Sunday afternoon."

"What's today?" Cole asked truly unsure.

"It's Thursday...well make that Friday morning now" said Albright.

"Guys, this is good," Cole said trying to contain his excitement. "Do we know what time dinner will be served on Sunday?"

"15:00 Zulu."

"That's 10:00 here and 18:00 in Yemen?"

"Correct."

"OK. Let's get a jacket ready, and we can brief McCune first thing in the morning. In the meantime, Amy, see if you can get the logistics going to get Darryl Capps assigned to us. He can join Amir and me to get over to Riyadh Air Base, Saudi Arabia.

"Then we will need CENTCOM to put us on the Regan if it is still out near the Gulf of Aden. We'll probably need to helicopter in close to the town."

"You'll be cutting it close on time. Fourteen to fifteen-hour flight to Saudi Arabia, then another three to four to get on the ship, set up with the Seal Team and run the ops?" Amy voiced her concerns about the logistics.

"Yeah, it'll be tight, so let's line it up, so we are ready to go when we get clearance. You sure you don't want just to have CENTCOM set it up with a Seal Team?"

"Look, no one knows more about Hasni than me. I need to be there when we grab him."

Hannah stood up and stretched.

"Since Jason and I are the domestic grunts we'll keep working Roslin with our teams in Arizona. But I think I should get up to New York and see if I can't find, Grant Ramsey." Now officially listed as a 'person of interest,' Ramsey was being sought for questioning by the FBI while McCune had designated a team of her own to hunt him down.

Albright contributed. "And I'm still sorting through the chemical data sheets from Roslin, I know you were focused on their VX project, but from what I see, they have all the precursor elements needed for others as well, VR and even that horrific Russian cocktail known as 'Novichok.'"

"I know, but the only thing in the vault that was empty was the Y44 containers. I think the containers had sensors on the bottom so there should be some data feeding to a status report of date, time, weights, temperatures, and things like that."

"Yeah, I was working down that path with all of the data we got when we were at Roslin, but there are a lot of corrupted files."

"Yeah, someone tried hard to scrub the system. It's going to take some time to reconstruct them," Amy said.

"Alright, look, I know it's late," Cole paused looking for Hernandez, then realized Raymond deserted them some time ago." Amy and I will finish the jacket for our briefing. Shouldn't take us much longer and you all can get on out so we can be somewhat coherent in the morning for our presentation."

Friday morning came very early, but the team methodically walked through their intel and hypothesis about Hasni's scheduled visit near Sayhut. McCune was hesitant but dialed Kingman's assistant, and in a few short minutes, the Director was on a video conference with them.

The team presented their findings a second time. Kingman was more decisive than McCune.

"Good, I'll get with CENTCOM, and we'll set up a drone strike and blow the bastard away."

"I think that would be a mistake, sir," asserted Cole. "Our theory is that Roslin was the first step and we are potentially looking at additional threats. Getting HUMINT at the location and snagging him alive would offer us the best chance of knowing what we're up against."

"I appreciate your take on it, but I know the President is facing political pressure to make a statement and a show of force against these sons of bitches."

"I understand sir, but if we miss this opportunity, we may just be striking a match. I mean, I don't think we can afford another Ash Shihr type incident. We should at the very least have visual confirmation on the target."

Kingman held up his hand interrupting Cole.

"Ash Shihr was a shit show, no doubt, and we have had to deal with that fallout, but I know this President, and he will want to push this so that he can interrupt the evening news declaring his victory to the world."

Kingman shuffled in his seat in front of the camera, processing his thoughts.

"That leaves about forty-eight hours to get him or the information you need, because I can promise you this, that airstrike will come, and you better be the hell away from there when it hits. I'll authorize the mission with that forty-eight-hour window, so get to it."

The monitor went blank, and McCune turned to Cole and sternly warned, "Don't screw this up," as she left.

"Copy that."

The phone in the room rang, and Amy answered. After a few seconds, she stretched the receiver toward Cole.

"Hmm…it's for you, Cole. It's Capps, and he is pissed. He just got back and was headed out on vacation."

"Tell him I'll see him on the plane."

"This ought to make for a very long flight for us," chided Amir in his Arabic accent.

Hannah joined Cole as he left the building.

"You be careful over there."

"Yeah, you watch your back too."

***

West Los Angeles, CA

Abu al-Himyari sat in the small and dimly lit apartment room surfing the TV channels searching for news coverage of his victorious blow to his sworn enemy. He smiled when he finally landed on a prolonged segment covering the Roslin event. He relished the media coverage as it hyped up speculations of additional attacks. A bright light broke through the dark room from the window.

"Close the blinds!" al-Himyari demanded.

"I'm just checking the front of the building, Abu," replied the young man as he obeyed the command.

"It is the same as it was the last time you checked."

Al-Himyari had become increasingly frustrated with his nephew over the last few days. Despite his constant reassurance the young man's nervousness and anxiety had him doubting the young man's ability to carry out his task when the time came.

It had been a week since Abu al-Himyari had initiated the first phase in a chain of events designed to unleash fury on the infidels. Hasni had handpicked him for this role, telling him that he was destined for greatness by the hand of Allah.

Surely, Allah's hand was upon him. After all, the border crossing looked derailed just when the Native American policeman showed up. *'Allah's providence,'* al-Himyari reasoned. And the attack at the Roslin Research Center could not have gone any better.

Hasni had promised the infidels would pay for the pain and suffering they inflicted on the believers. Both he and al-Himyari were well acquainted with suffering. After losing his wife and daughter, in what was considered collateral damage by the U.S., al-Himyari found a channel for his rage in Hasni's rhetoric and mission.

Hasni was not just a leader in words but also in action.

That is what he admired most. Even though Hasni was a man of action, he had proven disciplined as well. Strategically placing cells in the U.S. in crucial places and patiently waiting for the right opportunity to deliver a decisive blow.

Hasni was not merely seeking to strike fear in the hearts of the people. Instead, he desired the utter destruction and fall of the United States, but not before he delivered a personal message to those he held responsible for his loss.

When the godless Russians began discussions with Hasni, al-Himyari had objected. He felt they were as bad as the U.S. But Hasni had convinced him that only by working with the Russians would they realize their ultimate goal. To him, they were merely an instrument of war.

It was the Russians who provided them with information on Roslin and orchestrated the production of VX under the guise of a particular secret government project for Y44. It paved the path for Hasni's cells to deliver on his promises.

To prove their loyalty, they provided Hasni critical information on a covert operation in Ash Shihr. With that information, Hasni avoided capture and delivered a strike to the enemy.

"By the time they even know where to begin to look, Allah's vengeance will be felt by hundreds more," al-Himyari told his nephew as he turned the TV off.

"Let's get back to work."

The two moved to the kitchen, donned their chemical suits and masks and continued working with the precursor materials in their makeshift lab. Al-Himyari's nephew carefully applied the skills and knowledge he had gained as a chemical engineering student at UCLA. He went to the fridge and carefully removed the last canister labeled Y44.

***

Santa Monica, CA

William Garrison leaned back in his home office chair, dejected and exhausted. Dealing with FBI agents, ATF, and state and local officials in Tucson, in addition to the emotional burden of the tragedy had taken its toll. Adding to the weight was Garrison's overwhelming sense of guilt.

What had begun as an easy ticket out of his financial woes had escalated into unforeseen horror with the loss of lives he had not anticipated.

Grant Ramsey had caught Garrison at the most opportunistic moment in his life. The middle-aged man, pushing sixty was over-leveraged, and he had counted on exercising his stock options, but that required a transaction event.

His Santa Monica home was nothing compared to some of his peers in Bel Air or Brentwood. Still, it was well beyond his reach. He was certain Roslin was destined to be bought by a competitor, but the deal had fallen through.

On his third divorce and the heel of a failed buy out of Roslin, his was ripe for the picking when Ramsey offered him a way out. Garrison wanted to believe that at any other time he would not have been so easily swayed.

It was not supposed to go down like this. Grant Ramsey assured him no one would be hurt. His role was merely to provide access to Roslin for two men who were working with Ramsey. *'Corporate espionage,'* he was told.

Then Ramsey required that he provide additional clearance for Frank Alvarez, the VP of Research and Development and place suspicion on Clarisse Johnson to get her reassigned. Now, they were both dead.

Garrison knew it was only a matter of time before someone would be knocking on his door and he would have to account for his role in the events. He scribbled a note on his desk then opened the desk drawer and removed a Ruger .38 Special.

He flipped the cylinder open and verified the hollow point bullets rested in the chambers.

Garrison thought, *Now, time to end this miserable bastard of a life.*

CHAPTER 13

The Gulf of Aden

On the long fifteen-hour ride to Riyadh Air Base, Capps behaved just as Cole expected. It was as if he had to go through all five stages of grief over the loss of his coveted time off. Cole ignored him and stayed focused on planning the operation before finally getting some sleep.

They left Andrews Air Force base at 15:45 Friday and landed in Saudi Arabia at 10:33 Zulu Saturday. Between the fifteen-hour flight and the time zone change, Cole felt as if his forty-eight-hour window had collapsed considerably. They were pushing it.

The aircraft taxied and stopped near a V-22 Osprey aircraft with its crew ready. Its Rolls-Royce T406 engines were already running. The team stepped off the plane onto the tarmac, then directly onto the V-22. They strapped themselves in just as the tiltrotor military aircraft did a vertical takeoff.

As an aviation enthusiast, Cole marveled at the technology of the Boeing aircraft. It had the combined performance of a helicopter and of a fixed-wing aircraft. It can function as a helicopter with its rotors in a vertical position. Once the rotors are converted to a horizontal position, it transforms into a turboprop airplane with high-speed and high-altitude flight capabilities.

The aircraft's route took them east of Yemen then back west once they were in International waters. By 14:40 Zulu the aircraft hovered over the USS Ronald Regan and began its vertical descent onto the aircraft carrier's deck. As the tires touched down, a Marine liaison greeted the team and escorted them to a briefing room.

A familiar gruff voice came from the behind them into the room.

"I don't know who I pissed off to get stuck with you again." Capps and Amir recognized the Captain's voice.

"Sorry, sir, but I was thinking the same thing," Capps replied.

"Sir, this is Cole Cameron, this is his mission." Cole and the Captain shook hands.

"You know, I'm not your friggin' water Uber!"

"Yes, sir!"

"He's messing with you Cole," Capps offered Cole relief.

"The hell I am! Anyway, the Bravo Seal Team will be in shortly, you all can start your meeting then. In the meantime, let Officer Burke know if you need anything. Get this done and get it done right so you boys can get off my damn ship."

"Yes, sir!"

The team connected with CENTCOM via satellite transmission. They met Sara Wang who would be their eyes from the sky and voice in their earpieces. She uploaded satellite images on the screen while Colonel Fetterman laid out the mission details.

The District of Sayhut with a population near twelve thousand sat near the coast and west below a desert mountain range. The target was located in the Northwest part of the city. They identified the infill and exfil spots about ten kilometers from the target as well as the backup plan. There was debate over the best squeeze spot for snagging Hasni, but eventually, that was settled.

Three inconspicuous vehicles and drivers, who were in country assets, would be waiting for them in the mountain range. The drivers would then head south toward the small city, dropping off one of the Bravo team members that would set up a sniper position in the hills for overwatch.

The choke point for grabbing the AIJB leader was near the

center of the town which meant the three vehicles would be required to go nearly a kilometer back through the town in route to their exfil location. It was not an ideal situation, but given the time constraints, it would have to do.

✳✳✳

Counterterrorism Center – Langley

It had been a flurry of activity in the Titan Shield war room. Amy Wiggins and Jason Albright each sifted through a virtual forest of data looking for crumbs of clues that could shed light on Y44 and the Roslin guests.

Additional resources of equipment and a small team of analysts were added to the group. Their mission had priority status. Even with the other resources and mission priority, the work was overwhelming.

Amy and Jason worked with Hernandez to prepare another briefing for McCune. Kingman was looking for constant updates to keep the White House informed. There were many moving parts. Cole, Amir, and Capps were in Yemen for their mission and Jacobs was in New York City looking for Grant Ramsey.

The FBI field office in Tucson along with sources in the investigation had started putting some of the pieces together. They were both surprised and nervous when Director Henry Kingman and Charles Thompson from the FBI entered the room with McCune.

Amy Wiggins pointed at the screens on the wall and gave a summary.

"The Bomber has been identified as Yasser Nassif. Suspected AIJB cell member and was an international student at ASU from Saudi Arabi. The FBI is working on his known associates."

Albright jumped in, "Thanks to the quick grab of

129

surveillance video footage we were able to catch this…"

Albright clicked the video feed of the white van and three suspects dressed in chemical suits going in after the blast and coming out with cases and leaving the parking area.

"Looks like Cole's theory may be right," he added. "They were after something. The bomb gave them entrance and disguised their real objective."

"What the hell is in those cases?" Thompson asked with frustration.

"We're working on that, sir, but our hypothesis is VX or some other agent."

"What about the van?" McCune asked.

"We were able to get a read on the license plate as it was leaving and the team ran it through the system and got a couple of hits from automatic license plate readers. The Tucson field team and State Police were able to narrow the search range with the ALPR's data and found the van about three miles off of Interstate 10, but it was burnt out."

"Any way to ID the three suspects?"

"We don't have any footage of them without their chemical masks on," Amy replied, "but, we know that Nassif had requested to speak with Bashar, one of the Roslin employees killed in the blast. Our team combed through Bashar's social post and found photos of his parents and sister from Yemen." Amy continued after a brief pause, "and they match the hostage victim photos Capps took in Al Mukalla when he grabbed Abdul Mahib. Our theory is that Bashar was being forced to assist AIJB."

"Shanelle, how much longer before we need to dial into CENTCOM?" Kingman asked his assistant.

"You have about forty minutes, sir."

"It's going to be a long ass day," Kingman grunted to no one in particular.

***

Sayhut, Yemen

They shoved Hasni in the back seat between Cole and Amir. The driver, Kallah Majid, swerved to avoid hitting a woman in the street causing Sanders to yell out. "Easy man!"

They raced to keep pace with the lead car that had Master Chief Baker, Trujillo and Darryl Capps with the other driver. Cole was seated on the passenger side in the back seat and turned his head around to see if the third vehicle with the remainder of the team was keeping pace.

Sara Wang's voice came through the coms.

"Bravo team, be advised we see lots of activity on the streets. It looks like they may be trying to set up roadblocks. Take your next left."

"Copy that," replied Baker. "Boys keep your eyes peeled." Corey Sanders of the Bravo Seal Team looked to Amir and Cole in the backseat. "Be ready. This may get hairy."

Even in the scramble to secure him into the vehicle Hasni remained stoic. The operation had been pulled off without a hitch up until now. The squeeze was made easier due to the fact Hasni preferred to travel with as small of a security detail as possible. It was a tactic to stay off the radar of spying eyes. This time it had backfired.

The convoy of cars made a left onto the main road leading out to the north end of the town. Cole looked across Hasni to Amir.

"Why is he so calm?"

Hasni said something in Arabic. Amir had a puzzled look on his face as the driver of their car suddenly stopped the vehicle. The lead car with Capps and crew continued ahead now about forty yards in front of them.

Sanders was yelling at the driver. "What are you doing?"

Wang was yelling over the coms. "You have multiple enemy combatant inbound."

Cole turned to look for the proximity of the third car only to see it driving in reverse as over the coms they heard, "RPG!"

A loud explosion erupted near the front of the first car as it lifted the car almost perpendicular off the ground. The blast violently shook Cole's car as a second blast hit toward the rear car.

Cole could hear the sound of shots fired as Sanders left the front passenger seat to rush to the aid of those in the front car.

Just as Sanders cleared the front bumper, the driver in Cole's car quickly turned a hundred and eighty degrees and shot Amir in the head. He swung his arm left to aim for Cole but before he could get his shot off the .40 caliber bullets from Cole's Glock 22 ripped through and over the seat back, the final one hitting the driver in the head and sending him into the afterlife.

Cole tried to collect himself. He saw Capps working his way back but appeared wounded. There were faint sounds over the coms, but he could not make them out as his hearing had been impacted by the close-range gunfire.

There was no sign of Baker, but Trujillo and Sanders were laying down gunfire. He looked to the rear and saw the third car had avoided the RPG but was cut off. Cole knew he needed to get in the fight, so he quickly shoved Hasni's bound hands up to the handlebar above Amir's body, and zip tied him.

He jumped out of the vehicle and shouldered his M4A1 in the low and ready position and took cover behind the engine block.

The fight was a cacophony fully automatic fire. The enemy had them pinned in from various positions. The thick smoke, debris, and dust filled the air. That along with Cole's adrenalin made his breathing difficult. Still, at this point, he could only hear muffled sounds over his coms.

He aimed at his first target and with two shots put him down. He saw more coming from the rear of the vehicle, so he positioned himself to the front and began to fire. Another one went down. *Why aren't they shooting back?* Cole thought *they're afraid they will hit Hasni.*

"Sanders! Your 9:00," yelled Trujillo. Before Sanders could react, he was hit twice.

Cole saw the shooter and sent a volley of fire putting him down. He loaded a fresh magazine and raced to Sanders who was bleeding from his left shoulder and hip. Bullets flew around them as Cole pulled Sanders to Hasni's vehicle for cover.

"I'm alright. Go get Capps," he said.

Cole came around the front of the car, fired at the movement to his right and loaded a fresh magazine. He saw Capps shooting and reloading in a prone position near the rear tire of the blasted first vehicle.

Trujillo had worked his way to a stucco wall and was firing in the opposite direction. The wall was getting whittled with the barrage of bullets from the enemy. His cover would not last long.

"Capps, I'm coming for you. Cover me," Cole yelled over his coms.

Cole sprinted a few yards, took a knee and shot at the enemy. Hurried again, took a knee and fired. Before making the last sprint, he heard Trujillo shout over the coms, "Get Baker out of the front seat, we'll cover you." *Hearings back, thank God.*

Cole reloaded again on his way to the passenger side of the front car where he saw the blood-soaked and burnt Baker lying on top of the dead driver.

Shots were pinging off of the hood of the car. He heard Wang over the coms calling out to the team's sniper, "Rooftop, Bravo six, rooftop." He looked through the busted-out windshield to find the shooter and instead noticed an RPG swinging toward his position from the rooftop directly in front of the vehicle. He struggled to pull Baker up. Another glance to the roof confirmed Cole's fears as the RPG shooter to aim at him. Then suddenly the shooter's head busted like a watermelon.

"Rooftop clear," Cole heard the sniper's voice over his coms. *Thank God!*

Cole finally pulled Baker out and threw him over his right shoulder.

"Moving." He called out over his coms, grunting his way toward Hasni's car through a wave of screaming bullets.

As he passed Trujillo's position, he took a hit to his armor on the left side of his back. He heard a loud thump and felt the pounding as if someone had hit him with a sledgehammer.

It knocked him to the ground. As he stumbled forward, he attempted to stop his fall with his left arm, but the fall with the weight of Baker jammed his shoulder back into its socket.

Baker's body fell over in front of him. Cole worked to catch his breath from the shot to his back. He struggled with the dead weight of the warrior's body but finally was able to put him onto his right shoulder again as pain shot down his useless left arm now.

As Cole struggled to get back up, a bullet ricocheted into his left thigh. *Just a flesh wound. Burns like hell, still able to move*, he told himself, trying to will his body into submission and lift himself and the two-hundred-pound Baker.

Then he felt Trujillo help pull him up.

"Get moving! I'll get Capps!" Trujillo yelled.

Cole was still twenty yards from Hasni's car and began to think this might be his last day. He grunted, struggling to keep Baker on his shoulder. Those final few yards seemed too far to Cole, but he eventually made it to Hasni's car placing Baker in the back seat. He gasped for air and heard other team members over the coms.

"We're coming up on your six. Watch the friendly fire."

Fighting to the rear had dissipated, as the rest of Bravo team had broken through and advanced toward Hasni's car.

The third car pulled in tight to Cole's position. The seal team dispersed laying down a fury of fire on the enemy. In less than two minutes the fight was over.

They threw their brothers in arms into the vehicles and the

two remaining cars stuffed with passengers alive and dead raced to the extraction point.

Medic kits were out, and bandages applied to the wounds. They tried to revive Baker in vain. Cole looked over to Amir's body and then at Hasni. The man he had studied, analyzed and dogged for nearly four years was finally caught. *But at what cost?* He thought.

Hasni stared back into Cole's eyes.

"Are you prepared for a long dark winter?"

"It's springtime in America, asshole!" Sanders yelled out before Cole could answer.

The team carried their dead and severely wounded onto the chopper first and then assumed a tight formation as Cole took Hasni by the arm leading him to the helicopter.

When they approached the chopper door, Hasni's head snapped forward, and blood flew out as he fell to the ground.

"Sniper fire!" was called out over the coms. The shot was not heard over the sound of the helicopter.

Cole instinctively squatted down and was still holding Hasni's arm when the captain's voice shook him out of it.

"Get your asses on board! We've to get out of here!"

Nearly 1,000 yards away the deadly Russian sniper laid motionless in his covered prone position. Peering through the scope of his rifle, he confirmed what he knew the moment he squeezed the trigger. His target was neutralized.

As they lifted off the ground, Cole stared at Hasni's body lying at his feet on the floor of the helicopter. One of the Bravo team members who had been in the third car threw a brown leather satchel in Cole's lap.

"You better hope there's something in there to make all of this worth it," he said glaring at Cole. "Fucking spooks."

"Shut the fuck up, Reed!" yelled Trujillo.

"This spook saved my ass!" Sanders added.

"Bullshit! A drone strike would have been cleaner than this shit," Reed continued.

"All y'all better shut up before I throw you out of this bird," Capps ended the argument holding the bandage on his right leg.

As the helicopter flew over the ocean waves, Cole sat in silence contemplating the day's events. He had witnessed death most violently and suddenly. Amir, Baker, and even Hasni.

And there was the thought of the lives he had taken. He put down at least three of the enemy in the firefight with the rifle, but the first one was different. The driver in the car was at close range. He was confident the memory of Kallah Majid's eyes, as life left his body, would forever haunt him.

CHAPTER 14

Counterterrorism Center - Langley

Amy Wiggins stole an anxious peek at the eight clocks on the wall to her right representing the current time in some of the major parts of the world. She knew the operation in Yemen was well past its scheduled completion. Even enough time for mission debriefing had passed, by her estimation. As each minute clicked off without news, she grew even more distressed.

"You're worried about them." Albright gathered.

"Guys, remember the Border Patrol agent killed a few weeks ago? It was all over the news." Hernandez said interrupting Albright and Wiggins.

"Yeah."

"Well, you know they originally thought that the suspect had been killed but later discovered it was the body of a tribal police officer. The suspect had escaped. One of the captured coyotes had given a description of the suspect, indicating that he was not Latino but believed him to be Middle-Eastern."

Hernandez continued reading from the report he was now holding.

"Here is the sketch that we have, can we run it through the software flux capacitor thing a ma jig and see if we get a match?"

"Absolutely!"

Amy grabbed the paper.

"Flux capacitor?" Albright asked in disbelief.

"Either he is exhausted, or the veneer is finally coming

down," Amy whispered.

Hernandez looked around the room, let out a loud sigh as if he had accomplished his great task for the day and wanted to leave while he was ahead. So, he did.

"No, it's still him." Albright shook his head in disappointment.

"Guys, you're going to want to see this," shouted an analyst in the corner.

"What is it?"

"Putting it on the big screen now."

The monitor showed breaking news coverage of a 'Roslin Executive found dead in his Santa Monica home. Victim of an apparent suicide.'

"You better let Hannah know," Amy suggested to Albright.

***

New York City, NY

Hannah Jacobs slowed the black sedan to a stop and looked across the street to the apartment building where Grant Ramsey reportedly lived. So far, her trip to the Big Apple had been very frustrating. Her visit to Vistacom, Ramsey's employer, had tied up most of her day.

After dealing with an overly resistant gatekeeper, she finally met with the Chief Legal Officer, but only after a long wait. It was Sunday, and the executive did not appreciate having to make his way into the corporate office on the day he typically would be off or working from home.

She learned that they had not had contact with Ramsey for a few days and the company had not been overly concerned because of his role and frequent travels. But most importantly, Hannah was surprised to learn that Vistacom did not have acquisition plans for Roslin Environmental.

She was scheduled to check in at Langley soon. She was anxious to hear about Cole's mission but wanted to see what the search at Grant Ramsey's had turned up.

As she worked her way up the stairs of the apartment building, she received a text for Albright that read, *'Garrison found dead in his home, looks like suicide.'*

'Wow, call you soon, headed into GR apt,' she typed.

Jacobs met two other FBI agents who were at Ramsey's apartment, searching for clues of his whereabouts. Much like his corporate office, his apartment was neatly arranged and appeared to be used infrequently. She rifled through folders in his home office desk, trying to understand his actions.

"Agent Jacobs," one the agents called from the living room. "Over here."

The agent pointed to an eight by ten picture of a sailboat. "Take a look behind it."

✳✳✳

Sitting outside in a dark sedan, Grant Ramsey and his female companion watched on their tablet as Special Agent Hannah Jacobs approached the hidden lens.

"She is getting too close," Katrina Nikolin pointed out to Ramsey.

Katrina Nikolin was a contradiction in so many ways; she could be as deadly as she was graceful, as intimidating as she was irresistible and as chilling as she was attractive. While she favored the blond look, she was often brunette, light brown and even a redhead, but always beautiful.

Recruited by the Russian SVR from an orphanage as a preteen, the thirty-two-year-old was more than beautiful. She was desirable, intelligent, and skilled in ways to kill her enemy. She spoke three languages; Russian, English, and Mandarin. She had mastered the art of seduction and was one of SVR's most highly prized assets planted in the U.S.

Katrina used her talents to acquire intelligence from a

broad range of victims. From comfortable soft target politicians to hardcore high-ranking military officials, her efforts produced a steady stream of valuable intel for her beloved country.

She understood what was at stake for her native land. For her country to survive and flourish, they needed to subdue the greed and power of the U.S. She proudly played her role in sifting away the advantages held by her enemy.

Over the last three years, Katrina had worked on Grant Ramsey, prodding him along to this point. He was a reasonably easy target due to a broken marriage, resentful of those in command, he had a growing appetite in materialism, and of course, his insatiable thirst for carnal pleasures.

Initially, she had used Ramsey for intel, but when her superiors realized his weaknesses, they plotted even grander plans for him. It was the promise of wealth, and that the two of them would be together, that ultimately flipped Ramsey.

She noticed Ramsey's concern as the FBI Agent had discovered the hidden camera.

"Not to worry. Our friends left something behind for them," the beautiful Katrina told Ramsey.

The tablet's screen revealed erratic movement as Hannah flipped over the photo frame to examine the back side with the hidden camera.

Inside the apartment, Hannah quickly turned to the other agents, "did you sweep this place?"

"No, the warrant..." before he could finish Hannah interrupted him.

"Get Out! Get out!" she shouted, dropping the photo frame.

Katrina pulled out a cell phone and smirked, "Bye, bye, bitch."

As she began to dial the number, Grant reached across, "This isn't necessary."

Hannah had pushed herself into the back of the agent nearest her, driving them toward the main door to the hallway.

"I'm afraid it is my love," Katrina said in her subtle Russian accent, "We have so much more to do."

She completed the dial. A second later, a loud explosion erupted from the apartment. Flames and debris shot out of the corner windows.

✳✳✳

Counterterrorism Center – Langley (Sunday Afternoon)

Charles Thompson and Nancy McCune returned to the war room. The usually cool and calm McCune seemed visibly shaken. They had watched the CENTCOM satellite feed of the operation in Yemen. It was like watching someone play a video game but not having a controller and knowing the images weren't animated figures, but real human beings.

"The operation failed on its primary objective. Hasni is out of play," she stated.

"What about the team?" Amy asked.

"We lost one of the seal team members, and three other Seal team members were injured. Also, Amir was killed, and both Capps and Cole are also injured, although not thought to be serious. In fact, Cole is headed back to DC, Capps needed additional care before returning."

The crowded room fell quiet.

"I need to know what assets we used on the ground."

"We had the three drivers, and we moved Pearl Fahimi there from Al Mukalla."

"Contact Pearl. See if she can help get us photos or intel of the dead as they move them for burial. We can start crossing names off of the list. And there should be a lot to cross off. Then run a cross reference check on previous assignments for all four of them to see if anything pops out at us. I'm certain they knew we were coming."

The thought sank in on the room, then the analysts

resumed their activities.

McCune forced herself to move on, pressing the team for updates.

"Speaking of cross-referencing," Albright said to Thompson and McCune, "I've been reviewing the data related to VX and Y44. It seems that the reports were manipulated…"

"…and digital files scrubbed," Amy added.

"That's right," Albright continued.

"Amy was able to reconstruct some of the files and what we have pieced together looks like Frank Alvarez, the VP of Research and Development and Sameer Bashar were falsifying reports and disguising the additional production on VX into Y44 inventory. Y44 is what Cole found missing at Roslin."

"How much are we talking about?" Thompson asked.

"I can't say for certain, but so far, looks like maybe fifteen pounds worth. But from the chemical profile, whoever snagged the Y44 would need to have or add a precursor material to activate it."

"How difficult is that to do?"

"Not too difficult, I'm afraid, especially for someone with a chemical background," Albright reasoned.

"What kind of impact are we looking at," questioned McCune.

"That much could prove lethal with direct contact for hundreds, but if made airborne then thousands," Albright concluded.

"Like, the movie, *'the Rock,'*" Thompson said.

"Yes, but the movie took some liberties, VX does not have the corrosive effect you saw with someone's face melting off. You simply die through asphyxiation."

"Oh, just suffocating, that's all." Amy rolled her eyes.

The FBI Director started to leave. "Keep me informed, Nancy."

Thompson's assistant stopped him and whispered something in his ear. "There's been another explosion," he said to the room. "Do you have a news feed in here?"

McCune motioned for an analyst to put the news channel on the big screen. Thompson's assistant handed him his phone, and he conversed with the party on the other end while watching the screen.

Amy gasped when she saw the screen flash *'One dead and two injured FBI agents in NYC explosion.'*

Albright went to dial Hannah Jacobs when Thompson offered more details. Hannah and the agent she had pushed out sustained minor injuries, but the other agent that was in the kitchen near the explosive device when it detonated, was killed.

Both injured agents had suffered a concussion and were being kept in a hospital overnight for observation. After sharing what he could about the blast, Thompson dismissed himself.

McCune remained behind and attempted to refocus the team. "The best thing we can do now for our friends is to keep working the problem."

Jason Albright excused himself and attempted to call Hannah, getting her voicemail instead. He then texted her, *Are you OK? Call me.*

The hours dragged into the evening. The events of the day had shattered the team. The stress of the job was pushing everyone to their limits. McCune responded the only way she knew how, she was a constant presence, hovering and prodding the team along as if her efforts would speed the process.

"Anything out of that folder?" she asked pointing to an icon on Amy's screen.

"Ma'am, I have a system for processing these…"

"Excuse me, Ma'am, you wanted to know when the President was about to speak," interrupted Charlie, her administrative assistant. They turned the news feed on the screen.

Amy rolled her eyes and whispered to Albright, "Seriously, she's killing me."

The President of the United States addressed the nation

trying to calm their fears. He stated that the bombing in NYC did not appear to be connected to the attack in Tucson. Investigations were underway, for both and the government would not rest until all responsible parties were held accountable for their actions.

Along those lines, the President proudly announced that Hasni had died during a raid by U.S. Navy Seal team and military advisors. Unfortunately, the U.S. had suffered casualties, but the leader of the AIJB was dead. Though the mission had been costly, it had been successful.

CHAPTER 15

New York City, NY

We do make a great couple, Grant Ramsey thought as he glanced from the bed to the mirror on the closet door of the hotel room. Katrina Nikolin lifted her head as she knelt on hands and knees in front of Ramsey as he grunted and pushed from behind her.

She knew she owned him as she caught his look in the mirror and gave him her sultry smile.

"Give it to me," she demanded.

Ramsey grabbed her hair at the back of her head, pushed her down to the mattress, and obliged her request. It drove him mad when she played rough.

When Ramsey finished, he stepped off the bed and spanked Katrina's bare ass. She laid there finally releasing her grip on the bed cover. She moaned and flipped her blond hair as she turned over to watch Ramsey, admiring his physique as he walked to the shower.

What a shame, she thought, knowing *all good things must eventually come to an end.*

She made her way to the shower, opening the glass door to join Ramsey. She took the hotel soap and lathered up her body, teasing Ramsey as she glided the bar over her curves. Just as he made a move to touch her, she pushed him back against the wall, keeping him at arm's length, letting the warm water cascade over her body as she caressed herself.

She loved the control she had over men. She had never failed in her missions to get any of them to do what she wanted.

Ramsey leaned forward unable to resist, but she leaned back and pushed him downward. Ramsey knew what she wanted and again sought to give her pleasure as she grabbed the hair on his head and pushed him down.

When Katrina's needs were satisfied, the two of them dressed and prepared to leave New York. They would drive to DC to avoid the extra scrutiny at the airports and train stations.

"Have you heard from Yemen?" she asked, referring to Ramsey's planted asset as he took the car keys from the valet.

"Not, yet."

"Shouldn't he have called by now?"

Ramsey looked at his watch as he pulled away from the curb.

"We're still in the contact window."

Ramsey maneuvered the vehicle through traffic until he was finally heading south on I95. Katrina turned the radio on searching for a news station and catching the beginning of a broadcast related to the apartment explosion.

> *Officials are saying that a gas leak caused the explosion that killed one person and injured four others as it ripped through quiet upper east side neighborhood earlier today. Police have not released any information on the victims, but we have other reliable sources stating that victims included FBI agents and that the tenant of the apartment was not present. At this point, the police will not confirm any of these reports, but we will keep you updated. Reporting to you live from the Upper East Side, I'm Tracy Wells.*

"I thought I would have gotten all three of them."

Katrina sent a quick text on her phone. Ramsey looked over as he drove.

"What is it?" he asked.

"Just checking to see if our timetable has changed."

"Hey, we've earned our fucking money!"

"Calm down, dear. You Americans can be so dramatic," Katrina said putting her hand on his leg.

"Besides, we still have unfinished business, love." She knew that Ramsey was not looking forward to his final deeds. "Then we will get out of this cold and sail to tropical islands. We will drink the fruity cocktails, and frolic in the sand." She moved her hand up his leg to his crotch distracting him from unfavorable thoughts.

Ramsey followed the airport signs for EWR, Newark airport in New Jersey. They parked in an open area of the long-term parking lot and waited for the right kind of car to arrive.

A BMW 328i pulled in the next row over and once the driver left, Ramsey clicked the fob of his high-tech device. It unlocked the vehicle and disarmed the alarm and GPS device. The two loaded their bags in the new car.

Ramsey pulled his black SOG-TAC Automatic knife out of his front pocket and with the push of a button, the small black blade flew open. He used the knife to pry the EZ Pass reader off of the vehicle and dumped it into a trash can on their way out of the parking lot. The two returned to I95 and continued their southbound journey.

As they crossed the Maryland state line, Ramsey looked at his watch, realizing the communication window with the Kallah Majid had passed. *Not a good sign.*

"This is it." Katrina pointed to the rest stop area.

Ramsey pulled over in the first rest stop, inside of Maryland. He opened the trunk of the car, Katrina grabbed her roller bag and headed to the restroom while he searched through his luggage bag for his stash of sim cards. He exchanged the sim cards on the burner phone and sat back in the front seat.

After retrieving the hidden package and changing, Katrina returned from the bathroom in her new disguise. She covered her blond hair with a wavy brunette wig and librarian type eyeglasses. The SVR agent had changed from her trendy short skirt with leather boots into a more modest business skirt, dress shoes and dress shirt with a jacket. She threw the large manila envelope in the front seat and rolled her bag back to the trunk.

As she sat back in the car, she received a text and then dialed the number.

"Yes." She listened to her instructions. "Understood."

She opened the large envelope emptying the contents on her lap — a new batch of IDs, passports, and credit cards.

"The Hilton Capital, room 915."

"What about the equipment?"

"It'll be waiting for us there."

"You should go change, Mr. Ronald Jenkins," she said referring to his new cover name and giving him a look at his fresh set of IDs.

"Really?"

A few minutes later Ramsey returned to the car wearing a brown-haired wig covering his sandy blond high and tight cut. The hairpiece went over his ears, sported a side part, and he had to wear thick-rimmed glasses and a thick mustache.

Katrina snickered as he sat in the car.

"I look like a damn porn star from the seventies!"

"Yes, my Ronnie, and you are well-equipped for that role."

Katrina hoped to appease the man's wounded ego.

✳✳✳

Counterterrorism Center – Langley (Monday Afternoon)

Cole Cameron walked into the war room at CTC and Amy shot out of her chair to give him a big hug.

"Easy, easy!" His shoulder was hanging in a sling, and his back was bruised.

"Sorry."

"No problem, where's Hannah?"

"You don't know?" asked Albright.

"I've been in the air for the last twenty hours, and McCune wanted radio silence. I just rode over with the detail that was transporting Amir's body. What's going on?"

"There was an explosion at Ramsey's apartment in New York when Hannah was there…"

Cole was stricken with panic. "What? Where is she, I need to go…"

"No, no, she's OK. She's on her way back here. She was released from the hospital earlier today. She'll be here within a couple of hours." Albright stood to calm Cole down.

After Cole settled down, Amy asked, "What happened out there?"

Cole handed her Hasni's leather satchel.

"I looked through his notes, but to be honest, I'm not sure my head was in the right place. Nothing stands out to me other than a few pages with numbers in a grid. Maybe you guys can pick up some clues."

"Well, while you were out, we made some headway on data."

"Alright, give me the rundown. Wait, on second thought, let me go check in with McCune and make sure I'm still authorized."

Cole was halfway serious. In his mind, his mission had failed, Amir and Baker were dead, Capps was injured, and all he had was a leather satchel to show for it. He knew they were compromised, but not sure how. And the hit on Hasni was professional.

As Cole knocked on McCune's office door, he entertained thoughts that his own agency could have placed that sniper there.

Cole was taken aback by the hospitality McCune extended. She poured two glasses of Scotch and offered one to Cole with a light toast.

"I know it was rough out there, and from what I understand you performed admirably and losing Amir…well, that is most unfortunate."

Cole nodded.

They spent nearly an hour in McCune's office reviewing in great detail the sequence of events of the mission in Yemen.

To his surprise, McCune was empathic and appeared genuinely concerned for her team members. She asked him about his wounds. Cole explained he felt fortunate, the ricochet had just grazed his left thigh, only a surface wound. He lifted his left arm in the sling showing he had movement.

The 7.62 caliber bullet from the AK47, fortunately, had hit his armor plate leaving a grapefruit size bruise. A couple of inches lower and there would have been severe damage done.

"Well, I'm glad you made it. Maybe you'll think twice before requesting field assignments," she said with a grin.

"Have you spoken to your daughter, Jess?"

Cole was surprised. He had no idea McCune cared or even knew anything about his personal life. His surprised look gave him away.

"What? Not what you expected from the cold-hearted bitch, huh."

Cole wasn't sure how to respond. Everything that came to mind seemed disingenuous.

"It's OK. A woman doesn't get to where I am, worried about what others think."

"Jess isn't aware of the injury, ma'am," he was finally able to muster.

"I think I've learned a little more about you, Cole Cameron. First, I underestimated you and second, I think you're one of the good guys."

McCune sipped from her glass.

Cole sat at the chair in front of her desk and placed his glass down on the coaster.

"Thank you for saying that, ma'am. I don't feel like a 'good guy' right now."

"I know. That is exactly what makes you one. You know some people lose their soul in a job like this."

Cole nodded.

"Speaking of losing your soul," McCune said shifting the conversation back to a more business tone, "we've kept an eye on Grant Ramsey since he left the Agency, well actually, since Ash Shihr.

"He pointed fingers at everyone else for that mission, but we suspect he played a role in its failure. He is good at his craft and hard to find and pin down, but we think he was turned by this woman."

McCune slid a picture of a beautiful woman across the desk.

"Her name is Katrina Nikolin. Russian. We believe she is with the SVR. Have you ever seen her before?"

"She looks vaguely familiar, but I think I would remember if I met her."

"Yes, you would think so, as beautiful as she is. But don't count on it, she is very talented at disguising herself and playing different roles and capable of blending in."

"So, if Grant Ramsey is working with the Russians, where does the AIJB come in?" Cole asked. "Do you think Russia would covertly sponsor the AIJB. I mean I know the basics, but Russian politics are outside my wheelhouse."

Cole knew that McCune had served as Associate Director of European Operations and was well versed on Russian threats.

"Well Cole," McCune said using Cole's first name for the first time, "not everyone in SVR leadership is happy waiting around to see if they can outlast the U.S. My experience tells me, there are those in influential positions that if given the opportunity, would send our country back to the stone ages."

"You know, Ma'am..." Cole started to say.

"Nancy, please," McCune said before catching herself. She glanced out the glass door behind Cole and added, "as long as we're in private."

Cole nodded.

"You know, Nancy, sometimes I miss my former life of naivety."

He stood to leave, and his face lit up as he saw Hannah Jacobs making her way to the war room.

"I use to sleep better back then. If you'll excuse me, I'll get back to the team."

"Oh, I almost forgot," She said motioning him back in.

She opened her desk drawer and pulled out two tickets.

"Director Kingman wanted you to have these as a way of saying *'thank you.'* He's inviting you and your plus one to the Charity Gala in a couple of weeks. A real who's who in the political landscape."

"Thank you, Ma'am, but it's really not my kind of thing. And we've got so much work to do, why don't you keep these."

"I already have my tickets, and yes, we have work to do, but we have multiple agencies with teams working around the clock shifts that will keep the ball moving forward."

"Take a couple of hours for yourself; it'll remind of what you're fighting for. Besides, I don't think you want to tell the Director of the CIA that you refuse his invitation."

Cole took the tickets and shook his head and feigned a *'thank you.'*

"This late in the game, you'll have better luck getting your plus one on the acceptance list if he or she already has security clearance. You know, maybe someone with the FBI."

Cole said nothing, just nodded and left the office. *Damn it! I've got to work on my poker face.*

CHAPTER 16

Counterterrorism Center – Langley (Monday Afternoon)

Walking into the war room, Cole saw a few folks gathered around Hannah Jacobs, attempting to comfort her. She was not having any of it.

He watched Jason Albright approach her but before he could get to her, she put her hand up to stop him and then addressed the entire room.

"I'm fine everyone! Yes, we lost an Agent yesterday. But it was not me. I am OK. So, can everyone just go back to doing your jobs, before someone else dies."

"Hannah," Albright protested.

"Not now Jason!" she snapped back.

Cole slowly walked up and stood quietly next to her, both were looking at the split screens on the wall. Hannah, sensed Cole's presence and turned to her right ready to snap at him also but noticed his left arm in a sling and stopped herself.

"What happened to you?" she asked softening her approach.

"I think yesterday, was a terrible day for both of us."

Cole reached out with his right hand and gently touched Hannah's bruised and bandaged left hand. She stood shocked as he looked in her eyes and then reached up and softly touched the scratch marks above her left cheek.

"I'm happy you're OK."

Cole moved back over to Amy's chair.

It took a couple of seconds for Hannah to move as she stood in shock watching Cole walk away.

She was truly conflicted. Cole Cameron stirred something in her that she thought she would never feel. She had sensed the attraction when they first met, but she was most surprised by the unique chemistry that kindled between them. It was more intimate than she had ever experienced before. But while the chemistry was undeniable, they were professionals, and he put her in a most awkward situation.

In front of everyone there, he had touched her hand and then, *my God, her face*. It wasn't that he had taken her hand, it was how he had touched her, looking into her eyes, as if seeing the most vulnerable parts of her soul. He might as well have tweeted to the world, *I'm really into Hannah Jacobs, everyone!* She had worked too hard and sacrificed too much to get to this point in her career.

She had chosen poorly in the past and was content to keep her relationships at a superficial level. *The deeper the relationship, the deeper the eventual hurt*, she had reasoned. Most men had been incapable of dealing with her commitment to the Bureau, at least none that she genuinely respected.

"Cole, can I speak with you in private for just a second?" Hannah asked motioning for Cole to follow her.

Desk buddies Amy Wiggins and Jason Albright grinned at each other.

They walked out of the war room and down the hall a bit, and Hannah abruptly turned and pointed back to the room.

"Why did you do that, back there?"

"What?"

"You know damn well, what! Do you know how hard it is for a woman to get to where I am, and how easily it can all be taken away?"

"Whoa. Whoa," Cole said holding up his functioning arm for surrender.

"I'm really sorry if my touch was unwelcomed. But here's the thing Hannah, we both lost people yesterday, and we both nearly died. That does something to you."

Cole paused and adjusted his arm in the shoulder harness. He cast his eyes down, thinking that perhaps he had pushed her away for good.

"Life is short. I mean, I just…"

"Just what Cole?"

"You need to know, when I heard about the apartment explosion, my heart sank. It was as if someone had sucked all of the air out of the room. Then, just a few minutes ago when I was in McCune's office, I saw you walk in, and my heart jumped in my chest," Cole said holding his chest with his right hand. "You understand, I mean it literally jumped!"

Hannah was speechless, but before Cole could say another word, she leaned up and gave him a quick kiss, more of peck really, on his lips, smiled and quickly walked back toward the war room.

Cole was now the one in shock.

"Wait…" he said, reaching toward her as she briskly walked away. He stood in the hall, uncertain of what just happened.

"But that wasn't a real kiss," he mumbled quietly to himself. *Was that a friendly kiss or was that an 'I like you too kiss?' What the hell? She just ran off. Ah, the smile is the key. Yeah, she likes me.*

Back in the war room, Cole kept looking over toward Hannah, but she was not making eye contact. He pulled up a chair next to Amy and Jason.

"Sorry, Cole, I know you didn't mean anything by it," Amy said.

"Yeah, sorry man," Albright added. "We've been through a lot. She's just really pissed right now. Man, I bet she really let you have it out there, didn't she?"

"You have no idea, Jason," Cole deadpanned.

"Well, while you were getting your ass chewed out for inappropriate behavior, we ran Kallah Majid's phone data through the system and found that he made a call to a burner almost immediately after he received instructions to meet up with the team. You should also know Grant Ramsey is the one that brought him in as an asset."

"When was that?"

"Just before the Ash Shihr, operation."

"That's how they knew we were coming." Cole shook his head with regret.

"What about the moleskin notebook in Hasni's satchel?"

"Still working on it, but so far the most interesting piece is the grid pages. There are five of them, each with thirty lines of four-digit codes in two columns." Amy shared the digital image version with the large screen in the room so others could follow.

"Maybe pin codes?" Someone suggested.

"Maybe."

"What's the Arabic headings on the pages?" Hannah asked as she walked over to join the discussion.

"Colors," Another Analyst replied.

"Really?"

"Yeah, we've got blue, green, red, yellow and black."

"Sinha and Walsh are working on the grids, seeing if there is something to decode there."

Amy pointed to the corner where the two analysts were sitting at workstations. They each waved back to Cole. It dawned on him that there were several new faces in the room since he had left for Yemen. *Good more resources.*

"We think it is somehow tied to the Hijra system calendar," said Sinha.

McCune entered the room, placing her hands on her hips, and gazed at the screens.

"Did we get the data from Pearl sorted out?"

"I'll have it on the screen shortly, ma'am," a young female analyst replied.

"Thank you."

Images of the assailants from the Yemen operation filled the large wall screen. The room grew silent and jaws opened as more and more photos populated the screen. A few of the images were ghastly, due to headshots.

"Wow," Walsh said in disbelief.

"How many?" McCune asked.

"Twenty-seven confirmed dead, ma'am," the analyst

replied. "And Pearl believes that the number of the wounded to be at least a dozen."

"Does this include the photos Capps took in the grab of Hasni?" McCune asked, referring to Hasni's security detail that was neutralized.

"Yes, ma'am."

"Bridgette, can you highlight or separate the initial group received from Capps from the rest."

The young African American analyst who had worked with Cole in the past on assessing the AIJB grouped the images on the screen with the five from the initial operation to the right and the remaining twenty-two arranged on the left. Underneath each image data appeared for those, they had available intel. The data was updated in real time as more information became available.

"OK, what do you notice about the group on the right?" Cole asked hoping Bridgette would confirm his hunch.

"They're all unknowns, sir."

"Yep." Cole nodded.

"Maybe recruits."

"This doesn't make any sense. Who puts recruits on security detail?" Hannah questioned.

Bridgette stood up.

"All of our other intel on Hasni suggested that Jamil Rasul was always at his side, sort of his PA, right? And he typically would have one of his lieutenants around as well." She thought aloud.

"That's right, but if Hasni knew we were coming, then maybe he used expendables on the security detail and then set a trap for us on the exfil route."

"I don't see Rasul on the board at all," Cole said, recalling the previous study of the top AIJB players.

"But it looks like we took out Shakir and Zahir. Two of Hasni's lieutenants. Those are two heavy hitters." Bridgette pointed at the photos.

"Well, they definitely knew we were coming," McCune added. "My guess is they planned to torture and drag

American soldiers through the streets to celebrate their victory. If they knew CIA agents were there as paramilitary, I'm sure they would have loved to extract as much information as possible."

"Well, they underestimated us." Cole felt there had been a lot of that going around.

"They sure did." McCune picked up on Cole's reference. "And they paid a heavy price for it."

"Bridgette can you pull up the AIJB roster and let's look at the remaining leadership structure."

"Already have it cross-referenced, sir," she said as she posted on the big screen the revised AIJB org chart with the images of those eliminated dimmed out but still visible.

It looks like we have three remaining lieutenants, Jawahir, al-Samarrai, and al-Himyari.

Bridgette was ready with more information.

"Latest intel places Jawahir in Sana, Yemen, and al-Samarrai in Al Mukalla. But al-Himyari has been off the radar for almost four weeks now. The last known location was Medina in Saudi Arabia."

"Wait for a second," Amy said standing up from her seat.

"Steve, did you ever hear back from the NSA on the sketch Hernandez gave us to cross-reference."

"No," Sinha responded from the corner. "They said it could take a few days."

"What's going on?" McCune asked.

"The border crossing incident," Amy said excitedly.

"Hernandez gave us a sketch of the suspect to cross-reference. It looks similar to this guy. Don't you agree, Jason?"

"Well, maybe," Jason said unconvincingly.

Amy sat down and pecked at her keyboard and then the digital version of sketch populated the screen.

"Maybe." Cole said, "let's see what the technology of the NSA has to say."

He looked to McCune, and she knew his intentions.

"I'll go make a call and see if someone can't light a fire

under them over there," she said leaving the room.

"I thought you didn't trust 'all that technology,'" Amy said poking at Cole.

"Yeah, and I thought you did," Cole said, then he looked around the room, "by the way, where is Hernandez?"

Everyone just shrugged.

CHAPTER 17

West Los Angeles (Monday)

Abu al-Himyari's nephew threw a backpack over his shoulder and left the dark apartment headed to a lecture for one of his classes at UCLA. Al-Himyari was relieved to have some solitude finally. The two had stayed cooped up in the apartment for two days preparing the lethal vessels.

The devices were designed to fit in a large backpack or roller board and equipped with a pager that would trigger the release remotely when called. Upon discharge, the pressurized vessel would disperse its toxic fumes into the carefully targeted environment.

Al-Himyari concluded his morning prayers, rolled up the prayer rug and looked at the five canisters standing against the wall. The twenty-pound C02 aluminum canisters generally used for providing carbonation in soda fountain machines were perfect trojan horses for disguising the real weapon.

Each unit was about twenty-eight inches tall, eight inches in diameter and equipped with a standard looking sixty psi pressure gauge and valve. The only exception was that it had an additional valve in the stem designed to switch from real C02 to the VX. Having the ability to dispense real C02 if tested was his nephew's idea.

Al-Himyari's nephew had prepared the CO2 canisters before his arrival. He had cut the bottom out of the containers, leaving room to place a smaller 0.6-liter C02 as well as the deadly VX dispenser inside the hollowed-out aluminum canister before soldering the bottom back in place.

Al-Himyari sat in silence, pleased with the progress he had made thus far, but his mission was not over yet, and he suppressed his doubts and concerns about the movement. The infidels had killed Hasni. He had warned Hasni of being overconfident.

His leader had equated the partnership with the Russians to invincibility. His drive for retribution against the government that had taken away his loved ones was unapparelled. Al-Himyari understood his motivation, but Hasni wanted the individuals personally responsible to pay for their sins.

The Russians provided the information Hasni requested, and in return, his organization would play an essential role in helping usher in the *'darkness'* as the Russians called it. Neither Hasni nor al-Himyari understood exactly what that meant, but they both hoped and prayed for new world order.

Hasni used the information given and carefully plotted to exact vengeance on key individuals who had taken his family from him. He had the Russians kill the drone operator responsible for the attack in a staged car accident.

The CIA Officer, Cole Cameron, and his commander, Nancy McCune had been next on his list. Hasni was adamant that their deaths have a dramatic flair to them to serve as propaganda for his cause. The Russians had promised to take care of McCune, and al-Himyari knew Cameron was his responsibility.

Now al-Himyari had to get the canisters delivered to the assigned cells without suspicion. He planned for a university student from each cell to drive to Los Angeles to attend the upcoming International Conference on Islamic Cultural Issues hosted at the Los Angeles Convention Center.

Each was to travel by car with a specific make and model of a black large roller suitcase thirty inches in height by nineteen inches wide. They would stay in separate hotels under their real names. However, their alias' were registered to share a room at an appointed hotel. There the suitcases would be swapped out with an identical one containing the canister.

Four cells in all would take the deadly cargo back to their city and hit the predetermined target. The fifth device would be used in Los Angeles at an event hosted by UCLA. His nephew would be responsible for that attack. The AIJB had intentionally kept his nephew isolated from other cell members. His role was too important to risk suspicion.

Al-Himyari closed his eyes and tried to imagine the horror of his enemy, envisioning hundreds choking and suffocating to death. Bodies clamoring over one another. The recognition in their eyes that their lives were ending and they could do nothing about it.

A knock at the door interrupted his fantasy. The startled al-Himyari reached for the handgun on the end table and rushed to the door.

Before he could get to the door, he heard a key being inserted and saw the door handle turning. He lunged toward the opening door, pushing his foot at the bottom and abruptly stopping the intruder.

"Hasim!" the female voice shouted. "What are you doing?"

"Hasim is not here. Who are you?"

Al-Himyari kept the door ajar with his foot. He turned his head to see if the angle provided the intruder a view to the canisters and the chemistry mess still on the table. It appeared to be out of her line of sight.

"I'm Reen, who are you? Let me see Hasim."

"I told you he is not here. What do you want?"

"Who are you? What are you doing in Hasim's apartment?"

Al-Himyari placed the muzzle of the gun against the door, calculating the aim required to shoot her in the head. His heart raced, realizing the potential demise of his plans if she saw the material. If he shot her, he would need to move fast.

"Where is Hasim? I've been trying to reach him, and he is not answering? If you don't let me in, I will call the police. Hasim!" she yelled louder.

"Please, I am undressed," al-Himyari said. "I am Hasim's

Khal *uncle* visiting, please go away, I will tell Hasim you came by."

"I'm not leaving. He is not answering his phone, and now I find a stranger in his apartment."

"This is no way for a Muslim woman to behave."

"I am or was his girlfriend. Please let me in, or I will call the police."

"Miss, please, as I said, I am undressed. Where are your manners? His cell phone is not working. It is dead. I was sleeping when you knocked as I traveled a long distance to visit my nephew.

"Hasim is at the University. He left this morning for a lecture he was required to attend. Please, Miss, this is embarrassing. I'll have him call you when he returns."

"You have not told me your name."

"My name is Mohammed. Now please go!"

"Uncle Mohammed, I have class in an hour, if I don't hear from Hasim by four o'clock, I'll be back with the police."

Reen left the doorway toward her car and sent off a text to her roommate. *Some older guy is in Hasim's apartment. Says he's his Uncle. Acting weird.* Reen's roommate, also studying chemical engineering, had introduced the two. Reen sent a follow-up text. *Is Hassim in class with you?*

She paused hoping for a response when she heard the door behind her open.

"Miss, please I am dressed now, I have Hasim on the phone inside."

"That's OK." Reen was reevaluating her previous stance. She started walking away when her text message popped up. *Yes, he is here. Says his uncle is visiting.* A wave of relief swept over Reen.

"Miss, please he's on the phone inside. I insist. I feel terrible about the way I responded. I had been sleeping. Hasim said he wants to speak to you."

Reen grinned and bowed her head in deference.

"I'm sorry about making a scene earlier."

She followed al-Himyari back into the apartment to take

the call. As they entered, he closed the door behind them, and Reen's eyes grew wide as she saw all of the materials. She turned to leave, but al-Himyari leveled the butt of the handgun over her forehead, knocking her out cold to the floor.

A few hours later Hasim entered the apartment and immediately noticed the fresh carpet lines and the scent of ammonia from the full cleaning al-Himyari had given the place.

"Khal," Hasim called out.

Al-Himyari emerged from the bedroom drying his hands with a towel.

"Uncle, you did not need to clean up, I could have done it."

"Ibnu Al-Ukht *my nephew*, it seems the apartment is not the only thing I had to clean up after you."

Hasim's eyes widened, "What have you done? Where is Reen?"

"You did not tell me you had a girlfriend. She was quite disrespectful you know. My sister, your mother, would not have tolerated that sort of behavior."

"Where is she?"

He rushed into the bedroom, seeing Reen lying on the bed with her hands and feet tied with duct tape, her mouth stuffed with a cloth wrapped in more duct tape.

Blood had dried in her hair and along her face. Her right eye was swollen shut and the side of her face red and swollen. The sight horrified Hasim. He searched for a pulse and felt the beat on her wrist.

"Reen," he sobbed.

"Nephew, it is time for you to be a man and correct your own mistakes." Al-Himyari had taken his anger for Hasim's carelessness out on Reen. Beating her twice when she made a noise. Now she lied unconscious and subdued.

"What happened?"

She was not supposed to be here. She had gone home to San Francisco for her sister's wedding taking an extra week with the upcoming spring break to give her a little extra time. They had fought as she expected Hasim to join her. But he refused. He had things he needed to do and was falling behind on assignments. Hasim knew the break up was for the best. When his uncle arrived, he made him change cell phones out. Unable to reach him, she had returned.

"You got careless, that's what happened. Now she must pay for your carelessness. Carry her to the bathtub."

"Uncle!" Hasim cried, "No, please."

"Hasim, do it now!"

Hasim reluctantly lifted Reen. As she flopped in his arms, she began to awake. Her eyes rolled back and forth as if her mind was trying to make sense of what was happening to her. She began to mutter "Hasim" as he laid her in the tub.

As she became more fully aware, the horror of what was happening to her settled in, and Hasim could see the sheer panic in her eyes. She attempted screams through the duct tape gag and began kicking against the tub.

Al-Himyari handed his nephew the knife that he had used to slay the Border Patrol agent.

"Make it quick."

He left the bathroom.

***

Counterterrorism Center – Langley (Tuesday)

Cole Cameron entered the parking garage at Langley at 05:15 and sighed realizing he had just vacated the spot a few short hours earlier. It was dark, cold and wet. As he stepped out of the car, he took in a deep breath of the brisk damp air attempting to draw energy for the day ahead.

He was exhausted, and his sore and aching body reminded him of his limitations. He knew scores of analysts and team members from the various agency were working long hard hours as well, but he and his core team of Hannah, Amy, Jason, and Raymond were wearing down. He could sense it. *Well maybe not Raymond*, he thought.

Inside their designated war room at CTC, a handful of analysts sat scattered at various workstations. The techies had the room dark and quiet, just the way they liked it. Cole surveyed the room to see who was there, recognizing none of the core team had arrived yet he was glad, hoping they were getting much-needed rest. He also noticed Sinha working over in the corner. It was apparent he had never left.

Sinha turned, seeing Cole at the back of the room, he pulled out his ear buds and walked back to meet him.

"Morning," Cole said extending his hand for the analyst to shake. It was a habit from his business days he tried to break. The custom didn't seem to fit in this environment. Sinha seemed surprised by the gesture but shook Cole's hand.

"Good morning. Hey, I wanted to say sorry about not pushing harder on the facial recognition with the NSA."

"Don't worry about it."

"Well, the thing is I just heard back."

"And?"

"And...there is a possible match."

With what degree of probability?"

""Fifty-two percent. But also, they have pings on al-Himyari flying from Cairo to Mexico City, and then Mochis Airport in Mexico. So, he likely worked his way up to the Sonora desert area for the crossing."

"Shit!"

"Sorry, sir."

"Hey, you didn't have this until a few days ago. He had already gotten here. Let's focus on getting him now. Get the information over to the FBI and JTTF in Phoenix."

"I'm on it."

Cole patted him on the back as he left. It was going to be a long ass day, and now he wished the rest of the team was in to get the ball rolling. He logged into the nearest open workstation in the large room and began researching everything he could find on al-Himyari. Yes, indeed it was going to be another long ass day.

He looked at the refreshment table in the rear of the room. He needed caffeine. Cole never acquired the taste for coffee. Instead, he thought *maybe hot tea will do the trick*. He placed the tea bag in the paper cup and pressed the button on the hot water, nothing. *It's going to be a very long ass day.*

Over the next few hours, the war room steadily began to fill up. Cole had been in contact with McCune, filling her in on findings as she was scheduled for other off-site meetings. When Hernandez showed up, he inquired about the shoulder and sling, wanting to know details. Cole diverted his attention, by thanking him for the sketch and sharing what they had uncovered. Hernandez ate up the praise.

At 07:45 Cole was about ready to gather everyone around for a quick run-down meeting when he received a text from Hannah stating that she would be tied up at her office with a debriefing related to the New York City bombing. It was going to be a long day.

CHAPTER 18

INTERSTATE 40 – California

Al-Himyari double checked his rear-view mirror to make sure he wasn't being followed as he exited from Interstate 40 on Keebler Road. He followed the signs for Granite Peak in the Mojave Desert. He needed to dispose of Reen's body quickly before daylight.

They had taken her car to the oil fields in Inglewood, hiding it behind an old shed before going separate ways. Hasim had his part to do and al-Himyari his. The sooner he could get rid of the body the better. He needed to buy time for his nephew.

After a few minutes, he followed a turn off on a dusty road and searched for a spot. Fearing he would lose his way back he stopped, turned off the engine, listened and looked for any signs of activity. Satisfied that he was in the clear, he removed the army surplus tote bag stuffed with Reen's petite body.

He saw a large rock about twelve feet high and just as wide. *Perfect spot.* He dragged the heavy tote along the sand to the other side of the large mass of stone. The girl made him think of his daughter that he had lost. The thought of coyotes and other creatures ravaging her lifeless body did not sit well with him, but he had no time to bury her. He needed to get back on the road and fulfill his commitment to Hasni and Allah.

Al-Himyari dumped her out of the tote and walked back to the car. Then he had a change of mind and searched for something to use for digging. Nearly thirty minutes later as the sun started to peek over the desert mountain, a mound of sand sat butted against the rock. He felt better now.

Al-Himyari turned on the air conditioner of his car. He had worked up a sweat, his hands were grimy from digging in the sand, and his shirt was a mess. He needed to blend in, not stand out. A few minutes later he saw a sign, *'Essex Rest area'* and pulled over to clean up in the bathroom. As he hastily entered the men's room, he bumped into a heavy-set trucker.

"Easy, partner," the trucker said in his country drawl, turning his head as he caught a whiff of al-Himyari's body odor.

"Sorry, excuse me, please."

"No problem. You OK?"

He noticed the trucker eyeballing his appearance.

"Please, sir no problem. I had to fix a flat."

"Uh-huh."

The trucker shifted his Caterpillar trademarked cap and nodded. He gave a yank at his camo cargo pants and limped his way to his rig and climbed in for the long drive ahead. He cranked the engine and prepared to release the air brakes when his curiosity got the best of him.

He sat in the rumbling cab watching the bathroom entrance and then gazed up to a photo pinned in his visor. It was the picture of an Army Ranger, with a chest full of medals, his deceased son.

"Well son, if he heads east, he's going our direction, and we'll just trail him for a while."

"OK, OK," he said to the imaginary presence, "if he goes west, I'll leave it be."

Al-Himyari finally emerged from the bathroom, cleaned up and wearing a fresh shirt. The trucker watched as he got in the older model Toyota and pulled out to exit the rest area. The trucker released the air brakes and shifted the big rig in gear. The power of the diesel engine rolled the truck and its heavy trailer forward.

The Toyota turned right and headed onto the ramp for Interstate 40 eastbound. The trucker pushed his rig forward, the driver not wanting to get too far behind.

"I know, I know," the lonely trucker said to the photo. "We'll be alright, if he stays at the speed limit, we'll be able to keep up. Don't you worry, Johnny."

***

Los Angeles, CA

Hasim checked into the Los Angeles JW Marriott with the fake credentials and credit card his uncle had given him, courtesy of the Russians.

"I understand you have two separate rooms reserved?" The clerk verified.

"Yes, I have other family members coming but they will be joining later, and I am paying for both rooms."

"Would you like me to see if I can get adjoining rooms?"

"No, that will not be necessary. Separate floors are fine. Let me give you their names for when they arrive."

"Certainly."

"Also, I would like a key to the extra room as well. I have a gift basket prepared for them, and I want to leave it in the room."

"That's very thoughtful."

The clerk ran the cards in the machine, wrote the room number on the holder and handed the additional key card to Hasim.

"Enjoy your stay."

He rehearsed in his mind the details of the plan he had to execute. He had disappointed his uncle and taken his eyes off of the prize. Reen had died by his own hands, at first, he felt great sorrow but then came great resolve.

After all, it was the infidels who killed his father when he was eight and caused his mother's death after more than a year of living in the refugee camp when he was but ten years old. If it had not been for the infidels, they would never have been in that horrible camp.

A group of men had taken him under their wings at the refugee camp. They told him they knew his uncle, Abu al-Himyari and that Allah had grand plans for him. They fostered, protected, and provided for him until the wealthy family in Turkey adopted him.

The men told him that the new family would take good care of him, he was blessed with great opportunities and afforded the best available education. But these blessings meant that Allah would expect great things in return.

He asked forgiveness from his Uncle for allowing the distraction to come close to interfering with Allah's plans.

He had to come through now. His uncle depended on him for this critical role. Tomorrow four of his brothers would arrive for the conference. They would attend meetings, lectures and visit the booths of various groups represented, but first, they would each visit the guest room at the Marriott at separate designated times and leave with a different suitcase than the one they brought.

He was unaware of the specific details of the targets, and he understood why. But he knew the plan would be similar to his.

Cell members would use their maintenance or service positions at highly populated venues to bring in the C02 canisters for soda fountain machines. Only they would gain access to the air ventilation system, attach the assembly al-Himyari had built, open the value so that once triggered by a remote frequency the secondary valve would open dispersing the deadly gas for maximum reach through the air ducts.

Hasim opened the curtains and looked out the window of the twenty-third floor. The 110 freeway was to his right with a logjam of traffic. Staples Center was on the ground directly in front of his view and further up was the Los Angeles Convention Center only a five to ten-minute walk away. His thoughts drifted to Reen.

***

Counterterrorism Center – Langley (Tuesday Afternoon)

Cole arranged for lunch sandwiches and salads to be brought to the war room, allowing the team to work but reminding them to take breaks if they needed.

He noticed several of the analysts used the Pomodoro technique for focus and productivity. It was interesting to watch them as they broke their work day into twenty-five-minute chunks separated by five-minute breaks. After about four of these intervals, they usually took a long break of about fifteen to twenty minutes. From his observation, it appeared every effective.

Hannah Jacobs arrived while Cole was out and when he returned, he saw she had pulled up near Albright's workstation reviewing screen images while working her way through an Asian salad.

She always dressed well, but today she looked even better. She wore a dark blue suit and a white blouse, and her hair seemed to have a little more of a wave to it. She pulled her hair over her ear and jotted down some notes and then turned and smiled at Cole. He nodded and walked over noticing she had taken the bandage off of her hand.

"Hi, welcome back. Has Jason filled you in?"

"We were just working on that," she said in between bites.

"Well, McCune is on her way over for an update, so you'll get caught up. She's been out all day as well. I think you're going to like what you hear."

"What is there to like? A terrorist in the U.S." she said, sarcastically.

"Well, I mean…like the breakthroughs in the leads," Cole said unsure of how to take her.

She laughed. "I'm just messing with you."

McCune entered the room and stood at the back with Cole.

"What do we have?"

"Ma'am, we've had a couple of developments, I'll let the team share their findings." Cole motioned to everyone.

A volley of information came from what Cole had called 'the pit' where the analysts arranged their workstations.

Albright gave an update from the field surveillance on suspected AIJB members and the FBI's cyber team had uncovered that four suspected members were registered for the Islamic conference in LA set to begin tomorrow, and all four were members of an online group set up for discussions around the upcoming conference, hosted by a UCLA student, Hasim Rajar.

"Do we believe the student is connected with the AIJB?"

"He was not on our radar until, now."

"He could be a sleeper. If he is connected it would be a very deep plant," Cole offered.

"FBI counterterrorism has nothing on him. No radical online posts or downloads, nothing to suggest he has any strong political leanings. And Amy and I've been working AIJB for nearly four years and we've never seen anything cross the wire from the middle east. So, he seems clean. But we're digging. Bridgette," Cole said handing off the discussion.

"We should have a full background to review within the hour."

"OK. Four different members attending this conference in LA. I don't like it. Even if this kid at UCLA is clean."

"Exactly, we thought about having the FBI field agents pull them all in for questioning there in LA, but it could backfire. We think we should have active undercover surveillance of each target as well as the convention center."

"Makes sense."

"Did you get what you needed from our Israeli friends?" McCune questioned.

"Yes, thank you for making that call." Cole was referring to the text he had sent her earlier that day asking if she could work her connections to get additional intel on al-Himyari from the Mossad. He again nodded to Bridgette.

"Yes, ma'am. With the help of the Israeli Intelligence team, we were able to put some missing pieces in al-Himyari's background. We had known about his wife and children, but we also learned that he had a sister and family that suffered in Afghanistan as well. The brother-in-law was killed as part of the resistance early in Operation Enduring Freedom during a raid on the village of Ghazi Khan.

"The sister and nephew believed to be around eight years old at that time fled to Turkey as refugees. The sister died in the refugee camp; she was found beaten to death. Before she was killed, she had reported that men in the camp, presumably al-Qaida or early ISIS were attempting to influence her son, al-Himyari's nephew. The nephew disappears into the refuge orphan system, and that's the last we know about him.

"Oh, and we also discovered that al-Himyari was trained in explosives by Ibrahim al-Asiri before he was killed in our drone strike. So that could explain the ISIS bomb signature in Tucson."

"Al-Asiri was no joke." Someone vented.

Everyone nodded in agreement knowing the ISIS master bomb maker's reputation.

"And you have some information on the notebook?" McCune looked at her watch, knowing she had to speed this up.

Walsh, the analyst, teamed up with Sinha, jumped in.

"I'll keep it, brief ma'am. The four digits are the last four in preassigned burner phone numbers or numbers on sim cards. The five colors or pages identify the cell group associated with the phone numbers and the numbers one through thirty represent the day of the month that particular phone number would be live."

"How did you get the phone numbers?" Hannah questioned.

"We pushed area code and prefixes of the location on all of the numbers of the groups under surveillance and got matches from earlier this month. For instance, on the tenth of this month, a call originating from Yemen called this number which we have pinged in Seattle."

He pointed to the screen.

"Here on the blue page on the tenth, you see that last four digits match. We found calls to all five suspected groups. We assumed each group seems to have had a designated area code and prefix, so we pinged the numbers assigned for each group yesterday and today. Each ping landed us in the location. We believe each month of the Islamic calendar they had a new batch of numbers."

"OK. I think I understand the 'how' it was done now. Do you have any information on 'what' is being communicated?"

"The FBI has warrants coming through for the phone records, but I think that won't produce much that we don't already know. But now that we have actual numbers to reference, the NSA is working to scan any recordings of conversations."

"OK. Good work everyone. Sorry, I'm late for the JTTF call."

McCune tugged at Cole's good arm.

"Walk with me to my office please."

Fortunately, McCune's office was on the same floor, but it was nearly to the other side of the building. They strolled briskly to their destination.

"Any update on Grant Ramsey? Anything from the CCTV scans?"

"Nothing on my end, but I'll see if Jacobs has anything from the FBI."

"Cole, I'd really love for us to get to him first, but I've put other resources on Ramsey, so you stay focused on the AIJB."

"Understood." Cole's cell beeped with a text from Amy. "Excuse me, ma'am. I need to get back there."

"Keep me updated."

"Copy that, ma'am."

CHAPTER 19

Los Angeles, CA

Reen's roommate was frantically trying to get someone to pay attention to her pleas for help. Since she lived off campus, the UCLA police department referred her to the West Los Angeles Police station. There she tried to explain her concerns for her missing roommate. She gave her statement to the desk watch, and the female officer nonchalantly looked over the information.

"Ma'am, just leave the report with your contact information, and someone will get back to you."

"Are you fucking kidding me, right now!" she screamed causing heads at the station to turn.

"Look at the text message."

The officer sighed.

"Ma'am, I'm going to have to ask you to calm down. Leave the report, and someone will get in touch with you later."

"I'm not fucking leaving here! I need someone to help me! Why don't you get off your lazy fat ass and do something!"

The large officer stood up from her chair.

"Ma'am I've asked you nicely to leave, and I will taser your ass if you do not comply. Do you understand me?"

"That's bullshit!" came the shout from waiting area.

"You're threatening that skinny little white girl. I'm a witness to it." The gang banger pointed with his tattooed arm.

"That's right bitch," shouted his female partner. "You better set your ass down, or I'll file another lawsuit against this mother fucking place."

By now, other officers were stirring about, when a uniformed officer in his late thirties stepped into the fray.

"Everybody, calm down," he yelled with his arms extended gaining control of the room.

"I'm Sergeant, Bowman," he said extending his hand to Reen's roommate.

"Come with me, and I'll see if I can't help you."

✳✳✳

Counterterrorism Center - Langley

"You're not going to believe this." Amy had been waiting for Cole to come back in.

"What is it?"

Hannah jumped in, "I just got off the phone with Sergeant Bowman of the LAPD. A couple of hours ago he took a missing person report at their West LA office. The missing person is a UCLA student who was attempting to see her boyfriend, get this, Hasim Rajar."

"Are you serious?"

"Yes, it gets better, the girlfriend texted her roommate that her boyfriend's uncle was there and acting strangely. The police sent over a squad car; the landlord let them in, the place smelled of ammonia and bleach. When Bowman entered the suspect's name in the system, our POI popped up, and he called it in."

"You think the Uncle could be al-Himyari?"

"The age works," Bridgette said.

Hannah nodded.

"Well, Bowman said the apartment community had camera's up so we're trying to see if we can get a shot of Hasim or the uncle. I've sent a couple of agents from the LA office over to meet Bowman there."

Cole paused for a moment and slowly nodded his head in thought.

"Yep," Hannah said in agreement. "We need to get out there."

Cole looked at her bruised hand. "Jason and I can handle this."

"Screw that," Hannah said. "I'm officially your liaison, remember."

"I think I can get more done here, Cole," Amy said.

"I agree. Keep everyone moving along."

"You want me to contact Hernandez?

"No, we need to get moving. No time to waste."

"We have the plane again at Andrews," Hannah said.

"Really?" Albright asked.

"What can I say the logistics guys really like me."

"I'll say," Amy deadpanned.

Cole looked at Hannah's outfit.

"You guys have go-bags?"

"In the car."

"OK, I'll meet you at the elevator in ten minutes, going to try and catch McCune."

✳✳✳

Los Angeles, CA

Hasim completed the arrangements in the second room he reserved for the others. He left the large suitcases in place and hung the 'do not disturb' sign on the door. He sent a text to four designated cell numbers using a different sim card for each text, giving them the room number, 867 where they could pick up their device. He then removed the last sim card and battery from the phone and dumped them into the trash bin on the housekeeper's cart in the hall.

Back in his room on the twenty-third floor, he stood at the

window and panned the horizon. The sun was slowly setting in the hazy orange sky filled with the exhaust emissions of the gluttonous city. He ordered room service to avoid unnecessary public exposure.

Turning the TV on to the local news, he gasped when he saw his picture and that of his uncle as suspects in the disappearance of a UCLA student. He stared at the TV as they gave details. When the storyline moved to a different report, he switched to another channel trying to ascertain how much they had learned. *How had they pegged him so quickly?*

A knock at the door broke Hasim's thoughts. Anxiety rattled his body. *Had he been discovered?* He eased toward the door when a second knock hit.

"Room Service."

A small sense of relief rolled over Hasim. "Leave it at the door, please," he said peering through the tiny spyglass in the door.

"We really can't do that, sir," the server said. "Would you like me to come back later?"

"No, please I am not feeling well. I will need to cancel my order."

"I'm sorry to hear that. But no problem, we'll take the order back."

"Yes, thank you."

Hasim realized he was on borrowed time. The engineer in him demanded order and precision. He felt panicked at the thought of the intricate details of their plans that required revisions. He took deep breaths and reminded himself that his uncle warned him of unforeseen challenges.

Hasim recalled his three primary objectives:

First, ensure the devices get in the hands of the other members. Second, use one of the apparatus himself at UCLA on as large and influential of a population as possible. Finally but of utmost importance to Hasni himself, make sure that the UCLA attack results in the inevitable death of one particular student, Jessica Cameron.

Pacing the floor rubbing his hands, he contemplated his

options. He had been instructed to go dark after providing the room number of the devices to his associates. The decisions and the consequences were now all his. *What would Khal want me to do?*

The first objective seems safe now, he reasoned. The suitcases sat in another room. The room was booked under the pseudo-identities provided, not linking his name. He had worn sunglasses and a cap that should make it difficult for anyone to recognize him. His common features worked in his favor.

The plans for completing the attack at UCLA would need to change. His cover was still intact, but he would need to revise the timetable and target.

Originally, Hasim's assigned target was the audience attending a highly publicized speech by the former Secretary of State at the Pavilion. Jessica Cameron would be there as part of a requirement for her Poly Sci class.

He had researched the details and knew every step to complete to ensure success. The service van, uniform and access cards with the logo of maintenance service providers contracted by the University would still play.

But now, as a wanted man, the likelihood of lasting seven days for the scheduled event was not a wager he was willing to make.

His romance with Reen had cost him the advantage. He cursed her. His uncle had been right. He needed to figure out a way to accomplish his objectives and make restitution for his wayward behavior.

A thought came to him. He dug into his backpack and found the piece of paper from his original research. It would be risky, but it was a way forward for him.

***

Inflight

Before takeoff from Andrews, the three westbound team members changed into more casual wear and prepared for the long cross-country flight. The pilots estimated arrival at Los Angeles to be 21:50. Still late, even though they picked up three hours with the time zone change.

They were scheduled to be picked up by an FBI field agent and escorted directly to the FBI office on Wilshire Boulevard to work with the local team to prepare for the coordination of surveillance at the Islamic Conference and efforts to locate Hasim and al-Himyari.

On the flight over, they received updates from the team and continued working the leads. Cole could not help but think about his daughter a UCLA sophomore. This threat was too close to her for his comfort.

He sent a note to Grace, without giving her any details and suggested that Jess stay in DC until things blew over. He wanted her to be OK with the idea but knew it was Jess' call to make, and that would be a tough sell.

His body ached, his eyes were red, and waves of pure exhaustion came over him. He was getting edgy and tired of the friggin' sling for his shoulder injury and these long ass days were wearing him down. In frustration, he pulled the sling off and tossed it over his satchel in the seat next to him.

Jacobs and Albright sat directly across from him with the work table between them. Hannah gave him a concerned look and Albright, not knowing any better, said, "shouldn't you keep that on?"

Cole shot him a dirty look.

"I can barely type with two hands, trying to do it with one and a half is ridiculous."

"Wow, how old are you?" Hannah joked.

Another dirty look flew.

"Sorry!"

"Hey, we might have something," Cole said, opening the encrypted email.

"Amy says four of the five groups received a text to the numbers designated for today. Originating in LA, but the text is just a number, 867."

Hannah scrolled to the email on her laptop. "Yeah, interesting that it is the same number to all four but sent in separate messages from a different originating number."

"It sure seems like something's going down with these four, right?"

"Well, from what I understand there's a force of nearly a hundred people from the FBI. That whole area is going to be covered like a blanket. If something is happening, we'll get them," Hannah said with assurance.

Albright added, "The hotline in LA is getting flooded with calls related to Hasim and al-Himyari. The challenge is sifting through to find what's credible. A missing young pretty college student pulls at the hearts of people."

"Yeah, but we're starting to see some leaks about the Feds involvement as well. Hope this doesn't get away from us."

Cole sat quietly realizing his role was secondary now. The ball was in the court of the FBI to bring this to a conclusion. His purpose here was to advise on the AIJB group and assist in the questioning if suspects were apprehended. The Attorney General had made it clear that he wanted a strong case to prosecute in the court of law. But his thoughts drifted. They all resumed working individually on their laptops.

"I can't imagine," Cole said after a couple of minutes.

"Your daughter?" Hannah asked.

Cole nodded, then gazed out the window into the darkness with clouds illuminated by the moon and stars.

Soon fatigue won out. Cole's chin dropped to his chest as he fell asleep sitting upright. Albright and Jacobs chuckled. Albright eased up and removed a blanket from the back cabin and covered him up.

"Cute, I should take a picture of you two together,"

Hannah said.

"What?"

"Or you could see how many things you can put on his head before he wakes up."

"What? No way, he'd kill me."

She pulled her phone out and snapped a picture anyway. "Jason." Hannah motioned for Albright to join her for a selfie as they both leaned in with Cole in the middle. They got a good laugh, and she couldn't wait to use it on Cole.

Then Cole grunted, and the expression on his resting face turned to one of anguish. His eyes darted back and forth under his eyelids, and Hannah recognized the symptoms.

He sat in the back seat on the passenger's side. He saw the driver turn and fire the Ruger into the head of Amir. The loud blast deafening him and everything became a blur as he drew his Glock from his leg holster and in slow motion, squeezed round after round through the seat back and into the driver. He watched the drivers' eyes widen in horror as the brass bullets hit one after another into his torso and finally his neck and head.

A bump. He is on one knee with bullets flying in slow motion all around him, seeing his target through the red dot sight, he puts two in him, watching the body fall lifeless. Feeling the breeze of a bullet that just missed his head, he spins to his right and squeezes, the first bullet hit his target in the shoulder and spun him just as the second bullet hit him the back.

A bump. He's carrying Baker over his shoulder. Feeling the weight of the Navy Seal's body. His thighs feel like mush. Debris if flying around him. The stench of Baker's burnt flesh filled his nostrils. His chest is pounding; he is breathing hard.

A bump. There's the thump in the back, and a pain shoots through his left shoulder as he falls to the ground dropping the burnt blood-soaked fighter.

"Uaah!" uttered Cole as he was jolted out of his nightmare.

The plane had caught turbulence, and Cole was jarred against the window side of the aircraft. He rubbed his sore shoulder and tried to collect himself and felt embarrassed. *Probably sawed some logs*, he thought.

"You OK?" Hannah asked.

Cole reached in his bag and grabbed a prescription bottle.

"Pain meds?"

"Anti-inflammatory. Shoulder. Forgot to take them today."

"You sure you're OK? I mean…I know you went through hell."

"Yeah, so did you."

"I know, but I saw parts of the report."

"Huh? How did you get the report? It's classified."

"I didn't say I got the report; I just said I saw the report. Looked intense."

He gave her a wry look.

Cole grabbed the bottle of water sitting in the holder in front of him. He took a swig and shook his head. As he gathered his thoughts, he realized he had a blanket on him. He held the edges up, looked at Hannah and sheepishly muttered, "thank you."

"Psh! Wasn't me," she said pointing her thumb at Albright.

"Oh…thanks Jason," he said turning red with embarrassment.

"Yeah, I'm not really the care giving type, if you haven't figured that out already."

"That's OK, as long I've got Jason." Cole winked as he regained his composure.

"McCune wants you to call," Albright said.

"Geez, how long was I out?"

"Maybe an hour. We're landing in about thirty minutes. And the captain wanted to know if you would like to see the cockpit and get a set of wings."

"Oh God, I'm never going to live this down."

"She took a picture," Albright said, wanting nothing to do with it.

"And I recorded the snoring, too."

"What are you, twelve?"

"What are you, a hundred? You sure sound a hundred."

Cole raised his eyebrow. "Was it that bad?"

Hannah widened her eyes and nodded her head back and

forth. Albright shrugged, and offered condolences, "it wasn't that bad."

"OK, sorry about that," Cole said and then started packing things up for the landing. He fastened his seat belt, and Hannah smiled at him as she buckled in across from him. *This girl is an enigma,* he thought. *Either she is letting her guard down with playful banter, or she is trying to say we're just friends. I hope it's not just friends,* he thought.

It was nearly midnight by the time the team concluded the meeting at the FBI Division office on Wilshire Boulevard. An FBI agent drove them east on the 10 and then north on the 110 exiting just north of the Convention Center. They decided staying closer to the surveillance operation at the conference was a better option than somewhere near Westwood.

The FBI point team on the surveillance had set up a post at the Luxe Hotel and worked to establish camera feeds from everything around the Convention Center area. Between the conference and agency personnel, the hotels in the area were near capacity. The Hilton on Grand was the closest available option for their stay.

CHAPTER 20

INTERSTATE 40 - Arizona

For nearly half an hour, al-Himyari watched the same semi-truck get close and then fall back. He swore it was the same truck behind him that he had jockeyed back and forth with earlier that morning when he left the rest stop.

He decided to pull off at the next off-ramp, fill up the tank and let the truck pass. The mileage sign showed Winslow six miles ahead. Later came the billboard for a name brand truck stop. That will be his exit.

Al-Himyari pulled the car around to the pumps and began filling up. He kept his head down but watched as cars and trucks came and went, the drivers unmindful of the terror his network was destined to bring to their country.

What! That truck that he was concerned about entered the truck stop. He watched it drive over to the lot around the corner of the building and out of his line of sight. Al-Himyari released the handle of the gas nozzle and shoved it back in the holder. He quickly got in his car and drove around to the trucker's side of the large lot.

He eased around attempting to avoid being seen by the suspicious truck. He drove up a little further and saw an empty lane between two big rigs with long trailers. He looped around and pulled the car to the backend of the lane. From there he couldn't see the mystery truck or the entrance to the truck stop. *His car should be out of sight.* He thought.

Al-Himyari exited the car and walked behind the trailers three lanes over to find the wary truck. He did his best to look inconspicuous, but he knew he was in the open. He lifted himself to the driver's side of the large sleeper cab and peaked into the window.

Over on the passenger seat, he saw a Yeti cooler and aluminum clipboard with drivers log and manifest papers. He looked over the dash and up to the visor seeing a photo of a young man dressed in his army uniform. The door was locked, so he stepped down and decided to risk the exposure, going inside the truck stop. He needed to avoid the cameras as much as possible.

Donning his baseball cap and sunglasses, he kept his head down and went into the facility straight for the bathroom. He went to the urinal. As he was relieving himself at the urinal, a large man stepped up beside him. He glanced to his left and was stunned causing his aim to go off the mark. It was the trucker he had bumped into at the Essex Rest Stop in California.

"Whoa, you gonna to get some on your shoes," the trucker said casually.

"It's you. Are you following me?"

"Now why would I be following you? You seem sorta nervous there, partner."

"What? You have been following me. I've seen your truck go back and forth. I slow down, and you slow down, I speed up, and you speed up. Why are you following me?"

"Exactly, why would I follow you? You got nothing to hide, right?"

Al-Himyari left the restroom and walked toward his car, the trucker grinned and meandered behind him. Al-Himyari started his car and was ready to speed off, lose his follower and take a different route. But the news station on the car radio interrupted his thoughts as they reported on the story about a missing UCLA student and the hunt for two men.

A new plan, al-Himyari thought. He remembered the trucker's photo on the visor and thought of a different approach. He surveyed the paper map and found a place that would work. *Two birds, one stone.*

He needed new transportation, and there was something about the man's smugness that tore at al-Himyari. He could not stand the arrogant and smug Americans.

He continued east on I40 allowing the trucker to follow him. After some time, he pulled the car over under an overpass about a mile short of the Petrified National Forest exit. He opened the hood and waited. In a matter of minutes, the trucker approached, al-Himyari could hear the gears shift down as the trucker slowed. His trap had worked.

The truck pulled over to the wide shoulder in front of al-Himyari's car and the air brakes released. The driver looked in his side mirrors, opened his glove box and took out his Ruger LC9. He ejected the clip to check his 9mm ammo and reinserted it.

"Just to be safe," he said looking at the photo of his soldier son. He stepped down from the rig and slid the small handgun in the larger pocket of his camo cargo pants.

"Please, leave me alone. I don't want your help." Al-Himyari was determined that the cat and mouse game would be played his way.

"Look, we're just headed the same direction is all. I'm pretty good with engines and all, why don't you let me take a look."

"You think I'm an idiot?" al-Himyari said. "I'm also good with engines and can drive the rig just like you."

"Really? OK, amigo."

"That's right. I drove fuel trucks for the Kuwait army that kept your military's machines running during your first gulf war," he lied. He had driven fuel truck for the Iraqi's during that war.

"Well, I'm sure your country is grateful for your service."

"I was shot at and lost family members for your cause, and came to America and because of my appearance, I'm subject to your prejudice. All you see is an Arab man."

The trucker took his cap off and wiped his forehead with his sleeve. His son fought and died for people like this man. The old man's exterior was penetrated, and his heart was troubled that he had indeed been discriminatory.

"How can I help?"

"Are you sure?"

"Yes."

***

Los Angeles, CA (Tuesday Night)

Hasim wore sweatpants and a hooded sweat jacket with a towel from the fitness room wrapped around his neck. He pushed his sunglasses up the bridge of his nose and entered the guest business center of the JW Marriott. He plopped down into the office chair in front of the public computer.

The piece of paper rested between his fingers as he opened the internet browser. He shifted it to a privacy tab and typed in his web destination. Referring to the note, he entered a username and password in the appropriate fields on the screen and now had access to the personal calendar of Jessica Cameron.

Tabbing through course schedules and events for the next day, a morning class, study group, followed by two sessions in the afternoon. The impact would be so much smaller now that his plans required changes. Hasim hovered the mouse over the study group event on the calendar and recognized his opportunity.

The study group was scheduled to meet at the Covel Commons dining hall during lunch at 12:30. *Perfect.* It would be easy access and that time of day and the fifty-seven hundred square foot hall would be at near capacity.

The commons had been considered as a target but ruled out in favor of the higher profile event. Now as a fallback plan, it would do. The basics were the same. Place the canister at an air intake and release the gas into the ventilation system.

With his plan set, Hasim returned to his room and sought

to get some rest before the big day. He packed his bags and laid on the bed fully clothed and ready for a quick exit if needed. He stared at the ceiling. It was his moment in history — a moment that would send a message to the infidels and provide restitution for Hasni.

Once they executed all of the plans, the AIJB planned to release a video praising Allah and men who carried out his will. It would put the Western World on notice and send a specific message to individuals within the counterterrorism intelligence community to expect to pay a very high personal premium for their actions.

CHAPTER 21

Los Angeles, CA - LUXE HOTEL (Wednesday Morning)

At 08:30 Albright and Cole followed Hannah Jacobs into the large suite the FBI had blocked off. Dozens of agents flowed in and out of the room that hosted a slew of monitors and audio equipment. Video feeds from the area CCTV traffic cameras, and local businesses were scanned.

There was a large bay of monitors and tables in the center, but also four different banks of monitors, two to each side of the central area. Each bank had the name of the hotel it was surveilling written on a white paper on top. These were the four different hotels where the suspected AIJB members had reservations. None of them included the JW Marriott.

There were also camera feeds from the field surveillance. Each of the four members was carefully followed on their journey to the convention. Other agents had been positioned at the Conference Center itself with several in the security room monitoring events there.

Cole marveled at all the resources utilized. He asked the Special Agent in Charge, Adam Waltuch, how he could help and was pretty much told just to stay out the way. He gave Hannah a frustrated look, and she merely shrugged her shoulders. Time seemed to drag by.

He shot a text to his daughter.

"I'm going for a walk," he said, and Hannah nodded.

He left the Luxe hotel and took a casual stroll down Figueroa Street toward the convention center. His phone buzzed.

"Hi, Dad!"

"Hey, Sweetheart."

"Everything OK? I was surprised to hear from you."

"Yes, everything is fine. I just had a moment and wanted to call. I'm in LA for a couple of days. I was hoping to see you, in fact, I thought it would be great if you came back home with me and got a jump start on your spring break."

"What, I don't understand. I've got classes and a mid-term. I can't leave."

"I know, but…"

"I mean I'd love to see you while you're here, but I can't leave."

Cole decided this was better done in person.

"Yeah, OK. Maybe tonight, I'll see how this project comes along and give a call later."

"OK, Daddy. I love you."

"Love you too, Sweetheart."

Cole had reached the convention center and decided to walk through the Gilbert Lindsey Plaza around the front of the Staples Center. Moving felt nice to his weary and bruised body. He thought he would take a long way around to get back.

He crossed Chick Hearn Court with a moment of nostalgia remembering the Laker's announcer from his youth in Southern California. *Nothing like having Vin Sculley for baseball and Chick Hearn for basketball.* He scrolled through his emails as he walked up Georgia street lifting his head to see Olympic Boulevard ahead for his right turn to get back to Figueroa and the Luxe hotel.

There was a text from Grace. She had accepted an offer on the house, and it was going into a thirty-day escrow. *Great. This is all I need right now,* Cole thought of the hassle of moving while working on this mission. He put his head back down to respond and was startled by the honk of the service van that nearly hit him pulling out of the Marriott parking garage.

"Sorry, my fault," he yelled to the driver, putting his hands up for the van to pass. The young man in blue baseball cap and sunglasses put his head down and drove away.

Cole arrived back in the FBI suite, and Hannah waved him over. He stood looking at the monitors in the middle.

"We have our first arrival," she said pointing to the screen with a bouncing body cam following the suspect into the Convention Center. "He parked at the Conference Center."

The room began to scramble with activity.

"OK, where's the suspect staying?" Waltuch asked.

"He has reservations at Hotel Indigo," an agent said pointing to one of the designated banks.

"Shh, everyone. Turn up the audio."

The undercover agent following the suspect spoke through his coms, "Suspect is at the registration booth. Looks like he's picking up conference material."

The room watched the feed as the suspect walked right past the undercover agent who called out his handoff. "Number three, you have the ball."

"This is number three, I have the ball," came the reply and agents switched to her camera feed.

"Suspect appears to be heading back to his vehicle."

"This is number one; I have visual on the suspect, we are in position in the parking garage, ready to tail the vehicle."

"Copy that. Number five stay at the convention center. The second suspect may stop there first as well, he's about twenty minutes out. The team at Indigo Hotel will trail suspect number one when he arrives there."

"Number five, copy."

Waltuch got everyone's attention.

"OK everyone, let's get ready at Indigo."

"On it."

After a couple of minutes, the team watched the dash cam view of the trailing car.

"Suspect is turning left on Olympic."

"OK, he should be continuing up a couple of blocks and turning right to get over to James Wood, it's a one way."

"Copy."

"Hold on, the suspect's turning left on Georgia

Street…Suspect is turning into the self-parking for the JW Marriott."

"Shit!" Waltuch shouted. "Did he change rooms?"

An analyst in front of her laptop replied, "No digital evidence of that, sir."

"Shit! Who do we have at the Marriott?"

"Agents Wern and McCreery, sir. But they're in suits and not on our coms."

"Get 'em on the horn and tell them to keep their asses in that security room monitoring the cameras. We don't need them blowing this. Who is the closest UC?"

There was too long of a pause and no time.

"I got it," Hannah said grabbing the nearest laptop roller bag.

"Go! Go!" Waltuch said handing her a set of coms.

"Suspect is entering the parking garage elevator with a large black roller suitcase."

"OK one, stay put. Agent Jacobs is headed to the hotel lobby to intercept. Number five what's your twenty?"

"Ten minutes out."

"Shit!"

Cole knew she needed back up. "I'm going over!"

"No! You stay the fuck here. The last thing I need is a CIA officer getting in the middle of this."

"Fuck you! I'm going over." Cole followed after Hannah.

"Damn it!" Waltuch slammed his notebook down on the table.

Jacobs raced out of the Luxe and across busy Figueroa over to the Marriott, pulling the tie out of her hair to let it flow and take on a little different look. She slowed as she got to the main lobby and Cole caught her arm.

"I've got your back," he said holding the door for her. The two entered the contemporary lobby designed to promote conversation in a pseudo-intimate setting. They found a table and sat across from each other to have the best view from both vantage points. Hannah pulled some papers out of the roller bag as if she was having a meeting with Cole.

"This is Jacobs; I have a visual on the suspect."

"Jacobs we have our guys inside the security room on a line and will relay their information."

"Copy that," Hannah said smiling and handing a paper to Cole as if she was talking to him instead of her coms.

The suspect crossed from Hannah's line of sight to Cole's.

"Looks like he's headed for the registration desk," Cole said.

They waited a few long minutes.

"He has a room key," Cole relayed.

"This is Jacobs, the suspect has a room key and is heading to the elevators." After the suspect entered the elevator, Hannah jumped up.

"I'm checking with the front desk."

"Copy that."

As Hannah was gathering information from the front desk clerk, the undercover agent number five entered the hotel and calmly sat next to Cole. "Waltuch said to get your ass back over to the Luxe," he whispered.

Cole just nodded '*no.*'

"Your funeral."

Number five spoke into his coms, "Affirmative, message relayed. Negative, not complying."

After a few minutes, Hannah walked back and sat down with number five and Cole.

"Sounds like your needed back at the Luxe," she said referring to the barrage of insults that Waltuch was spewing over the coms.

The defiant Cole said, "I'm good here."

Number five chuckled. Hannah shook her head in disbelief.

"Let me guess, room 867," Cole said.

'The text message," Hannah agreed. Then she held up her hand, listening through her coms.

"He's on his way down."

"We've got him from here," number five said.

"This is Jacobs, Cameron and I will check out the room, it

was under a different registration and prepaid by another party. I'm sending the names over in text."

They headed to the elevator.

"Hold tight Jacobs," she heard through the coms as they stopped at the elevator doors. "Let the boys run back the video feed. Make sure no else is in the room."

Then the door opened, and the suspect exited with the black roller. Hannah and Cole needed to do something instead of just standing there.

"After you," Cole said casually, holding back the sliding doors.

They entered the elevator and headed to the eighth floor.

"Just tell him you lost coms in the elevator," Cole said.

"Jacobs do you copy, stand down!" Waltuch screamed.

She grabbed Cole's arm. "Cole, let's wait."

"How long?"

"This is Jacobs how much longer for clearance?"

The elevator doors opened up to the eighth floor.

"Give us two more minutes."

Hannah held up two fingers to Cole. The two stood near the elevator area on the eighth floor waiting in awkward silence.

"Do you like to dance?" Cole asked just as a businessman entered the hallway from a few doors down and came to the elevator.

"What?"

"Do you like to dance?" Cole repeated slowly.

The businessman glanced at the two of them from the corner of his eye forgetting to push the button. Cole reached over and pushed the down button for him.

"Yeah, I guess. Do you?"

"Uh, hell no! But I've got this thing I've got to go to, and I thought…" the elevator finally opened and the businessman distracted Cole with a devilish grin as he entered with the doors closing behind him.

"…Well, I thought, I sure would like for you to come with me."

Hannah looked surprised and started to speak, but instead held her hand up listening over the coms.

"OK, we're clear."

They drew their weapons as Hannah used the key she had gotten from the front desk and opened the door to room 867. Cole cleared the bathroom and joined Hannah in the guest room. She handed him a set of latex gloves.

Three large identical suitcases were lined against the curtains of the glass wall. A fourth suitcase was positioned on the opposite side of the bed. Hannah took a few photos with her phone and sent them to the Agent in Charge.

Cole lifted the suitcase that was separate from the others onto the bed and carefully examined it before slowly opening it. He pulled out bags stuffed with rags and tee shirts. He then went through the liners.

"Nothing."

"OK, let's check out this one on the end here," Hannah said pointing to one of three lined up against the curtains. Cole again scrutinized the outside before opening. As he opened the top of the suitcase, he saw the C02 Canister.

"We need to get Albright over here," he said, removing bags of rags and clothing cushioning the canister inside the case.

"This is Jacobs, we have a potential device here. Request Agent Jason Albright to examine."

"Copy. Albright's on his way. I've got Division piped in on our coms, give us your assessment."

"Sending pictures now."

Cole gave the run down.

"Aluminum canister, looks over two feet tall and maybe seven to eight inches in diameter. Has a sixty-psi pressure gauge and valve and some sort of electronic gadget like a pager on the valve, I'm guessing the trigger."

Hannah relayed the information in her coms.

"Looks like the bottom was recently soldered."

Cole then carefully moved and opened the other two cases. "Same story here."

"This is Jacobs; we now have three devices."

"Copy."

"What's the play, here? Are we evacuating, bomb squad coming in?"

Jacobs motioned to her earpiece.

"It's chaos."

Albright knocked at the door, Hannah brought him in, and he joined Cole to examine the devices.

"Can you disarm it?" Cole asked.

"I need some time," he said removing a handheld cell phone jamming device to prevent remote detonation.

"We don't need a telemarketer dialing the wrong number. The coms should be fine on a different frequency."

"Now you tell us," Cole deadpanned.

"What the hell is going on over there anyway?" Cole said pointing toward the Luxe.

"There's concern that if we evacuate and snag the first suspect, it could trigger other attacks."

"What?"

"They have the HMRU team and CIRG standing by in the basement," Albright offered.

Hannah continued, "the AG is arguing that we would only have a circumstantial case against the other three suspects. He's wanting us to explore ways to capture the suspects while in the act of retrieving the devices."

"Are you kidding me? There's no time for that."

"You're right about that. The next suspect just pulled into the parking garage," Hannah said holding in her earpiece.

"How much longer, Jason?"

"I need more time."

"We need a few minutes, sir," she said over the coms.

"Quick, put everything back," Hannah said. "He's at the front desk getting the key."

"You gotta be kidding me!" Cole protested.

They swiftly moved everything back in place and straightened out the bed and moved to the hall. Hannah banged on the door of the room across that had a 'do not disturb' sign inserted in the key slot.

"We don't have time," Cole said watching for the elevator down the hall.

"I'm busy!" shouted the voice inside the room.

"FBI, open the door, now!" Hannah shouted as she banged again, holding her badge to the peephole.

A middle-aged man in his boxers and sleeveless tee shirt opened the door. "What's this all about…"

Hannah pushed him into the room, and the others cleared the hall just as the elevator doors opened. Motioning for the man to be quiet. "Sit over there and don't move." Seeing his intruders with guns in their hands he complied.

The three stood quietly just inside the room, Hannah peered through the spyglass and saw suspect number two enter 867 across the hall.

"Copy that," she said quietly in her coms. "We're taking the suspect down, alive, when he exits. Alive, Cole."

"Me, what about him?" Cole asked offended that she had singled him out.

"Hey, what's going on out there?" the hotel guest asked.

"Shut up!" all three quietly shouted back.

"What about the others?" Cole asked.

"They're getting apprehended as soon as this guy goes down."

"About time."

"Let's get in position in the hall."

"If he's looking through the door, he could spot us."

"You're right."

"I think we rush out when he opens the door. He'll have one hand on the suitcase and the other on the doorknob. Got to make sure he is halfway out so he can't close the door."

"I'll go to the left, Jason you take the right, and Cole you stay in front at this door," Hannah said.

They heard the hefty hotel door lock turn and Hannah watched the suspect look both ways down the hall and then pull the suitcase forward letting the door ride behind it. Before the door had fully closed, they burst out from across the hall shocking the suspect.

"FBI freeze!"

The suspect gathered what had just happened and then reached inside his coat. Cole dove across the hall with a full body tackle sending him and the suspect flying back into the room. Hannah and Albright joined the fray and subdued him.

Cole sat on his knees, holding his left shoulder that was throbbing from the body tackle as two other FBI agents joined them in the room.

Hannah shot up and began scolding him.

"Are you crazy! I could have shot you."

Cole grunted as he stood.

"You said 'alive,' right?"

She started to continue and instead responded to the call coming over her coms.

"That's affirmative; we have the suspect in custody."

"So, how about that dance?"

Hannah couldn't help but smile and then suddenly held her earpiece again. She grabbed her phone and scrolled through the photos she just received.

"Copy."

"The guys in the security room have been digging through the hotel videos for the last two days. This is our guy," she said showing a picture of Hasim in cap and sunglasses.

Agents from the FBI Hazmat Team and Critical Incident Response Group entered the room and took over the disarming of the devices for Albright. The three moved toward the hall to give the response team room to work.

"Shit! I think I saw him this morning. I was distracted and almost walked in front of a service van. He was driving it."

Hannah relayed the information over the coms, then she and Albright listened for a long while.

Cole hated not being in on it.

"What's going on?"

Hannah and Albright looked at each with dread in their eyes.

"We've got to go!"

"What?" Cole asked as he followed Hannah and Albright down the hall.

"They have a video of Hasim on the guest computer in the business center. The cyber team uncovered his tracks." The elevator opened.

"Cole, he accessed your daughter's schedule."

"What the...how did he..." Cole couldn't finish.

"Her next event is a lunch meeting with a study group at Covel Commons. We have teams headed over now."

"We've got to go now!" he shouted.

"I know. I know. We'll get to Jessica. She's going to be OK."

Cole knew that was a promise Hannah should not make with so many things out of her control.

"What the hell am I doing over here on the wrong side of this fucking town. That's an hour drive this time of day."

His sense of helplessness was overwhelming. His eyes darted back and forth as his mind raced to find solutions.

An agent in a dark suit was waiting in the lobby to guide them.

"We have a helicopter inbound for the heliport near Staples Center. We're better off on foot right now. And here is a set of coms for you."

The group ran toward the Staples Center and could see the inbound helicopter sitting down.

"Let's go!" Cole yelled to everyone racing to catch up to him.

Finally, onboard and gasping for air, the group ascended over the towering buildings and headed west. Cole scrolled through his phone, searching the campus map. "Where are we sitting down?" he spoke through the aviation headset.

"UCLA Medical Center is closest helipad for us, sir."

"That's not going to work. That's too far away. This thing will be over by the time we get there." Cole brought the phone to the co-pilot.

"Can you put it down on the field at Drake stadium here or the intramural field?" Cole asked pointing to the spots.

"If there isn't much activity, maybe. Show the captain; it's his call."

The captain called out the exchange of flight controls, "You have the controls."

"I have the controls," the co-pilot replied.

The captain looked at the spot. Cole recognized his hesitation.

"The resources are on the other side of town. This will go badly, please, it's my daughter."

"We'll clear it out and sit her down, sir."

"Thank you," Cole said with a pat on the shoulder and tears in his eyes.

He sat back down and strapped himself back in and redialed Jessica's number. Straight to voicemail. He shot her another text. No reply.

"I can't reach her."

"I think Division is jamming the cell towers to avoid remote detonation."

"How'd we get the helicopter?"

"Waltuch says your welcome!"

CHAPTER 22

Los Angeles, CA – UCLA Campus

Hasim pulled the service van into the loading dock area of the Covel Commons shortly before noon. He placed the twenty-pound C02 cannister on a dolly but still needed to assemble the electronic trigger. He allowed for plenty of time. His uncle had equipped this device with a timer in addition to the pager.

He planned to set the timer for 12:45 and place the device at the air intakes in the maintenance area of the basement of the commons. He wore a maintenance uniform and matching cap but in his backpack was his light jacket and his blue LA cap if needed.

A supervisor at the loading dock saw him and did a double take as Hasim rolled the dolly with the small canister into the dock area.

"I thought they used hundred-pound tanks for the dining hall?"

"They ordered a backup tank," Hasim replied and continued moving.

Instead of the dining hall, Hasim made his way to the basement and searched the schematics on his phone to guide him to the right spot. He entered the door just as a couple of workers were leaving for their lunch break.

His uncle was right; a uniform made hiding in plain sight easy. He was a wanted man. His picture was plastered all over the news, but no one saw his face, just his uniform.

He found one of the primary air ducts that directed airflow

to the dining hall and swiftly assembled the trigger device onto the gauge. He set the timer for 12:45.

✱✱✱

Los Angeles, CA – UCLA Campus – Covel Commons

Jessica Cameron pulled her long straight blond hair back over her shoulders as she lifted her laptop out of her bag and took a seat. Sitting around the table were three other classmates in her study group.

"Where is everyone?" one of the students asked. Jessica looked around.

"I know Jen is coming, I saw her down the hall," she said.

"You got big plans for spring break?" asked Chase, with his flirtatious grin.

"Not really, just going back to my Dad's in DC to see old friends," she said smiling enjoying the attention of the young charmer.

Chase chewed on a straw in the corner of his mouth.

"Maybe I can come with you, and we can get better acquainted."

Oh boy. Here comes the full court press, she thought.

"I don't think my Dad would like that too much."

"Ahh, come on. Do you always do what your dad wants? What is he like an old-fashioned codger or something?"

'Thwup-thwup-thwup-thwup' was the increasingly loud sound that interrupted the two. The thumping of a helicopter rattled the windows as it circled of commons before descending. Everyone rose to watch it over the rooftops of the adjacent building. Jessica stood to peer out the window. The five-foot ten-inch tall coed raised herself up on her toes to see over others that were watching the scene.

"Or something," she mumbled.

"Uhh?"

"Wow. Did you see that?" Jen said pulling everyone back to their table.

"Looks like it went over by Drake Stadium. Should we go check it out?"

"I don't know, what the heck is going on?"

"I don't know. Maybe one of our star athletes sprained an ankle or something," Jen joked.

"Hey Jess, can I borrow your phone?"

"Why?"

"Mine's not working for some reason."

Jessica handed her phone over to Jen. She gave it a try.

"Nope. Yours isn't working either."

Jessica felt uneasy. *The helicopter and now cell phones not working.*

"Chase, is your phone working?"

"Why? You want to upload some wicked and naughty photos for me to remember you by over the break. I prefer video over still shots."

"Ugh! Stop being an asshole and just check your phone!"

"Whoa, you look so hot when your tense."

"Eww! Check your phone you-disgusting-perve!" She spaced out the last three words for emphasis and shot him the Cameron look.

Chase saw a side of Jessica he had never seen before, causing him to be both aroused and terrified at the same time.

"Uh…it's not working," the confused student said.

✳✳✳

Hannah Jacobs and the other agent with them took the loading dock area, while Cole and Albright raced to the front entrance.

Outside the Commons, several campus police officers were just starting to tape the area off to prevent additional foot traffic. Cole and Albright converged with two FBI agents and other campus police near the entrance.

"We've got a visual on the van," they heard Hannah say over the coms.

"Damn it!"

"Did you evacuate the building?" Cole asked the campus police at the steps.

"We blasted out the emergency text to all students and faculty. We didn't know if it was safe to go in there."

"Are you kidding me! The cell signals are jammed. Start moving them out of the building, now!"

"Jason, on me," Cole directed as he sprinted into the Commons.

"We're moving to the food court," he said through the coms.

"When we get there check the C02 canisters at the soda fountains," he told Albright as they hustled up the hall shouting for people to get out of the building.

"I don't think so, boss."

"What?"

"If it were me, I'd put it in the ventilation system."

They turned the corner in the dining hall and stopped.

"OK, get help with the schematics and get there. I hope to God you're right. I'm finding Jess."

Hasim turned the corner in the loading dock and ran right into the two FBI agents. He tried to break away, but the other agent with Hannah pinned him against the wall and subdued him. He realized he was caught.

"We've got Hasim!" Hannah called out over the coms.

"Find out where the device is!" Cole shouted back.

Hannah and the other agent were working Hasim. They held him against the wall in the loading dock and searched his pockets and his backpack. They pressed him for information.

"I said, Where's the device?"

His eyes drifted over her shoulder then he grinned. Hannah turned and saw the clock on the opposite wall. 12:42.

"It's on a timer! Get out! Get out!" she yelled over her coms.

Cole frantically searched the crowded venue looking for

his daughter, his body language telegraphed dread. The diners stared at him in confusion. He pulled out his Glock 22 and held it high in the air and began yelling.

"Everyone out! Everyone out, now!"

Some stood in awe, others took the floor. Two rounds were fired from the Glock into the ceiling. *Now they were listening* and began running out.

"Jess!" he yelled.

Albright came over the coms, "I think I found it."

"Dad!" Jess screamed back, gawking in disbelief as he ran toward her.

"Oh shit!" Chase yelled, choking on his straw and stumbling to the floor as he tried to get out of his chair. "I'm sorry, I was just messing around. I'm sorry, sir," he cried with his arms over his face.

Cole grabbed his daughter and yelled for everyone to leave. Chase was still on the floor with the crotch of his shorts wet with his urine.

"Get your ass up, let's go!"

"What's going on Dad?" Jessica frantically asked.

"No time! No time! Everyone out!" Cole pushed them along.

Albright came over the coms, "I've got it, pulling it out of the intake now. Moving it to the mechanical room to enclose it in case it's triggered."

"Leave it Jason, get out!" Cole hollered over the coms.

Albright moved the canister from the intake and quickly carried it to a nearby mechanical room with a metal door and concrete walls.

"Oh shit," he said with a sad resignation in his voice.

"Jason, get out of there now!" Hannah screamed.

"Move it, Jason!" Cole yelled.

"Honey keep going. I've got to go back. Tell the FBI agents out there who you are they'll take of you."

"Dad, no!"

"Sorry, sweetheart, I love you." He ran back through the nearly empty dining hall, motioning and yelling at stragglers to get out of the building as he found them.

"Jason, do you have your atropine with you? Jason come in?" Cole knew the nerve agent would induce asphyxiation and kill his friend in a matter of minutes.

"Hannah?"

"Negative, Cole. Back at the Luxe."

"What does the scum bag have on him," he said, stopping to get his bearings on the building layout.

"His backpack has an air mask but no atropine."

"Meet me at the basement stairs with the mask, hurry!"

They met at the stairs going to the basement.

"Give me the mask," Cole said. He pulled back the strap and lifted it over his head but was jerked backward by two men in white suits and air masks while two others pulled Hannah away.

"You both have to get out of here now! We've got to contain this," the leader of the Hazardous Materials Response Unit from the FBI yelled.

"Our, guy is down there!" Cole protested violently.

"We're sealing the door now. I know it's a shitty deal, but it was the only way."

Cole fell to his knees as he watched Hannah cry out and pull away from the chemical crew. Someone helped lift him back up to his feet.

"You need to go back out through the loading dock to the designated safe zone." One of the suits tried to retake Hannah's arm, and she yanked it away.

"I've got her, I've got her," Cole said. He put his arm around her and led her away.

✼✼✼

INTERSTATE 40 - ARIZONA

Al-Himyari slid down the embankment at the overpass

back at the spot where he had set his trap for the trucker. He was sweaty and dirty again. He climbed into the cab of the semi-truck and started it up. *Just be careful at the scales*, he told himself.

Al-Himyari killed the trucker as he was looking under the hood, slicing his throat with his faithful knife. The hardest part had been getting him in the car without being seen by the traffic passing by. He almost gave up at one point, thinking of leaving him in the ditch, but he needed to buy more time.

Instead, he put him in the car and drove into the National Park that circled back around to the overpass where he had parked. He had found a turnout about half a mile from the bridge and pulled the car off. He took all of the trucker's identifications and wiped down the car to remove his fingerprints.

As the truck rolled down the highway, he began to sing with his Arabic accent the Willie Nelson hit, *'On The Road Again.'*

He gazed at the photo of the soldier in the visor.

"Say hello to your papa." He snagged and crumbled the picture tossing it out the window to be carried by the desert wind.

Al-Himyari flipped on the satellite radio, it was tuned to Fox News Channel. The broadcasters were discussing the breaking news of the attempted terror strike on the UCLA campus. After hearing a few details, he knew the plan had failed.

"Hasim!" al-Himyari yelled pounding his fist on the steering wheel.

He used the trucker's cell and called his Russian contact.

CHAPTER 23

Washington, DC

"How was your stay with us, Mr. and Mrs. Jenkins," the desk clerk at the Hilton Capital hotel asked.

Grant Ramsey just stared at the young man.

"It was delightful, thank you," Katrina Nikolin said to appease him.

"OK, here's your receipt and let me get that package you were looking for." A moment later the clerk returned with a large Tyvek envelope.

"Here you go."

"Thank you."

Grant and Katrina left the lobby and walked a block down K Street to the coffee shop on the corner. Katrina grabbed the corner table, and Ramsey ordered her latte and his coffee.

They carefully reviewed the documents in the envelope. Another set of credentials, phones, and a car key fob. They put their old items in the packet and dumped them in the trash.

"Damn it!" Ramsey belted as he took a sip.

Katrina placed her hand on his, "What's wrong dear?"

"I hate this mustache!"

"I know dear. It won't be long now."

"Any idea where we're going?"

"The GPS in the car is set to our destination."

"And where's the car?"

"Third level of the Colonial Parking Garage just down the

street."

They picked up the car and the GPS directed them out of DC along the Potomac River on George Washington Memorial, catching 123 and then heading west on 267. After about an hour of driving, they passed Dulles International Airport and continued westward until hitting James Monroe Highway south for a while. The GPS then put them heading west again off of Highway 15.

"We're getting out in the country now," Ramsey said breaking the long period of silence.

Eventually, they turned into a long winding gravel driveway leading up to an older farmhouse with white wood siding.

The thirty-four-acre farm provided ample privacy, and the equestrian setting was purely picturesque. The farmhouse looked like something from the mid-twentieth century, and the grounds were hemmed by dark brown picket fences that defined the pastures.

Ramsey drove the car around the gravel circle to the front porch where they were greeted by two big, athletic men who decided to frisk them both. The one beast spent extra time on Katrina, causing Ramsey's blood to boil.

"Knock it off, Meathead!"

The bodyguard shot a dirty look toward the American and stepped toward him when a voice from the porch stopped him.

"Dmitry, enough! These are our guest."

The heavy-set middle-aged man looked toward the sky and then stepped back toward the door, attempting to avoid any surveillance from above.

"They've had a long drive. Please, you come in now."

"Katrina, my love, it has been too long," he said kissing her cheeks and hugging her as she entered. Ramsey noticed the man's hands going down her back to her ass.

"And you must be the famous Mr. Ramsey?" he said shaking Ramsey's hand. "I'm Gavriil, please, why don't you freshen up and get comfortable. We have much to discuss."

"Dmitry, show them to their room. Filipp will take care of the car."

The bodyguard left Ramsey's bag outside but carried Katrina's up to the stairs to their bedroom. Ramsey retrieved his bag quickly not wanting to leave Katrina with Meathead any longer than necessary.

As they situated themselves for an indefinite stay, Ramsey inquired about Gavriil as he removed the mustache and hair piece. Katrina explained that Gavriil Medvedm is her handler and had worked with her since she was brought to America.

What she did not tell Ramsey was that Medvedm was the number two SVR man in North America. He had risen in rank over the last decade mainly in part to Katrina's valuable intelligence gathering. She did the work, and he took the credit.

"I'll sometimes call him 'Bear' because that is the literal meaning of his name," she said.

"How appropriate for such a big guy, I was thinking more like, 'fat bastard,'" Ramsey's comical reference was lost on Katrina.

"Don't be rude, dear. Think more of a grizzly bear in the woods and not some fairy tale fluffy animal."

Ramsey smirked.

"I'm serious, he is not to be trifled with."

"I don't care what you call him as long I get my fucking money."

Medvedm was part of an emerging group of nationalists who grew weary of the slow progress being made to catch the West. The Kremlin's policies reflected, in their opinion, a misguided belief, that the West was on the verge of collapse, due in some part to the technology efforts of the SVR.

Teaming with China, Russia had been instrumental in influencing elections in the US and the UK with misinformation tactics, and affecting the economic policies pushing the countries deeper in debt and marching them toward hyperinflation.

But for Medvedm and his group, the progress was too

slow, and by his estimation, he would be gone and buried by the time any real results were seen.

Instead, he proposed a more radical approach. Rather than a gentle nudge, his plan called for a hard and fast punch. One that would knock his opponent out of the competition. But before he could actualize his dream of power, he needed certain obstacles removed.

Medvedm served behind the deputy of SVR for North America. In his mind, the deputy was soft and too subtle for his position of power. He had sought to undermine his authority on several occasions resulting in a few confrontations. But Medvedm had clout with the Kremlin due to the valuable intel he had produced over the last several years. His superior was stuck with his insubordinate, egotistical assistant deputy for the foreseeable future.

Medvedm sat in a large leather back chair and stoked his cigar waiting for the couple to join him. The house carried the noise from their movement, and he heard the mumblings of their conversation.

Katrina was his crowning achievement. He had taken the caterpillar and transformed her into a beautiful butterfly. The Bear knew she would always be loyal to him. *The clueless American was eating out of the palm of her hand*, he reasoned. Seeing his guest come down the stairs he motioned for them to join him in the parlor near the fireplace.

"Please, help yourself," he said pointing to the table with Vodka and Whiskey bottles.

"Our friend from Yemen arrived in Virginia a couple of days ago. He is eager to complete his mission as I am sure you are as well."

"Yes, I am very eager to get paid for my services," Ramsey said. "I've made all the preparations as requested. The equipment at the hotel is secure and ready for the meeting. I believe we agreed that payment would be made in the form of bearer bonds."

"That is correct, but we have a bit of a problem."

Ramsey didn't like where this was going,

"What sort of problem?"

"Our friend has requested one more task that I need your help with."

"Spit it out Bear," Ramsey said with growing frustration, sensing he had been misled.

The Russian man's veins bulged from his fat forehead. He sought to contain his contempt for the American. Smoke from his cigar floated above his head, he reminded himself that he still needed the bastard.

"Mr. Ramsey, please, you will have your bonds as we agreed. We simply have a need that matches your unique skill set."

"Go on."

"In addition to the bonds, I'm prepared to offer another four million in cryptocurrency for your inconvenience."

"And if I say, 'no'?"

"We are not animals Mr. Ramsey, you are free to go with your bonds." The large man drew another puff and released circles into the air.

"But Katrina, on the other hand, belongs to the State and she will be required to carry out the mission without you. Oh, and of course her half of the bonds will stay with her as well."

"That's bullshit," Ramsey said turning to Katrina. "Kat?"

"What he says is true. I can't leave without completing the mission."

Ramsey had an idea where the Bear was leading him but also realized that he already had blood on his hands and that staying ahead of the CIA or the SVR for that matter would be an expensive endeavor. He and Katrina needed the money.

"OK Bear," Ramsey gave his wry reply. "I'm in, but I want half now and the remainder when the job is completed. I will expect the balance of the cryptocurrency to be transferred before my feet leave the states. And one more thing, Katrina and I never want to see you or Meathead ever again."

"As you wish."

"OK, which one do I have to kill?"

CHAPTER 24

McLean Virginia

Cole scrambled the eggs in the skillet and turned over the slices of Canadian bacon. He sighed thinking about the hellish nightmare he and those close to him had experienced. It had been over a week ago that the team was in LA, working with the FBI frantically trying to stop the terrorists. And they had. The devices were secure and the terrorists arrested. But success, as Cole had learned, in this field was always costly.

Jason Albright was a great young man with a bright and promising future. His parents were presented with the FBI Memorial Star for his selfless act of courage that saved hundreds of lives.

He tossed the eggs and Canadian bacon slices on two plates. Albright had saved his beautiful daughter, Jessica, from a horrific act of vengeance.

"Breakfast is ready," he hollered.

"Morning Dad," Jessica said, peering out the front window before shuffling back to the kitchen island in her pajamas.

"Hey, Sweetie. What are you looking for?"

"Just seeing who was out there," Jessica said referring to the FBI agents parked outside to help provide security.

"Here you go. Best eggs you'll ever have." Cole slid the plate over to her.

"And he's not out there."

"Who?"

"You know who. Agent Kincaid."

Cole had seen the way Jessica looked at the young agent and more concerning to him was how the agent looked at his daughter.

"These are good. But you cook 'em the same way every time," Jessica said changing the subject.

"Oh, I thought you liked them this way. Not that I can do other ways, but you always liked them."

"Oh no, they're great, but I like variety too."

"OK, I'll make a note of that along with a million other things I'm learning about you."

He smiled and kissed the back of her head as he pulled up the stool next to her.

"You hear from your friends at school?"

"Yeah! You're like a freakin' hero. Everyone chatting about it. I can't believe that was you in the helicopter."

"Hey what about the kid in your study group? You know, Mr. Wet Pants."

"Dad! That's so mean." She slapped his left shoulder.

"Easy, easy."

"Oh yeah, I forgot sorry."

After a few bites, she shifted the subject.

"Dad, I'd really like to get back to school as soon as possible. I mean next week is spring break but after that, I want to be there when classes start back."

"We talked about this, Jess. Until they find this guy, I can't let you do that."

"Dad, I'm nineteen. Technically I can do whatever I want. I mean you can't stay home forever and how long is someone going to be parked outside our house watching us."

"You didn't seem to mind when Kincaid was out there. And for a young guy, he seemed to have a weak bladder. I mean how many times did he come in the house to use the bathroom?"

"Dad! I'm serious."

"Jess, until I know you're safe. And I do have to go in today, but I've asked Darryl to come by and stay with you." Capps was on medical leave recovering from his leg wound.

"Oh my God, Dad! I don't need a babysitter! How embarrassing! It was bad enough you had Mr. Capps, here when you went to the funeral the other day. I mean, he's really intimidating and grumpy. And he's injured, how much help could he be?"

"Hey, Darryl could kick most people's ass with just one good leg. And is it really such a bad thing to want you safe."

"Dad, in this world I'll never be a hundred percent safe. You of all people should know that. They may never find this guy. But I don't want to stop living my life. I mean, it really isn't fair."

Cole knew she was right.

"OK, I get it. I can't treat you like a little kid but before I go today, we're going to go through some dry firing drills with the XD and Darryl will be over."

"Ugh! You should have had a boy!"

"No, that's my terms and their final, oh and you do the dishes."

***

Counterterrorism Center – Langley

Cole arrived at CTC early for the Friday afternoon meeting that McCune had requested. He used the extra time to check in on Amy Wiggins. Amy had worked closely with Jason Albright on the project. The two had spent hundreds of hours together over the last few weeks. Their workstations always side by side. To Cole, they seemed to have their own techie language, and by the end of their first week together they could finish one another's sentences.

He last saw Amy along with Hannah at Jason's funeral just two days ago. They both seemed so distraught and affected that Cole worried for them. But with Amy, who was such a bright light of positivity, he feared that her soul would be so scarred with grief that her natural illumination would be permanently dimmed or even extinguished.

He understood this pain. He had felt it several years ago when he lost his brother. And then after his experience in Yemen, he felt that he had somehow become hardened and callused.

Jason Albright had died saving him and his daughter and perhaps hundreds of others. He truly enjoyed working with Jason. The kid looked up to him. Cole smiled at the thought of the blanket that Jason had put on him on the flight to LA.

But Cole struggled to understand why he was not feeling deep sadness, like Amy or Hannah. It seemed surreal to him. Maybe his soul was forever hardened. He thought of the implications and hoped it would not be true of Amy.

Her back was to him at her workstation as Cole entered the war room and stood next to the empty chair and workstation of Albright.

"Hey girl," he said putting his hand on her shoulder.

She seemed distracted, but got up and hugged Cole.

"Sorry, I must have zoned out. Just digging through Jason's data. It's tough."

"Why don't you have someone else do that?"

"No, I understand how he works and it's best if I do it."

"How's Jess?"

"We're good, thanks. FBI's got a security detail helping watch for now."

Cole motioned to the skeleton crew and some tech guys moving equipment. "I really wish we could have wrapped this up ourselves. Al-Himyari is still out there."

"The FBI's got it now. He's rapidly ascending the most wanted list."

After the takedown of the suspects and the additional devices, the FBI concluded that al-Himyari was on the run. Hasim and the other four cell members were in custody but refused to cooperate with authorities. The manhunt was generating thousands of leads for the Bureau to qualify, but the most promising came from the southwest region in

California and Arizona. Some speculated that al-Himyari had worked his way back across the border into Mexico to escape.

"I know, speaking of the FBI, has Hannah been by here lately?"

"I haven't seen her since the funeral. But she said she was taking some time off."

"Hmm," Cole nodded. "I've got to meet with McCune, call me if you need anything."

McCune sat at her desk combing through emails, she waved Cole in when she saw him at the door. He closed the door behind him and took the seat in front of her desk. She held one finger up requesting another minute of work before they spoke.

"Sorry about that," she said turning her attention to Cole.

"No problem."

"How's your daughter?"

"She seems OK. I don't think she's fully absorbed how close she came or how dangerous the situation could be. To make matters worse, she's just at that awkward age?"

"Brace yourself, that awkward age for most women is between the ages of twelve and thirtysomething."

Cole laughed, "Yeah, I guess so."

"The key Cole is for you to stop being her manager and become her consultant."

"I'll keep that in mind."

"When do you feel you'll be ready to get back into the fight?" McCune asked with a more serious tone.

"As long as the FBI continues to provide security detail, I feel like I'm OK getting back in. Jess is spending a lot of time with her friend and pushing to move on, I think she'll be going back to school after the break next week."

"OK, I'll make a call and push to keep resources allocated for the security detail until she leaves. Take the rest of the weekend with Jess and feel free to take some time next week with her home but I'd like for you to come in on Monday to start your new role."

"Beg your pardon, ma'am."

"You've been promoted Officer Cameron, well, effective Monday," she said handing him a folder. "You'll need to take this over to personnel."

Cole opened the folder, "Wait," he said in disbelief. "This is for Assistant Director of CTC."

"That's right. But really, it's just a title. We have something a little more creative in mind. This just gets your pay grade where it should be with the added responsibility."

"Ma'am I'm not sure."

"Nancy, please."

"Nancy, I have to tell you before this whole thing with the AIJB, I was ready to resign. In fact, I think the letter is still in my case. I'm sure some more worthy candidates have been waiting for an opportunity like this."

"Oh yes. There are plenty of candidates scrapping at the next rung on the ladder, and you'll need to watch your back, for sure. That, I can tell you from firsthand experience."

Cole dropped his head thinking about the prejudice he had shown McCune.

"But none of those have the kind of experience that you have. Do you realize what all you've been through in the last couple of months?"

Still surprised, Cole sat silent for a moment, then asked, "So what is this new role entail?"

"Let's leave the details for Monday. There's too much to get into, and I'm booked solid. So, unfortunately, we need to wrap this up."

Cole rose to leave.

"Be sure to wear a nice suit and tie on Monday. You'll want to look good for the photograph," McCune suggested.

"What photograph?" asked the puzzled Cole.

"You're being awarded the Intelligence Star. The Director himself will be here to bestow the honors."

"I don't know what to say." Cole searched for the right words. He understood the significance of this award. The Intelligence Star is awarded by the Central Intelligence Agency to its officers for 'extraordinary heroism.' It is the third-highest award given by the Central Intelligence Agency, behind the Distinguished Intelligence Cross and Distinguished Intelligence Medal.

McCune held her hand up to the door signaling her PA to wait. "Between your work in Yemen and Titan Shield efforts, you've earned it. Although the public will not hear about Yemen."

"Amir and Capps?"

"Intelligence Medals, Amir posthumously and Capps will have another Jock Strap Medal." McCune was referring to the Intelligence Medal that is given in secret due to the mission. "And of course, Amir's will have a spot on the memorial wall."

"I'd feel better about this if al-Himyari was found."

"That's why I like you, Officer Cameron," she said opening the door. "We think alike. That's exactly what I told the Director. But then he reminded me Hasni is dead, a terrorist attack was averted and you ran in when others were running out. You deserve it."

Cole assumed that the Director was looking to capitalize on the recent public events to generate a more favorable impression of the Agency.

"So, this is a public ceremony?" Cole dreadfully asked.

"Yes, it is Officer Cameron. Bring your daughter. I'm sure she will be proud," McCune said as the admin assistant entered the room.

"Ma'am, the Gala?" Charlie said pointing to Cole as he exited the door.

"Grab him and ask him yourself," she scoffed.

"Officer Cameron!" the admin shouted trying to catch him.

"Hey Charlie, what is it?"

"The Director's office called again, looking for your plus one info for the Gala."

"Oh yeah. Sorry about that. Can I let you know on Monday?"

"I don't know if I can hold Shanelle off over the weekend.

She's a beast," Charlie said referring to the director's PA. He stood to wait a minute, then gave in, "Monday. 09:00 at the latest."

"Great, thanks. I'll text you if I have it sooner," Cole said.

Strolling the hall between cubicles toward the elevators Cole became acutely aware that things were different. Looking back, he realized there had been subtle changes along the way, ever since the Titan Shield team was formed but especially after the Yemen operation.

Colleagues in the CTC building who previously ignored him or showed little interest now offered friendly nods and smiles. *I guess all it took to get a little respect was getting shot, killing a few bad guys, nearly getting poisoned with nerve gas, watching two of your colleagues get killed and having your family targeted by a terrorist.*

As he stepped into the elevator, he sent a text to Jessica.

You OK if I invite a friend over for dinner tonight?

Sure, she replied.

Good, can you prepare a salad and prep for my Chicken Pasta dinner?

CHAPTER 25

Washington, DC –Wharf District

C ole walked up the stairs of the mid-rise condo building in the Southwest waterfront neighborhood on 4th street. Over the last few years, the area had seen significant redevelopment attracting an eclectic mix of residences. Hannah Jacobs' building was on the modest side to that mix.

Reaching her apartment number on the sixth floor, he knocked at the door. He thought he could hear movement, but waited before giving the door another tap with his knuckles. On the other side of the door, Hannah Jacobs looked through the peephole and saw Cole.

"Shit!" she whispered to herself, looking at her reflection in the mirror. She felt like she was a mess having spent the last few days locked in and grieving in her home, leaving only for the funeral and a walk to the groceries.

Her image in the mirror wasn't very flattering in her mind. She was braless and wearing a thin white tee shirt and shorts. She plucked at the chest of the tee shirt in a futile attempt to hide the obvious.

"Shit!" she whispered again, hearing the second knock.

"Not a good time, Cole."

"Sorry to surprise you," Cole said through the door, "but you haven't responded to my text or calls."

"I know, I'm sorry, but..." she paused, "I'll call, I promise." She peered the tiny fishbowl lens to see Cole's confused expression.

"Hey, it took a little effort to get your address, and I fought traffic on a Friday afternoon to get here. The least you can do is let me in."

Suddenly, Cole thought of the possibility that she was with someone else. *Damn it.*

"Oh, it must have been a rough ride in your Range Rover." She grinned, taking pleasure in watching his uncomfortableness without him being able to see her.

Then she realized it was her uncomfortableness that she was most concerned about. How would Cole respond to seeing her in this condition? Her hair was a mess, not to mention she was wearing the same tee shirt and shorts she had been in since getting home from the funeral two days ago.

"What?" Cole asked growing a little annoyed, "what about the Range Rover?" He was clueless.

One more peek out the door, and she couldn't resist. He was like a little puppy dog pleading with his eyes for attention. His expression coupled with the distorted view from the fishbowl lens was just too much.

"I'm going to unlock the door but count to ten before you come in. I've got to put on some clothes," Hannah said peering through the hole. She saw a big goofy grin come over Cole's face.

"Shit!" she whispered again.

She unlocked the door and dashed to the bedroom closing the door. She tossed her tee shirt in the hamper, threw on a bra and frantically looked for the right clothes to wear. Cole made it to five. She heard the door open.

"Coming in!" Cole called out.

"Shit," she muttered repeatedly.

He walked in and saw a hall that leads to a closed-door directly ahead. He assumed it was the bedroom and to the right that was the door to the half bath. The condo was nicely remolded creating an open floor plan with light hardwood flooring throughout. He entered the open area to his left taking in his environment.

The home was furnished in a modest contemporary style.

The small condo's kitchen had nice white shaker cabinets and granite counter tops followed by a dining table with four chairs and a living area with a grey sofa and side chair.

A large glass window and sliding door led off from the living area onto a patio overlooking the courtyard area. Cole pictured himself sitting with her at the teak patio set and enjoying an evening. His world had changed, and he wanted Hannah to be a part of his new life.

Cole could hear drawers opening and closing in the other room. He swore he could hear the word *'shit'* being mumbled with each drawer closing.

The bedroom door opened and Hannah's voice carried down the hall.

"Make yourself at home. I may have something you like in the fridge. Just help yourself." The door closed again.

Cole walked over yelled down the hall, "What are you doing?"

"Never you mind. Just give me a few minutes," Hannah yelled back, holding a shirt up to see herself in the mirror.

She looked closer at her puffy eyes, threw the shirt on the bed, ran back into the master bath and started frantically brushing her hair and applying mascara to her eyelashes.

"Shit," she muttered thinking about how this all was going down. She grabbed her electric toothbrush and shoved it in her mouth.

"Shit," she said again, spraying the toothpaste foam on her mirror. She wiped the mirror and rinsed with mouthwash.

Cole recognized the grey smart speaker on the wall table behind the couch. He had an idea.

He thought *It's now or never.*

He gave a verbal command to the device to play 'Unknown' by Jacob Banks on all speakers." The device repeated the order and complied. It was a song Jessica had put on his playlist, and for some reason every time he heard the haunting rhythm, he thought of his yearning for Hannah.

Hannah stood by the bed still undecided about what to wear. She buttoned the blue striped shirt when the small round smart speaker on her nightstand began playing the soft melody.

"Shit," she whispered, frozen by the surprise of his forward move.

"Oh shit," she whispered again, recognizing the intentionality of the song selection and hearing his footsteps on the hardwood floor coming toward her door.

She thought *It's now or never*. She held her hand to her chest and felt her heart pounding. There was a soft knock on the bedroom door.

"Shit," she said softly with resignation, yielding to the draw of her heart as Cole slowly opened the door and moved to her.

He said nothing but slowly leaned in and passionately kissed her. She stood on her toes, wrapped her arms around his neck, her emotions racing as she invited him into her heart.

He leaned her against the wall and braced himself with his right arm. She held his face gasped for air between their kisses. He unbuttoned her shirt and explored her body with his left hand as she grabbed his collar and pulled him in. Their bodies bumped against the wall driven by desire.

She gently pushed him back, to catch her breath before saying, "Cole, it's been a long time for me…"

Cole put his finger to her mouth. "For me too," he said, taking her by the hand to the bed to satisfy each of their cravings.

Later, they laid together on the bed fully depleted, looking at the ceiling. Hannah rested her head on his right shoulder. Cole pulled her dark hair back to see her face. Words were unnecessary. They simply enjoyed the moment.

Eventually, Hannah broke the silence, "I'm starving."

"Me too!"

"Sorry, that's not much in the fridge."

"No problem. That's why I came. I wanted to invite you to my home for dinner."

"Oh Cole, I don't know, your daughter may not like that

idea." Hannah got up from the bed to dress.

"Well, I mean I was inviting you over because I wanted her to meet the woman I'm taking to the Gala. That was before all of this," he said waving his hand across the bed.

"What Gala?"

"Remember? I asked you out, twice I believe. And you conveniently never gave me an answer."

"You asked me to 'a thing' as I remember. It was right in the middle of you tackling a terrorist. We were sort of busy, you know."

"I know. I know. Wait, is that a 'yes?'"

"Sure, I'll go. I've never seen anyone work this hard to ask for a date."

"Come on, get dressed, Jess is going to have everything prepped."

"You sure she's going to be cool with this?"

"Positive," Cole said pulling his pants on.

Hannah looked at the clothes tossed on the bench at the foot of the bed.

"Shit!"

"What's wrong?"

"I still don't know what to wear."

✳✳✳

McLean Virginia

The dinner did not go as expected for Cole. Evidently, Jessica assumed his friend would be Mr. Capps or some other male colleague. She had failed to decode his message. As a result, the three struggled to shuffle food around their plates and words from their mouths.

"This sauce is delicious Jessica. What do you use?" Hannah attempted yet again.

"A jar," came the tart reply.

"Well, it's good. I really like it."

"And, it's not just any jar," Cole stepped in trying to break the tension, "tell her what our favorite is, honey."

"It's Newman's Sookarooni," she said with a fake smile.

"Oh really?" Hannah said trying to muster some enthusiasm.

"Are you enjoying studying at UCLA?"

"Sure, it was great until you guys all showed up and a terrorist tried to kill my friends and me."

"Jess!" Cole scolded. "Where's this coming from?"

"May I be excused?"

"No, hold on. What's going on here?"

"You said you were having a friend over. I even cooked it and everything," Jessica said throwing her napkin down.

"Hannah is my friend."

"Maybe I should leave," Hannah said starting to get up, but Cole reached his hand out.

"Wait. She is my friend."

"Well, I thought I was cooking for Mr. Capps or somebody else. I didn't know I was cooking for your date. How long have you two been dating anyway?"

Cole and Hannah looked at each other. "Well, I guess since today."

"Oh my God, Dad. You brought her here on your first date!" then she turned to Hannah, "Wow, isn't that a little quick."

"Jess! We've been working together for a couple of months. It's not like we're strangers."

"You work together? Isn't that against the rules or something."

"Jess! Stop it now!" Cole said slamming his hand down on the table startling both Jessica and Hannah.

"Listen, yes we've been working together for a couple months, but only on this project. Hannah is with the FBI, which you would have known if you would have listened to our conversation or shown interest in someone other than yourself."

Cole stood up from the table.

"I'm sorry. I really am. Hannah and I have been through a lot together in a very short time. And now that our task force is over, I wanted to see her."

He dropped his head, lowered his voice and slowed his speech.

"I know it's hard for you to understand, but we've both had near misses with death. Do you get that? We've both lost people close to us. People we cared about are dead."

He saw a tear run down Hannah's cheek and his eyes teared up as well.

"My God Jess. Can't you see we're both hurting so bad? But somehow in the midst of all the sadness when I'm with Hannah I'm happy."

Jessica looked at Hannah who was drying a tear. She saw her Dad's pain and Hannah's as well and dropped her head in shame.

"Look, a lot is changing. And I'm sorry for the way this happened. I really should have been clear in my text."

"Yes, you should have!" both women said in near unison, throwing Cole off his train of thought. He chuckled and then received a death stare from both of them.

"OK Jess, I told you about the Gala, and you asked me who I was taking. I told you I wasn't sure yet. Well, I had asked Hannah, but with everything that went down, we had not solidified our plans. Today she said yes, and I wanted her to meet you. That's why I texted you."

Everyone sat quietly.

"Hell, if I were inviting Darryl Capps over, I wouldn't text you to help with dinner, we'd just get pizza."

"I bet right now, you wish you would have invited Capps over instead?" Hannah said blowing out her cheeks.

Cole saw a slight grin on Jessica's face, and with it came a little relief.

"Hell, right now, I wish I would have invited him to the Gala!"

The tension broke as everyone laughed picturing the

possibilities.

"He's a big man, I'm not sure you could handle him," Hannah said laughing.

"Oh my God, he is so intimidating!" Jessica chimed in. "Dad had him stay here when he went to the funeral. He kept telling me *'girly, get away from the window,' 'who you calling now, girly,' 'your daddy needs an ass whipping, girly,' 'he done ruined my vacation.'"* Jessica mocked Capps' deep, gravelly voice, leading to a good hard laugh by all.

"Cole, you should take Jessica to the Gala," Hannah suggested.

"No. No. You guys go. Besides, Dad would probably just try to embarrass me."

Hannah nodded toward Jessica, prodding Cole to push harder.

"You know, you're right. I'm not sure I want to make a fool of myself on a dance floor with Hannah, why don't you come with me like she said."

Jessica's face lit up with an idea.

"Do you have extra tickets?"

"What? What do you mean?"

"Well, if you had two extra tickets, you two could go, and I could get a friend to go."

"A friend?" Cole questioned, unsure if he liked where this idea was going. He saw the sheepish grin on his daughter's face.

"Oh no, Kincaid is off limits!"

"Wait. Kincaid. Is that the rookie agent we met outside on the way in?" Hannah asked smiling at Jessica. "Well, I certainly see the attraction."

Jess smiled.

"Ladies, please," Cole said clearing his throat.

"Dad! No. I was thinking of bringing Brittany. Please."

"Yeah, I guess I can ask for the extra tickets. Hannah is that OK with you?"

"Well, it would be a dating first for me, going on a double date with a father and his daughter."

She paused sipping her wine as both of the Camerons waited for her response. *She's his daughter alright,* she thought.

"Sure. I'm in."

"Good you can take Hannah, and we can have David drive us."

"Who is David?" Hannah asked.

"Agent David Kincaid," Cole replied in a stare down with his daughter.

Hannah sipped on her glass of wine and tried to watch out the corner of her eye to see who would blink first.

"One more thing," Cole said breaking the stare, "there will be a little ceremony Monday morning near my office. Jess, I'd like for you to be there and Hannah if you're free maybe you could meet us there, as well."

"What kind of ceremony?"

"Evidently, someone thought I deserved to be awarded the Intelligence Star for our recent work."

"Wow, that's a big deal. It's like the third highest award in the CIA," Hannah said.

"I think they're just trying to get some good press out of the situation," Cole said pouring more wine for Hannah.

"Is that where they put a star on the wall?" Jessica asked.

"No, that's for those who die in the line of duty." Cole paused and thought of Amir. He explained the differences in the medals and awards in the CIA and that many are given secretly. Cole also shared that he was receiving a promotion, although he wasn't sure what the new job entailed. He was moving forward.

As he discussed the promotion, he noticed Hannah's body language, she had a very subtle look of concern. He knew he would need to explore that further at a later point.

Later Jessica was on the couch texting with her friends while watching a reality show. Cole and Hannah stood at the sink doing the dishes that Hannah had insisted they do since Jessica had prepared the meal.

She handed Cole a plate to dry and looked up at him and narrated in a whisper their previous exchange.

"She asked, *'are you sure your daughter is going to be cool with this?', 'positive,'* he said not skipping a beat." She handed him another plate and shook her head.

"Well, I think it ended alright," he said.

"Yeah, crises averted for now," she whispered looking over toward the couch.

"Thank you for tonight. I think I'm ready to get home."

"You sure?"

"Yeah. Where did I put my phone? I'm going to get an uber."

"No. No. I'll drive you back."

"Nonsense, you should stay with Jessica."

Jessica overheard their whispers.

"It's OK Hannah. Dad should drive you back."

Hannah was facing Cole with her back to Jessica when she heard her call out, her eyes widened and gave Cole a look that said, *you're killing me.* "Oh no Jessica, that's not necessary," she said turning to the living room.

"No please, take him," she said with an eye roll, "he'll just make me watch 'Last of the Mohicans' for the hundredth time, or 'Hoosiers,' actually, that one's not too bad."

She stood and walked over to them.

"And please, call me Jess…and…I'm really sorry about tonight. I was way out of line, and you should know that my parents raised me better than that. I was just caught off guard, it was not your fault."

Cole was proud that his daughter had recovered her maturity.

"Thanks, Jess," Hannah said giving her a hug. "I think your Dad is a special guy, even if he is a poor communicator."

"Hey!" Cole said taking the brunt of the joke.

"Well, you must be a special woman for him to bring you here to meet me. I'll see you on Monday."

Cole and Hannah pulled out of the driveway, he waved to the agents sitting watch in the car across from his home. As he drove down the street, he said to her, "See, I told you I was *'positive'* everything was going to be great."

"Uh-huh."

"Oh, I forgot to tell you, the kid has superhuman powers when it comes to hearing. Seriously, especially when you are whispering. I mean, the TV going, texting, multitasking, doesn't matter, she'll pick up everything. I swear I don't know how she does it."

"Uh-huh."

Cole was getting a little nervous that it was all going to be too much, too fast for Hannah.

"Hannah. You OK?"

"Hears everything, huh?"

"Yeah, it's crazy."

"I guess we'll be spending a lot of time at my place, then."

CHAPTER 26

Washington, DC

The weekend went by way too fast for Cole. He had broken away from the house on Saturday to visit Hannah. This time she was prepared for his arrival, and he could barely pull himself away from her. On Sunday, he and Jess were growing stir crazy in the home, so they drove downtown and walked parts of Arlington Cemetery and then went to the Lincoln Memorial.

Cole had taken Jess there a few times over the years when he wanted to have father-daughter talks with her. They stood in the Memorial looking over the engraving of the second inaugural address.

"What is it about these places you like so much?" Jess asked.

"I guess it's the thought that such great sacrifices were made for freedom and it reminds me to respect and honor those sacrifices made by men like your uncle Jack and Jason Albright."

He looked over to Lincoln and put his arm around his daughter appreciating the time they had but realizing as she grew older there would be less.

As they walked back to the car, Jess saw her Dad, texting. "Why don't you invite her over again tonight. I could use a mulligan from Friday night," she said.

"She's not going to trust that I've communicated well enough. I mean, you're not the only one needing a mulligan."

"Call her."

"You sure?"

Jess nodded.

Cole obeyed and dialed Hannah's number, but before he could bring the phone to his ear, Jess had snatched it from his hand, wanting to personally deliver the message to avoid any misunderstandings.

"I was just thinking about you," Hannah said in a soft sexy voice as she answered the phone.

Jess freaked out and shoved the phone back to her Dad. Cole shrugged his shoulders questioning Jessica's reaction.

"She's thinking about you," Jess whispered and shook herself as if gross insects had just crawled all over her body.

"Cole, you there?" Hannah asked hearing muffled sounds.

"Shit!" she quietly screamed clenching her fist in the air.

"Hannah," Cole said trying to remain cool.

"She heard that didn't she," Hannah gritted through her teeth. "Oh my God, she does hear everything."

"Umm, well, hey, Jess wants to talk to you."

"Cole!" Hannah yelled. Then blew her cheeks out.

Cole handed the phone to Jess who had regained her composure.

"Hi, Hannah. My Dad and I wanted to see if you wanted to come over tonight. We're probably just going to watch a movie or something."

"Ahh...thanks, Jess, that's very kind, but I'm not sure. I mean, I know your Dad really wants to spend as much time as possible with you before you go back to school. I don't want to get in the way of that."

"Oh please, come. It's my idea, seriously."

Jessica walked a few steps away from her father.

"I know my Dad really wants to see you and besides I thought maybe you could help me pick out something for the Gala as well."

Hannah agreed.

Later that evening the three enjoyed conversation over dinner and learned more about each other. Afterward, Jess grabbed her iPad and asked Hannah to join her on the couch.

She scrolled through images of formal evening wear she had narrowed down to a handful of favorites. "This is the one my Mom likes the most," Jess said showing the picture to Hannah.

"Oh yeah. That's beautiful. I think you'd look great in that." As the two reviewed other selections and pointed out nuances of each, Cole dismissed himself to his study for a while.

He sat at the desk and flipped through encrypted emails, preparing himself for the upcoming week. He had appreciated the time he had been given to take care of his daughter, to grieve and to connect with a remarkable woman. But he also missed the work, the productivity, the sense of accomplishment that he had grown accustomed to over the last few weeks.

He was anxious to see what McCune had in store for him in his new role, but none of the recent emails gave any details on that. After a while, he decided it was movie time before it got too late.

"OK, girl time is over!" he said entering under the barrel archway back to the family room breaking up the fashion conversation.

"Which one?" he asked picking up the smart device remote.

"Oh my God, Dad, no. Really?"

"Which one, what?"

"He wants to see something like 'Last of the Mohicans' or 'Hoosiers,'" Jessica explained.

"Hey, I tried to get you to expand your entertainment choices years ago, but there's only a dozen that you let me use."

"Dad, you really should have had a boy," she said.

"Hannah when I was a kid, he would make me watch these 'guy' movies with him. 'Gettysburg,' 'Saving Private Ryan,' 'Band of Brothers', 'the Rock,' I mean you get the idea. So, I agreed that each time I come home I would sit through it at least once and tonight is it."

"How long ago did you start this," Hannah asked.

"I was probably around ten."

"Wow, isn't that kind of young?"

"Hey, parental discretion is just that, and besides you didn't mention 'Brian's Song' or 'Pride of the Yankees,'" Cole said defending himself.

"You mean the ones you tear up in. Then tell me it's your allergies acting up."

Hannah laughed trying to picture Cole in that situation.

"Oh, my Mom, hated it," Jessica said. "But when he quotes these lines at least I know what he's saying."

Hannah shook her head, "Yeah, guys really like to quote movie lines, I don't get it."

"OK, if you two are done now," Cole said handing the remote to Jessica. "Jess, you pick it, I'll start the popcorn."

Jessica scrolled across the icons on the screen and said, "We've got to work you up to 'Last of the Mohicans.' I don't think you're ready for that yet," she said as she searched other options.

"Hey, I'm an FBI agent, bring it on!"

"OK, blood and heartbreak it is," Jess warned.

"Good choice," Hannah said with a smile. *I really like this girl, after all*, she thought.

"Let me help you, Cole," she said joining him in the kitchen and sneaking a kiss.

"I'm having a good time," she said taking his hand and reaching up to kiss him again. This time their lips smacked a little, and she covered her mouth.

"I'm starting the movie!" Jessica said with a hint of *I can hear you* carried in her voice.

"Damn the open floor plan," Cole joked in a whisper.

Later, near the end of the movie, Jess had fallen asleep, and Hannah snuggled up close to Cole who was seated in the oversized chaise part of the couch. She laid her head on his shoulder and thought about how their lives were so different, but at the same time they seemed to share the same values, and for her, they really seemed to fit well together.

She had tried other relationships in the past, but nothing seemed to fit as he did for her. He was confident, but not arrogant or pretentious, he was fearless and yet humble at heart, and he was modest yet had shown that he could be strong-willed. She admired his relationship with Jess, not an easy feat for any man.

Perhaps that was another quality that pulled at her heart. Cole reminded her a lot of her own father. An honorable man, worthy of respect, who had taught her not to settle for anyone who did not deserve her love.

She had failed to heed that advice a few years earlier when she was swooned by a tall young medical doctor quickly advancing his career. Her ex attempted to spoil her materially, which to her, proved he really didn't know her.

She paused on that thought and scanned her environment. Cole lived in a great neighborhood, in a very nice home, drove a luxury car. But it really wasn't his identity, like it was for her ex. She had the feeling Cole's contentment was not determined by his possessions.

Her ex had also insisted that she give up her career at the FBI. It started out as a big turn on for the guy, telling all his friends he was dating a *'hot young FBI Agent'* fresh out of the academy. It seemed innocent enough in the beginning, but the warning signs were there for her if she'd just had eyes wide open. She had caught him sending a compromising photo of her to one of his friends early in the relationship. She nearly ended it then, but he charmed his way out.

Then there was the way her parents were around him. While they were always polite and never said an ill word, they just behaved differently with him around. Deep down she knew her father did not like the man. Visits to their small fifteen-acre farm in the East Tennessee mountains always felt therapeutic to her except during the time she was with her ex. The tension made the visits uncomfortable. Her father could never hide his emotions very well.

Hannah had pushed her father for his thoughts before the marriage, and he had cloaked his concerns about the man. He had peppered her with questions like, *'how does she know he's the one? And does she have any doubts? Why him?'* Finally, she remembered him saying, *'when you know it, you really know it, you won't have to ask if it's right.'*

At twenty-seven years old, she tried to understand that but didn't fully comprehend it until she experienced it for herself. Now at age thirty-four, she wondered if life had given her a second chance.

She had watched her parents over the years. They had served as a great role model of a successful marriage and family. She felt blessed and appreciated her good fortune. But evidently, it had not helped her in choosing men.

The relationship with her ex became increasingly toxic. Eventually, they were in constant bitter arguments usually centered around their two demanding careers. At one point, the ex even followed her on an assignment accusing her of cheating. It was then that she realized that she was just another one of his possessions. She filed for divorce and never looked back.

After the divorce, she made a couple of other attempts at relationships, but they didn't stick, and she made a commitment to herself that the next man she brought to meet her parents would be a keeper.

She put her hand on Cole's chest feeling his heartbeat, and it hit her, she remembered her Dad describing how he felt when he was dating her Mom and worked on the oil pipeline in Oklahoma. He had been gone for months, and when he came home and saw her on her front porch, he said his heart *'nearly jumped out of his chest.'*

Warmth filled her heart as she recalled what Cole had told her that day when she kissed him. She quietly giggled and thought aloud, "Dad was right, when you know it you really know it."

"What?" Cole asked quietly, not wanting to wake Jess as the credits to the movie scrolled.

"Oh, nothing. I guess he's the last Mohican, right?" she said referring to the movie as she raised herself up and pulled her hair back over her ear.

"Wait, your eyes are little wet."

"Damn allergies."

CHAPTER 27

CIA Headquarters - Langley

"You look so handsome, Dad!" Jess said adjusting her Dad's tie as they waited alone in the media room next to the large lobby at CIA headquarters.

"Thanks, sweetheart. I'm glad you're here."

Cole saw Hannah being escorted by security into the room. He waved to the guard at the door as Hannah entered and kissed him on the cheek.

"God, you look great!" she said, giving him the once over.

"That's what she said," Cole replied creating an unintentional pun.

Both women gave him a dirty look.

"No, really, that's what she said," pointing to Jessica. Hannah shook her head thinking of the retraining of her man that might be required.

"You look great, too."

The ceremony was pretty straightforward and relatively quick. It was Cole's chance to score the two extra tickets though, and he took advantage when the Director offered, "let me know if there is anything I can do for you."

Cole saw his opening and introduced the Director to his date for the Gala and his daughter and requested the two extra tickets to Gala.

"Absolutely! This pretty young girl will be the talk of the party. Shanelle, get officer Cole two extra tickets for Saturday night would you." He said, leaving Cole with the PA glaring at him as if she wanted to strangle him as she gathered the details for security clearance. *Charlie was right*, he thought, *she is a beast.*

As the media room cleared out, McCune greeted Hannah and introduced herself to Jessica.

"You must be very proud of your father."

"Yes, Ma'am," Jessica replied. She was enjoying the attention and perhaps for the first time realized the importance of her Dad's work. It was also a sobering thought that she had been fortunate that they had gotten to her and her friends in time.

McCune congratulated Cole again and said, "See you at the office, later."

"Dad, I'm so proud of you," Jessica said as tears began to flow.

"Hey, honey, what's wrong?"

"Nothing. No, I just don't think I realized…I didn't realize how lucky I am."

"Ahh. Thank you, sweetie. I feel pretty damn lucky too."

They held each other for a moment.

"I hate to leave you both, but I've got to get to the office."

"Oh Dad, I forgot I need some money for the dress. I asked Hannah to go with me to help me try on some things."

"I thought you'd already picked it out," Cole said, regretting the words as soon as he had spoken them, receiving the look again.

"Just use your credit card, I'll reimburse you."

Jessica wrapped her arm around Hannah's arm and pulled her away toward the door. "Wait," Cole said. "Jess give us a second."

Jessica let her go back to the media and stayed in the lobby to give them some space.

"You sure you're OK with this?" Cole asked, concerned that things were moving too fast for her.

"Yeah, I might find something for myself…wait…what do you mean? Are you OK with it?" she asked, now concerned that things were moving too fast for him.

"I'm fine," Cole said, looking toward the door to make sure they had privacy.

"I mean, I know you've got this week off, I want to make sure this is how you want to spend your time."

"I'm good…if you are."

Cole smiled, "I'm more than good, you have no idea. But I don't want you to think…"

"Think what?"

"You know, that maybe I was moving too fast or…look I have not been single long. I mean I went on a few meet and greets with the divorce, but I don't know what the rules are."

"There are no rules." She took his hand. "Cole, the day you knocked on the door of my home, and my bedroom," she said whispering the last part, "I saw you walk in and *'my heart jumped in my chest.'*"

She patted her chest with her right hand repeating Cole's words from the day at CTC when she had first kissed him, "you understand, *'I mean it literally jumped.'*" she quoted.

He had never felt such a deep connection as he sensed at that moment. He had experienced love before, at least he thought he had. He had given love, and he had received love. But today there was a deep, undeniable stirring in his soul, something like he had never had before. It fulfilled his longing and left him wanting at the same time.

"My God," he wanted to continue and say *'I love you,'* but instead what came out was, "this could get really complicated."

"I think it will be easier than you think." She kissed and left the room.

There was so much he wanted to tell her, and so much he wanted to learn about her. And it was incredible how Jess had taken to her. Now, he wished he'd requested additional time off to be with her. He had a sense that he was about to get buried with work in his new role.

***

Counterterrorism Center - Langley

Cole learned a little more about his new responsibilities, though much of it was still vague. He was assigned a temporary private office just a couple doors down from McCune. Charlie had already arranged for his technical needs, and the computer and other essentials had been set up.

His personal items from his cube were in a banker's box. Charlie was unsure how long he would be in the office before McCune showed him his new 'work center', but the primary objective of the week was to begin the build-out of a hand-selected team of specialists.

He was given a short list of specialists to review. He would need a cross-section of capabilities with the highest degree of competency in their field, driven to see results even at the expense of protocol if required, and above all else, trustworthy. They had to fit into a strict profile matrix that the psych division had developed.

He reviewed the team's budget parameters and was amazed at the resources that were being entrusted to his new team. He would be able to offer each person a substantial pay grade increase. In return, there would be high expectations and considerable demands on this team.

Part of his briefing that day included a visit with the Chief Legal Counsel who personally showed the secret Executive order and the classified Congressional approval for the establishment of the team. Also, he met with Deputy Director Friedlander. The way Cole was reading the tea leaves, Friedlander was the next Director of the CIA and McCune was in line for Friedlander's current role of Deputy Director of Operations.

As a mission center team, they would sit under the Counterterrorism Center umbrella but would work closely with external agencies to leverage all available analytical and operational support to take on some of the most pressing national security problems. It was a sobering responsibility in a game where the stakes are high, and the margin for error is slim.

On the surface, the team seemed similar to Titan Shield. As with his recent experience, Cole would need liaison relationships with domestic agencies to support their mission, but he fully expected some of their work would be off the books. They would be expected to be a disruptive force in fighting terrorism. With Titan Shield, they had to play defense, from what Cole was gathering, this team would take an offensive posture, and he liked the idea of taking the fight to the enemy.

It had been another long ass day, but the newness of the work invigorated Cole. He was reviewing personal profiles when McCune knocked at his door.

"Heading out, but wanted to check in," she said looking around at the barren walls. Cole did not realize how late it was. He had not even checked in with Jessica.

"Easy to lose track of time when you don't have an outside window."

"No kidding," he said. "It really got away from me today."

"I know it's your new baby and you're probably ready to go balls to the wall, but a word of advice?"

"Please," Cole motioned for her to sit, eagerly ready to soak it up.

"Slow it down, make sure your team selection is solid, it'll make you or break you."

"Copy that. From CTC, I like Amy Wiggins, Bridgette Robinson, Steve Sinha, and Darryl Capps if cleared medically, to start with. And I've got a lead on a sharp candidate over at CENTCOM, I'm following up on." Cole was referring to Sara Wang who was nearing the end of her military career."

"I can see that, their tops in their area. Get 'em started on the full assessment with the Support Group. If they pass, you'll be off to a good start. Oh, but hold off on Capps he's still pissed you ruined his last vacation."

"Nah, Darryl will be fine. Ma'am, I'm sorry but what's the mission?"

"To be the tip of the spear. You build the team and the missions will come."

Cole thought his brother Jack would have been proud.

McCune turned and added, "Go home, your daughter heads back on Sunday, right?

Cole nodded in agreement.

"Right behind you, boss."

He spent the next few days interviewing team candidates and sent several of the finalists to the Support group for full evaluation sans Darryl Capps. He was sure Bridgette and Sinha would pass with flying colors, but he was worried about Amy's ability to stay composed. He loved having her positive energy around, and she was extremely skilled in her work but what he liked about her personality potentially would keep Amy from this team.

By the end of the week, Cole was feeling good about his progress. He had spent a lot of time at work but made sure he was home each night with Jessica. She actually seemed to enjoy the home to herself during the day and with her friend Brittany. Her security detail now seemed a natural part of their environment.

The decision had been made to release the FBI security when she returned to LA. Cole was a little uneasy about that, but understood a detail following Jess around at school would not go over well. Capps had offered to spend some time with her in self-defense training over the last week and the two bonded as they both had a common target for their jokes.

Hannah had dropped over in the middle of the week, he asked her to stay over, but she insisted on going home.

Cole looked at the still barren walls and thought, I should at least put a clock up. When McCune jumped in.

"Walk with me."

"Yes, ma'am."

They walked at a brisk pace to the elevators, and she asked Cole to swipe his card on the elevator control.

"B three," she said. The light illuminated, "Good you have access, now."

What the hell have I gotten myself into? Cole stood silent for the ride down.

The doors opened to a sterile twelve-foot-wide hallway. The bathrooms were immediately visible to the left. On the right, what looked like the only glass in the hall, allowed visibility into a large break room. The rest of the hall had plain off-white concrete windowless walls and windowless metal doors.

The place looked more like a prison than an office. Again, the thought hit Cole, *What the hell have I gotten myself into?* It was eerily quiet as they walked. Finally, someone exited a door to the left and headed toward the elevator.

"You saw the bathrooms and breakroom near the elevator. Your team will be located on the fourth door to the right when they're not in the field." McCune allowed Cole to take it in.

Cole recognized the retina scanner, he swiped his badge and stood for the eye scan as well. As the door unlocked, he opened it and saw the space was divided into a large open pit area with workstations and a closed off area behind glass walls. Systems were still being set up, and wires hung from the ceiling.

The open area ran forty feet long and was about twenty feet wide. To the right of the pit was a glass wall running the forty-foot length with a large private office in the middle and conference rooms on each side of the office.

"Your office is there in the middle," McCune said.

"Ma'am how does the team handle the dungeon feel of the workspace."

"This is your designated workspace, you and your team are free to make it as homey as you want, no one's going to bother you down here."

They walked the floor space and turned into his office.

"You will be completely and literally untethered. You still in?"

"I'm ready to make a difference, ma'am."

"That's what we're counting on. Now let's discuss something else." They sat at a small table at the corner of the private office.

"What's that, ma'am?"

"I need to tell you about Grant Ramsey."

CHAPTER 28

McLean Virginia

It had been a busy Saturday at the Cameron house. Jessica's friend Brittany came early that day bringing her bright personality that mirrored the Spring sunshine into their home. Brittany was Jess' best friend ever since the Camerons moved to the area. She was like a permanent fixture in the house. Her parents had split, and both traveled professionally, leaving Brittany with them so much that she was like an adopted daughter for Cole Cameron.

Jessica had repeatedly asked for her to spend the night during her visit, but Cole only allowed a few daytime visits since they were still accepting FBI security.

The girls were seated at the island in tee shirts and shorts munching on snacks in rhythm with the loud, fast beating music blasting from the wireless speakers.

"Hi Mr. C," Brittany said greeting him as he entered from the mudroom near the kitchen carrying his tux he had picked up at the cleaners. "Thanks for the ticket to the Gala," she said giving him a hug.

Cole smiled remembering the fun times his daughter had with her close friend. They always knew what the other was thinking. Cole recalled how as teenagers they had nearly morphed into one, having the same mannerisms and they sounded the same over the phone with the valley girl flavor of 'what' being drawn out.

"You're welcome, sweetheart. I'm the lucky one that gets to go to a Gala with three beautiful women," he yelled over the music.

Cole gave the verbal command to the music device, "volume three."

"Dad, we can't even hear it now."

"Volume three or one of my playlists."

Jessica redirected the music device with her own command, "play 'Dad's oldies' playlist," Jessica said rolling her eyes.

"Ha, ha. Very funny," Cole said and then was surprised when the device gave confirmation and begin playing the Crowded House song, '*Don't Dream It's Over.*' Throughout her intervals of boredom over the past week, Jess had taken the liberty to build a new catalog of playlists for her Dad.

"Oh, that's cool," he said nodding his head to the song.

"Volume six," he ordered the device.

"Hey, that's not fair!" Jess said.

The girls watched him as he sang while he built a sandwich for lunch. He threw his head back and sang along to the chorus, causing the girls to erupt in laughter.

"Volume eight!" Cole shouted.

"Oh my God, Dad!" Jessica bent over laughing at her father's goofy effort to be cool.

Undaunted by their ridicule, he grabbed Jessica's hand and pulled her up, singing and dancing with her as she laughed.

Brittany grabbed her phone and videoed the two until Cole reached over and pulled her into the dance with them. The girls burst into laughter at Cole's exaggerated moves. They all sang the words out loud, danced, and laughed until the song ended with a big group hug.

It had been a very long time since Jessica had seen her father this happy. She knew Hannah was a big part of his newfound happiness. Jess also knew that things were changing. She was getting older, and he had now completely moved on from her mother.

She was both sad and happy at the same time. Sorry that her parents had gone separate ways and divided her time, but happy for her Dad, knowing that maybe they each had a shot at happiness.

"Volume three!" Jessica shouted as the next song played. "Dad, you're crazy," she said still laughing and hugging him.

"Ahh, honey, I'm going to miss having you around here," he said kissing her blond head.

"I'm going to miss you too. And this house," Jess said. "Have you found a new place yet?"

"No, but I guess I have to get on that."

"Hey Mr. C, I talked Jess into coming back this summer," Brittany said excitedly.

"Really, you're giving up the beach this summer."

"Well, we have a plan," Brittany said.

"Oh brother," Cole sighed.

"No, no hear me out," Jess said. "I'm thinking I can fly back, stay with you for a week or two and then Brittany and I can drive to California. You know like a road trip."

"Yeah, that will be so cool!" Brittany said clapping her hands.

Cole sighed heavily, not wanting to discuss it, knowing that the two of them together were a formidable opponent. He was sure that they must have done an Internet search on '*how to win arguments with your parents.*'

He couldn't resist, "I don't know if it's safe."

"Dad, Mr. Capps was here all this week, by the way, he's really a nice guy after all. Anyway, he trained me on self-defense techniques, like you wanted. I mean he is really good."

"Yeah, she showed me one of the moves," Brittany said, going up behind Jessica to demonstrate. "Show him, Jess."

"That's unnecessary. I don't want anyone to get hurt."

"Mom, already said yes as long as it's OK with you."

And there it is, he said to himself.

"We'll talk about this more, later on. I've some things I need to take care of before we have to get ready."

"Oh my gosh, Jess! It's 1:30! We've got to get ready," Brittany shouted.

Cole suddenly remembered why he always felt worn out after she visited.

"What? You all aren't leaving for another five hours."

"Dad, this is a full day affair," Jess said as they cleared the kitchen island.

Brittany took her turn on the device, "play *'California Dreamin'* by Sia," she yelled.

"Volume six," shouted Jess as they headed through the barrel archway to the foyer to go upstairs to her bedroom.

Cole shook his head as he watched sensing what all fathers of grown daughters sense, impending doom. Walking before him were two kids at heart with the bodies of grown attractive women. He wanted desperately to push the clock back and have more time to dance, laugh and watch sappy movies with her, but he knew he was on borrowed time.

Tomorrow she would leave him again, and he would have to deal with the empty house all over, and by the time of her next visit, he would most likely be living somewhere different as the house was set to close escrow in a few days. But tonight, he intended to fully drink in all of the enjoyment that the experience would offer. He knew he would have to keep his protective emotions in check, as Cole fully expected her to draw more attention than he would be comfortable with.

✱✱✱

Washington, DC –Wharf District

Cole arrived at Hannah's condo, thirty minutes early and chided himself for being overly prompt. It was a chilly evening as the sun began to set over the adjacent building. He took the steps two at a time in anticipation of seeing Hannah.

Hannah had suggested an uber, but Cole reserved a professional car service to the event and would leave his car at her place, hopefully allowing for time together beyond the superhuman hearing capabilities of Jess.

He knocked at her door but didn't get a response. He tried

again, still nothing. He checked the door, it was unlocked. He opened it knocking again hearing nothing. His heart beat faster as all sort of possibilities flowed through his mind. He looked to the left into the open area from the kitchen to the living room. The usually very tidy room had a few clothes and towels tossed around.

Cole removed the Glock 22 from his shoulder holster and went back to the hall walking toward the closed bedroom door. He glanced in the half bath to the right, it was clear. He walked softly to the bedroom and slowly opened the door.

He saw open a couple of open drawers and more clothes on the bed, he went around the foot of the bed to the other side to check the master bath. He braced himself against the door frame to allow his muscles to relax.

Hannah was wrapped in a large white towel, bent over, her leg up on the closed toilet seat. She was nursing a razor nick on her beautifully toned leg. Cole holstered the gun and stood there admiring her, knowing she was oblivious to his presence.

He heard her mumbling *"tell me that you want me, tell that you need me…"* She seemed to be making up her own words to the song he played in the room a week earlier.

"Shit," she said taking a quick look at her watch. She made one last dab and turned to find Cole at the door. She jumped and screamed.

"Agh! Shit! Shit! Shit!"

Cole stepped forward to calm her down but instead received a barrage of fist pounds to the chest as a reward for his early arrival.

"Oh my God! You scared…"

"…The shit out of you it sounds like," Cole deadpanned. "You really need to expand your cursing vocabulary."

She gave him one more slug for good measure and pulled the wireless earbuds out. He gave her a big hug feeling that her heart was still beating fast.

"How did you not hear me knocking?" he asked kissing her. "The door was unlocked, so I just came in and when I didn't see you and well, you really scared me too."

"I thought I could get ready so much faster. I haven't done anything this fancy in a long time. It's been a nightmare."

"No, you're fine. I'm just early."

"No, I'm really late and need my space," she said pushing him to the door, and the abruptly covered her mouth.

"Oh, I forgot about the laundry. You're right. You are way too early. Go wait in the living room."

He opened her closet door and grabbed a clothes basket.

After the laundry was folded, Cole sat at the counter nursing a beer, it was not lost on him that she had stocked up on his favorite brew. He sent a text to Jess to see how they were fairing, evidently about the same as Hannah's situation as reply said it all, *not now dad!* So, he did what most men must do in these situations, wait.

After a while, he heard Hannah's voice command the music device, and soon the familiar song that been woven into their love began to play. Cole smiled, remembering their connection. The sound of graceful footsteps in high heels on the hardware floor indicated she was coming to him. His anticipation grew, but nothing prepared him for what he saw.

She seemed to glide around the hallway toward the table in her long black evening gown that swayed with her movements. The slit on the right side revealed her long, toned leg. Her dark hair was worn up, wrapped in a Dutch braided low bun with a stylish brooch that worked well with her long diamond earrings that dangled from her ears. The vee neck front was low and revealing. She looked like she had just stepped off of a magazine cover. Cole was speechless.

She turned to give him the full view of the bareback dress. Strings crisscrossed the lower back. He then realized why her hand was behind her back.

"This is where I need your help," she said softly as their song played. Cole tied the back strap.

He was overwhelmed. He had always thought she was out of his league. All doubts to that fact were now removed, he now knew for sure, Hannah was beyond him in so many ways.

"My God Hannah, you are simply stunning."

"Thank you," she replied as they kissed.

"Is the car here?"

"Yes, but he can wait. I just want you all to myself for one minute before the eyes of everyone start to devour you."

"Cole," she said patting his chest and feeling the hardware underneath the coat.

"You're carrying your gun tonight?" she asked, surprised.

"Yep. Taking some liberties with my new position."

"Yeah, I want to hear more about that but not tonight. I want to enjoy this special evening."

He leaned across and kissed her. *God, she loved his kisses.* "OK, now I have to reapply, so maybe you should get one more before I do that."

"With pleasure." *God, he loved her kisses.*

CHAPTER 29

Washington, DC Hilton Capital Ballroom

Cole and Hannah lingered near the entrance of the ballroom shaking hands and making introductions as they waited for Jessica and Brittany to arrive.

"She should have been here by now."

"She'll be here. Just relax," Hannah said in between greeting strangers.

He noticed three men in their thirties standing across the room, looking toward Hannah a little too often for his liking. It wasn't that they looked at her, it was the way they looked at her.

"Geez, act like you've been here before guys," he mumbled to himself.

"What was that?"

"Ahh, nothing."

The three looked over again, and then they laughed. *Oh, there it is, the adolescent guy joke*, keeping his thoughts silent this time. He recognized one of the men as a young congressman with an abhorrent reputation for womanizing. The congressman started walking toward them. *Are you kidding me?*

Hannah stood to his left and saw the sleazy politician come their way. She put her arm in Cole's and braced herself.

"Shit," she said under her breath. Cole felt something was off but couldn't put his finger on it.

The congressman walked over eyeing Hannah up and down the entire way, not even giving Cole an acknowledging look until he was directly in front of him. Then he finally looked over to Cole and extended his hand.

"Congressman Scott Shepherd."

Cole wanted to deck the putz right there but felt Hannah's tug.

"Cole Cameron," came the cold reply. Before he finished saying his last name, the congressman was on to Hannah with his outstretched hand.

"Hannah, darling, so good to see you out again."

What a smug ass punk, Cole thought.

"Congressman Shepherd." Hannah nodded, but never offered her hand.

"Oh, you know to call me Scott," he said turning to Cole to rub it in, "Hannah and I go way back, don't we sweetie?"

He looked at them recognizing they weren't carrying drinks. "Oh, someone's failed to take care of you. Let me get you a drink."

"We're fine, thank you." Hannah fought to maintain her composure.

"Nonsense," he said waiving over a server walking around with a tray of drinks.

"Congressman," Cole said trying to get bastard's attention.

"Uh-huh," the congressman said feigning interest and instead he looked over and winked at his guy pals.

Cole had dealt with too much crap over the last few weeks. He had dealt with terrorist attacks, the stress of a firefight, his daughter's life threatened, and he had seen death too close. He wasn't about to take shit from this punk. Not tonight.

"Hey, asshole!"

Shepherd spun around. *That got his attention*. Hannah gave another tug at his arm.

"We said we don't need a drink," Cole spoke calmly.

"Who did you say you were?" Shepherd asked, putting his finger on Cole's chest. "Do you have any idea who I am?"

"I've got a pretty good idea, and I suggest you stop touching me now."

Before Shepherd could respond, CIA Director Kingman stepped between them.

"Officer Cameron, so glad you made it. Agent Jacobs," he said taking her extended hand.

"The pleasure is ours, sir. Thank you again for the tickets," Cole said.

"Where's that darling girl of yours?"

"On her way, sir."

"Well, bring her over when she gets here. I want to be sure to say hello."

"Will do, sir."

The Director turned to the young congressman who was salivating like a dog for an opportunity to pucker up to the powerful public servant.

"And you are?" the Director knew the congressman, but couldn't resist crushing his ego.

"Congressman Shepherd," he said surprised, "we spoke at the security briefing a few weeks ago."

"So sorry, I don't recall that," the Director said, winking at Cole. "If you'll excuse me, I've got some folks to meet. Oh, but a word of advice congressman."

"Oh yes sir, I'm all ears."

"Careful how you treat our American heroes. The voters take stock of that sort of thing."

As Kingman moved on Cole watched Shepherd stomp off to lick his wounds. Hannah's tug finally got his attention.

"What?"

"Well, if your pissing contest is over, your daughter is here, and she looks amazing."

Cole looked toward the doorway and saw his tall, slender daughter grace the floor with her dark blue gown that complemented her long straight blond hair and blue eyes. She was luminous. Literally making heads turn.

Stepping in next to her was her petite friend, Brittany, wearing a beige gown 'so that they would not clash.'

"Damn," Cole said as he exhaled.

"I know, Cole. She is striking." Hannah agreed.

Cole looked over to the congressman and his two buddies. They were eyeing Jess and Brittany, like wolves sniffing out fresh meat.

"Yeah, and I have a feeling it's going to be a long night if I have to put up with assholes like that."

"About that," Hannah started.

"Nah, not tonight. They're not going to ruin our night. Let's say 'hi' to the girls."

Cole was enjoying a fantastic evening, aside from the run-in with the congressman, the night had gone splendidly. The charity event benefited a Children's Research Hospital in the DC area. He and his three lovely companions sat with six other guests at their table.

During dinner, short speeches were given, and pleas for additional ongoing support were made. The Director's wife, as a long-time significant contributor, had orchestrated the event. After concluding her gracious remarks, she offered the Director an opportunity to say a few words. True to form of most seasoned public servants at that level, he understood politics as well as he understood any aspect of the agency he ran.

"My wife and I are grateful for your support to this worthy cause," he said. "Many of our friends and associates understand the motivation for our support. We'd like to think that our giving can mean that someday maybe a young child can avoid the kind of suffering that our dear granddaughter, Abbey had to experience. Your giving will mean so much to so many. Thank you for your generosity."

The audience applauded as he stepped away from the podium. Cole looked two tables over and saw McCune checking her watch. She seemed distracted.

Before the applause had died down, the Director returned, and said, "Folks, I'm sorry. One more thing. I'd be remised if I didn't acknowledge a couple of special guests we have tonight. All of you are acutely aware of the recent attacks against our country."

"Shit," Hannah whispered.

"Yeah, shit is right," Cole whispered back.

"Earlier this week the CIA awarded the Intelligence Star to

Officer Cole Cameron for his role in stopping the attempted terrorist attack in Los Angeles. And he is here tonight accompanied by Special Agent Hannah Jacobs who was one of the Agents that apprehended the terrorists in Los Angeles. Officer Cameron, Agent Jacobs, would you please stand and allow us to show our appreciation for your bravery and courage."

The two stood, and the Presidential Ballroom with nearly six hundred attendees began to roar with loud applause. As the intensity grew, everyone rose to their feet. Cole and Hannah humbly nodded and mouthed *'thank you'* to the room.

The crowd continued the roar. It was getting awkward for Cole. "That's why he gave us the tickets," he said to Hannah understanding the Director had used them as props for good PR. He had enough of it and sat down, and Hannah followed his lead. He looked over and saw tears rolling down the cheek of his daughter.

"Dad, I'm so proud of you," she said crying, "You too, Hannah."

"Hannah, you're like a badass," Brittany said.

As the room sat back down Cole caught the look of the three men from the earlier altercation. One of Shepherd's friends whispered in his ear and gave a smug look over to the table. *One day me and that guy are going to go at it.* Cole thought.

After dinner, a cover band began playing hits from different eras. The girls were quickly up and on the floor. Cole dreaded this moment. It was one thing to be a fool in front of his girl and her friend at home, it was another to dance with the woman he was falling for in a room full of people who all knew him by name now. But he had brought her *so by God, he was going to be the one to dance with her.*

"Shall we?" he asked Hannah taking her hand as they stood.

"Actually, do you mind if I freshen up first."

"Sure," Cole said, happy to procrastinate making an ass of himself.

"I'll walk with you. I need a break myself." On the way

out of the hall to the restrooms, they ran into McCune.

"You heading out?" Cole asked. Hannah excused herself and headed to the restroom leaving the two to talk.

"No, actually heading upstairs. I've got a meeting. Hey, your daughter is so beautiful."

"Thanks."

"Everyone having a good time?"

"It's been great, thank you. Even if the price of admission was a little bit of my dignity."

"You mean the PR move back there."

"Yeah, not really comfortable with that."

"I know but the country needs some good news, and right now you're it."

"God help us!"

"You said it." McCune saw Hannah returning.

"If I don't see you again, you two enjoy the rest of the evening, and I hope you don't mind me saying this, but you two really do look great together."

"Thank you, Ma'am," Cole said, and Hannah tilted her head and smiled.

"You ready," Cole said holding his arm out for Hannah.

"Absolutely! I am so excited to see the moves that Jess and Brittany told me about."

"Oh no," he said knowing he was in trouble.

They got to the floor and fortunately for Cole it was a slow enough song that he could take Hannah in his arms and keep it simple. But that didn't last, by the third song, Hannah seemed to be dancing with Jess and Brittany as much as she was Cole. In those breaks, there was always someone coming up and saying thanks or congratulations on the Star.

He saw all three of the girls conspiring and then Jess ran up to the band leader as they finished a song.

"This one for Officer Cameron, courtesy of all three women you brought to the Gala tonight. Whoa, what a stud!"

Several laughed, but Cole wasn't one of them.

"Easy Ragweed, that's my daughter," he yelled back.

"Even sicker man!"

The band leader got more laughs then strummed the strings of the guitar, as the drums joined in then and Cole recognized the tune. The girls came to him dancing as the band sang the Crowded House song, *'Don't Dream It's Over.'* Cole found joy again and let loose and began singing the lyrics and dancing with each of them.

As the band rested between sets, Cole took a break and stood at the urinal in the men's room when Shepherd's two cronies pulled up beside him, one on each side. Both had been served too much, and it showed.

"You think your hot shit don't you," the one to his left said.

"Yeah, three hotties hanging on an old fart like you," the one on the right said.

"Speaking of farts, you two really stink. I thought it was your personality that was repugnant, but really, quite literally, it's your odor."

There was a chuckle from one of the stalls, and Cole zipped up. That really pissed the boys off. He washed at the sink as the two moved in behind him. The first one getting really close to his ear.

"We have connections shit bird. We can make your life miserable. But not until we take turns on all three of those girls."

Wisdom told Cole to just ignore them and walk away, then the second one added his thoughts.

"You might want to get a checkup tomorrow if you are porking the FBI girl. I hear she's like a petri dish." The man in the stall cleared his throat.

Cole spun around.

"I'm going to pretend for your sake that you never said that. Now step aside."

"Hell, I thought the FBI girl was hot shit until the tall blond strolled in." The first one was back at it. They weren't letting up. Cole knew and braced himself for the inevitable. *Just like tenth grade all over again.*

"Talk about fresh, I can't wait to have my way with her. I

bet that's some sweet pus…" before he could finish the word Cole had decked him with a solid punch to the nose. Blood spewed out as the man fell against the wall screaming in pain.

The second stepped up to throw a swing, but Cole ducked and raised up with an uppercut from his left hand connecting under the jaw of the assailant. He too flew backward.

Cole felt a shooting pain in his left shoulder as if someone had just shocked him. It was the shoulder injury from Yemen all over again. Before either of the two could recover a hotel security guard arrived breaking it up.

A small crowd had gathered near the restrooms as the three were pulled out into the hall. Cole saw Shepherd off to the side with a smirk on his face. Hannah ran up to see the guards and crowd, then she saw Cole being taken to the security office. His Glock 22 in the guard's hand.

"Where are you taking him?"

"He's going to the security office, the police have been contacted, they'll question him and determine if any charges are to be filed."

"Are you kidding me?"

"Hannah, there was a guy in a stall, who heard everything. You got to find him. I think Shepherd set this up," Cole said being hauled into the security room.

"Shit!" Hannah shouted, this time in anger.

Hannah returned to the hall near the restroom, she surveyed the people and spotted Shepherd working his manipulation on the guards. She walked straight up and confronted him in front of everyone.

"You set this up you little bastard," she said and slapped his face.

She turned and saw a man giving a statement to one of the guards. They pulled him away from the event, and the guard pointed to a seat and told him to wait there for the police. The man who looked to be in his late sixties complied with the directions and rested on a sofa with his phone in his hand.

Hannah came over and played coy asking, "Oh my gosh, what happened in there?"

"That guy from the CIA they talked about tonight opened a can of whoop ass on two drunk assholes."

"Really?"

"Yeah, they were asking for it too. I mean those guys were very vulgar ma'am."

"Wait, aren't you the one that was with the CIA guy?"

"Hannah Jacobs, FBI."

"Oh wow, Miss you need to know that man defended your honor and that of his daughter as well."

She smiled. "I'm afraid, Officer Cameron might be in trouble because of it."

"What's wrong with this world?" the man asked shaking his head, "Who goes up to a man in a bathroom and asks for a beating and then when they get one, they call the law?"

Hannah saw police entering the building and knew her time was short.

"I'm sorry I didn't get your name."

"Samuel Meade, but you can call me Sam, Agent Jacobs."

"Ahh...thanks, Sam," she said rubbing his arm. "Is there anything else you can tell me?"

"Well, the guard told me that a congressman wanted to talk to me and I guess the police as well. He left before I could tell him, I think I've got all of it on a recording right here, well, most of it anyway."

"Can I see that? Do you mind if I send a copy of to myself?"

"Oh, I don't know about that."

"Sam, this is Washington, I'm with the FBI, you know."

"Yeah, I guess, go ahead."

Hannah saw Shepherd working his way toward them, she quickly uploaded the audio file to her cloud account. Then tapped her phone and saved a file on her device as well.

"Sam, the congressman that's coming to talk with you, is not a good guy. The two in the bathroom were his buddies doing his dirty work."

She stood up and kissed his cheek. "You be careful."

The old man lit up. "Ma'am you are the prettiest FBI

Agent I've ever seen, and I'm talking about the ones on TV, too!"

"Thank you! You're such a sweetheart!" she said with a big smile.

She walked down the hall passing Shepherd and drew back her hand as if she was going to hit him. He flinched big time, nearly tripping over his own feet.

"I have the recording, so think twice before you have twiddle dee and twiddle dumb press charges," she said.

She found Jess and Brittany wandering the halls looking for them.

"Where's Dad? What happened?"

"Over here, over here, your Dad's alright, follow me." Hannah motioned for them follow her into the hotel lobby looking for a place to sit. The three attractive women in formalwear drew a lot of attention.

Finally finding a couple of seats together she played the recording of what had happened. At first, Brittany laughed at Cole's quick comeback, but as the tone grew intense and hearing the sounds of the scuffle, she realized the seriousness of the situation.

"Who does that? What major assholes!" Brittany said.

"Yeah, I hate to say it, but there's a lot of them out there like that," Hannah cautioned.

"Is Dad going to be in trouble?"

"I hope not Jess, but he shouldn't be, they really backed him into the corner."

"He kicked their asses, didn't he?"

"Yeah, he did, but I could see he was in pain. I think it was his shoulder. Let's go to the security station and see if the police are there, maybe this recording will be enough." Hannah attempted to conceal her worry for Cole.

Chapter 30

Washington, DC Hilton Capital Ballroom

Cole sat in a small office with a security guard who sat across from him. They had locked his Glock 22 up in the desk drawer. He had been watching all of the hotel monitors outside the office in a large open room. A dozen monitors rotated vantage points. Two security guards in front of the monitors toggled to different cameras sometimes zooming in.

The guy sitting across from him seemed like a decent man. Cole explained what went down. But was destined to wait for the police.

"What's your name?" Cole asked.

The guard just pointed to his name tag on his uniform. *Mike Kilroy.*

"Mike? You got kids Mike?"

"Yep."

"Daughter?"

"Three."

"Ouch, sorry man it's tough. It's harder when they get older."

"For what it's worth sir, if that's what truly happened, I'd kicked their asses, too."

Cole smiled and caught a glimpse of Hannah with the girls on one the monitors. *What have I done? I really messed up.* Cole thought about the implications of charges being filed against him.

"Hey, there's my boss," Cole said.

"Top monitor on the left," He said helping Mike spot it.

"I didn't really like her at first, but now I think she's kinda cool. What is that the Presidential Suite she's headed into? Is that on the top floor? What is there like fourteen or fifteen floors here?"

Cole didn't know why he was talking so much. Maybe he was coming down from the adrenaline of the fight, or maybe Mike just looked like a guy that you could talk to.

"You ever do any bartending?"

"Uhh"

"Hey, there on the bottom toward the middle. The three girls. The one in the black dress, she's my girlfriend, badass FBI Agent too." Mike looked over at the monitor. "The one in the blue is my daughter and the other one is her friend."

"Mike, why do those guards keep zooming in on my girls?"

Mike got up and went into the monitor area to see which person was toggling the control.

"Hector, knock it off."

"Thanks, man," Cole said as Mike came back.

Cole stopped talking and watched the camera on the door to the Presidential Suite as three men arrived. One person entered, and the other two stayed outside the room. *Shit. Something big is happening up there.* He thought.

A few minutes later a camera caught a dark figure ascending the stairs.

"What was that?"

There it was again. It was apparent to Cole that whoever was ascending the stairs was working hard to try to avoid the cameras.

"Mike, something is going down."

"Mr. Cameron please."

"Listen to me man, you know what I've done. My job is to spot threats…there it is again!"

"Mike, east stairway, man in a hood, heading up the stairs."

Mike opened the door, "Hector scan the east stairway." The guard populated the monitors with different views.

"There it is!" Cole yelled. Mike saw it this time.

"Twelfth floor. Damn, where did he go?"

"Mike, this is a professional. Let me out. I've got to get up there. Pull the alarm, do something."

"I can't just let you go and as far as we know this is just someone exercising or something. We have guards at the doors of that floor tonight. They'll stop him if he gets too close."

"Damn it! Mike, give me my gun. Let me out. There's a high-ranking CIA officer up there."

"Oh, Shit!" Yelled the other guard at the monitors. The camera feed from that floor went out. "I think the dude took the guard out just before the cameras went out!"

"What are you talking about! Playback the feed!"

"Look!" he replayed the scene at the door of the suite showing one of the Russians shot the other.

"Mike, the gun now!"

"Get Rogers up there," Mike ordered and nervously opened the drawer and handed Cole his gun.

"Which floor is the presidential suite on?"

"Fourteenth."

"I'm going with you," Mike said. "Service elevators will be the fastest."

"We got to move fast."

The two ran out of the security office toward the service elevator. "Take it to the thirteenth floor," Cole yelled.

"There is no thirteenth floor."

"OK the floor below fourteen then, Geez!"

The elevator lifted them up, Cole checked his ammo. "Check your weapon," he told Mike. "Is your safety on?"

"Yeah," Mike was breathing heavy.

"Take it off, your finger is the safety. Shoot only the bad guys."

"How will I know who is bad?"

"If they're shooting at you, shoot back."

The elevator stopped on the eighth floor.

"Shit." A housekeeper stood at the door with her cart.

"Get out" Cole yelled waving his gun. "Get your guys on the radio, find out what's happening on the monitors."

"Radio's not working."

"They're jamming signals."

The elevator was moving again, and the fire alarm was ringing now. *Finally,* he thought. This time the service elevator stopped on the tenth floor.

"We're on foot from here." They pushed their way past another server with a cart.

"Which side is the Presidential suite on?" He yelled over the alarm ringing.

"It's in the middle across from the elevator hall."

"Of course, it is! I'll take the east stairway where we saw the guy, you take the West."

"Got it," Mike said as he started to run down the hall.

"Mike, no matter what, make sure you go home to your girls tonight."

Mike nodded his head, "Yeah, you too!"

Cole scanned the east stairway and hustled up to the next levels. Two guards had been taken out with headshots. He wondered what Mike had found on his side. He got to the fourteenth floor and in the stairway outside the hall laid a female CIA agent. Cole checked for a pulse but found none. He went to ease open the door to the hallway, but it was locked. *Shit.*

Cole hustled back down to the guards and found a key card. Soon he was back up at the hall door of the 14th floor. He hesitated, knowing that he would be an easy target down the narrow hall. He saw no other way. Waving the keycard over the scanner, he pulled the metal door back about an inch. He heard someone say something in what sounded like Russian.

He threw open the door, falling to his right knee and using the door frame to shield his body. Bullets flew into the metal door just above his head, as he saw two men, guns raised, charging down the hall at him. Two taps and the closest one went down. He ducked back for cover.

He heard other gunfire. Not like the suppressors that were shooting at him. *That's got to be Mike.*

He leaned back in now to see the second man had darted into the elevator hall across from the entrance to the suite.

"Hold your fire, Mike!" Cole yelled.

Cole and Mike raced quickly to converge on the second target in the middle.

"Mike he's going to get on that elevator." Cole motioned for Mike to lay down two cover shots.

Mike nodded and fired two shots toward the suspect near the elevators. As return fire was directed on Mike's side, Cole leaned in from his corner and nailed the big Russian with a headshot.

"Mike, we got him!" He turned to see his new friend gasping for air.

"Damn it!"

"Mike, hang in there!"

Cole examined him then dragged the big man to the elevator and selected the first floor. He sent him down praying that he would make it.

Cole entered the double doors to the spacious fifteen hundred square foot Presidential Suite and braced himself for the worst. He grabbed a decorative piece from the table in the entryway and jammed it under to door to keep it open.

He saw the long couch and side chairs directly in front. To his left, a closed door to perhaps the bedroom. To his right, he had a partial view of the large dining table, and McCune taped and gagged in the chair at the end of the table. She appeared unconscious. *What the hell went down here?*

The rest of the dining area was a blind spot sitting out of Cole's view behind a wall. He quickly moved to get to McCune, when he cleared the wall and saw the man he had watched enter the room on the monitors back in the security office. He too was strapped to a dining chair. Blood covered the wood table where the man's right eye had been cut out.

Cole felt for a pulse on McCune. It was faint. Then he checked the man, he had none. He went back to McCune and cut her free, checking her over for wounds. He looked for a room phone to call for help knowing the cell signals were jammed. As his eyes bounced around the room, he saw the bedroom door that had been closed was open.

He started to clear the rest of the suite when he heard from the open door the elevator ding and what sounded like an army of footsteps. He quickly laid down his Glock and put his hands over his head wincing at the pain in his left shoulder.

"Freeze! Police! Move, and you're dead!"

They had him pinned to the floor, he felt the full weight of the person over him driving their knee into his back. The cop pulled both arms back to cuff him. The jerking motion felt like it pulled his left shoulder out.

It was mass confusion until someone removed all of the non-essential personnel, realizing they had a crime scene. Cole tried to explain the situation, but in all the chaos no one was listening.

"Check Nancy McCune by the table, she needs medical attention immediately. She's an Associate Director at CIA. She needs help!"

Finally, Hector arrived with someone in authority and pointed Cole out.

"How's Mike doing?" He yelled to him, Hector just shrugged.

"You the guy that sent him down the elevator?" The man in authority asked.

"Yeah, is he alright?"

"Doesn't look good, but he told us you were up here and needed help." The officer uncuffed Cole.

"What the hell went down in here?"

"I'm not sure. I just knew something was going down and we needed to get here. Did you guys get anyone else? There was a least one more."

"No, it was a shit show with the guests leaving, everyone trying to get out with the alarm. Sorry man looks like you were too late."

Cole nodded and hoped it was not too late for McCune.

"FBI and DC police are down in the lobby they're going to want to talk to you. Someone get that damn alarm turned off!" he shouted turning away from Cole.

When Cole arrived at the hotel lobby, he saw a madhouse of hotel employees, police, firefighters, and the FBI windbreakers everywhere. He searched the hotel entrance for the girls. The guests and Gala attendees had all spilled out of the hotel, he could see outside the lobby doors that both sides of 16th street were packed with people, and the street was blocked off with response vehicles.

"Cole!" he somehow heard over all the noise. It was Hannah pulling her ID out of her small black purse to get past police. She and Kincaid dragged Jess and Brittany by the hand. He saw the concern on their faces and realized that his white shirt was bloody.

"It's not mine. I'm fine." They all gathered and hugged.

"Let's get inside," Cole said. He noticed Jess seemed a little shaken up but was holding it together. Brittany, however, continued to sob.

"Look, I'm going to have to be here for a while. You all should go home."

"I'll see to it, sir," Kincaid said.

After tonight's events, Cole was in a hyper-protective mode for his daughter. "Agent Kincaid, I think it would be best if someone else escorted them home."

"Dad!" Jessica said knowing her Dad's motivation.

"Cole," Hannah reached out putting her hand on his arm.

"Sir, can I speak with you privately," Kincaid asked.

They stepped away from the girls. "What's on your mind agent?" Cole asked.

"Sir, we all know what happened in the bathroom earlier. I'm not like that, sir," he paused. "My younger sister is the same age as your daughter, Jess..." he corrected himself, "...Jessica is a lot like her. If a couple jerks acted like that with my sister, I would...well, let's just say I completely understand and I am damn proud to be of service to you and your family."

The girls watched the conversation from a few feet away. Jess continued to try to comfort Brittany.

"Hannah will you stay with us tonight," she said nodding her head toward Brittany. "Brittany's folks are out of town, and I think she should stay with us. Would you mind convincing Dad to let her stay over?"

Hannah nodded in agreement.

They saw the two men shaking hands and returning.

"Agent Kincaid is going to take you two, now. I'll be along as soon as I can. Hannah, I'm sorry, why don't you take the car service, and I'll catch up later."

"Nah, we've got a better plan," Hannah said, surprising Cole.

"The girls asked me to stay with them tonight, we're going to have Brittany stay as well."

Cole saw Jess nodding in agreement.

"David, can you take us by my place first so I can pick up a few things." Just like that, she was in control.

Cole's world had become a landslide of intensity and high-strung emotions, but standing before him were two of the most refreshing and soul healing forces he could ever imagine. Well, three if you count Brittany.

Cole looked at his cell phone.

"It's Capps, I've got to give him a call."

He said his goodbyes with regret, and they left. The perfect evening had spiraled out of control. He had imagined enjoying his time with Hannah, fully appreciating her captivating beauty and their undeniable connection, but for now, he would have to wait.

He was happy to know she would be waiting at his house, but he knew it would not be the same. There was a tug on his coat sleeve as he walked away. He turned to see her standing in the long black gown, looking into his eyes and somehow in the midst of everything, smiling at him.

"Cole Cameron…" she said with a deep sigh and tearful eyes. She wanted to say '*I love you*' so badly. He looked back into her eyes and read her mind.

"Me too," he said and kissed her. They held each other for a moment.

He whispered in her ear, "I've been thinking all night about how nice it was going to be to help you out of this beautiful dress. I'm sorry the evening was ruined."

"Well, what's underneath will still be there," she whispered back with a seductive smile.

Jess cleared her throat.

"Shit!" Hannah hissed covering her mouth as her face turned pale. "Please, tell me she didn't hear that?"

Cole shook his head.

"Nah, she didn't hear that," he said unconvincingly. "Bye." He kissed her again as she drummed up courage, spun around and joined the others.

CHAPTER 31

McLean, Virginia (The Cameron House Earlier that Evening.)

Abu Al Himyari had patiently waited for the opportunity to exact Hasni's vengeance. His nephew failed to deliver Allah's judgment upon Cameron's seed. Allah had willed instead for Abu himself to be that instrument. By Allah's providence, the Cameron daughter was at her father's home. Now he would be able to show Cole Cameron firsthand how suffering and loss truly felt.

The Cameron house sat in a newer fifty home neighborhood with the homes ranging from three to seven thousand square feet. The homes were well placed blending in with the natural topography of a small creek and woods that coiled its way around the neighborhood providing the large lots with ample privacy, uncommon of similar communities in the area.

Cole's five-year-old, thirty-eight hundred square foot craftsman style, two-story home was on the smaller side for the neighborhood, but it was well designed with its large open floor plan and a great patio area with a fire pit and built-in BBQ. It was more room than they needed, but they felt like they were buying at a good time and building something new allowed them to put their own flavor on it.

Grace and Jess had both argued for a pool, but Cole stood firm, not wanting the extra expense. He tried to carefully manage his investment proceeds from the business he had sold.

One of the things Cole liked most about his home was its

location in the neighborhood. They were early enough in the development to grab a premiere spot. The lot was situated with a natural buffer of thick woods in the back and along the left side of the house as you enter it and it was raised with about a ten-foot incline above the street. They had a neighbor thirty feet to their right and another that sat to the right corner of the backyard where well-placed landscaping provided privacy there as well.

The thick woods behind Cole's home provided Abu al-Himyari with cover as he waited for the FBI agents to escort the girls to the event. He knew from his previous reconnaissance that the rear of the home was equipped with bright motion sensor LED lights and the Russians, who had their own plans for the evening, had provided the necessary information on the home security.

The Russians also allowed al-Himyari to look at the dossier they had on Cole. He was impressed with the plethora of intel compiled and the details not only about his past but his current interests, habits, and record of operations at the CIA that he was believed to have been involved with.

Abu recognized in his profile the impact of his brother Jack's death as well as a much earlier agony when they had lost their second child at birth. The write up suggested that was the starting point of the deterioration of his marriage. It did not escape Abu that perhaps Cole Cameron had tasted pain and suffering after all, but what the CIA Officer had experienced in the past would pale in comparison to the sorrow and misery he would face before the sun rose upon his house.

In return, for the additional resources and intel provided, al-Himyari committed to lead the former Hasni network and continue the alliance formed with Gavriil Medvedm. With the failed VX attacks, he was convinced Hasni had been right, after all, they did need a partner with sophisticated capabilities such as the Russians. Abu knew the Russians had their own plan and his network would be called upon and play a significant role.

Outside the home, two agents remained on watch seated in their car. But with the house set high above the street level, it put them at a disadvantage to view the backyard. Even so, the watchful agents had positioned the car up the street as far back to the left as possible to gain a better view.

As he waited, al-Himyari reflected on the fact that his mission had failed. The VX and key cell members, including his nephew had been captured, and Cameron and his daughter remained alive. For Abu to have any remaining dignity and an opportunity to assume Hasni's leadership role, he would need to eliminate the Camerons in the dramatic fashion that Hasni had envisioned.

He planned to catch them in their sleep. First, he would take the daughter and secure her, then he would surprise Cameron, have him sit bound and watching, as he slowly and grotesquely takes his daughter's life. It was important for Cole Cameron to know what that loss feels like. Even if he would only know it for a short time.

Al-Himyari drew satisfaction from knowing in Cameron's last state of consciousness, he would be forced to face the reality that he was alone and helpless to save who he loved most.

Finally, the agents had left with the daughter. Al-Himyari made his way from the woods up the lawn, and he did indeed trip the floodlight at the rear of the home, so he moved quickly to work the lock.

Outside in the car, Agent Sanchez caught the light and asked his partner, "Did you see anything?"

"No. It's probably the damn cat from next door," the older agent in the driver's seat responded.

"You mean 'Mr. Strawman'?" The agents had learned Jessica's nickname for the neighbor's cat that seemed to prefer Cameron's landscaping straw for his litter box.

"I'll go check it out."

"Nah, let it ride, the neighbors are already giving us shit about being here, and it doesn't help if we keep poking around with flashlights. I heard we're being pulled off tomorrow anyway."

"Really, man Kincaid's going to be pissed."

"That kid better watch himself."

"Still, I'll go check it out, anyway. Be right back."

Al-Himyari finally had the back-patio door free and quickly jumped in pressing the keypad on the wall. The outside light flicked off, and he breathed a little easier. He started to step forward when the light flicked on again.

Abu pressed himself against the wall next to the door. The agent had come around from the right side of the home, between the neighbors looking for Mr. Strawman, the cat. He walked to the back patio shining his bright flashlight beam through the glass patio doors. The light searched the kitchen area to the left, breakfast table straight ahead and large living area to the right finding nothing disturbed.

To the right of Abu, the living area had four large windows to the backyard side. The windows were covered with plantation shutters, tilted open from earlier in the day. At the end of the living area, the gas fireplace sat in porcelain tiled floor to ceiling, without a mantle. A large screen TV was fixed to the wall above the fireplace.

In most homes, the cutouts next to the fireplace were great places for built-in bookshelves and storage. But because their house was positioned with woods on the side as well as the back, Cole had large forty-inch-wide windows placed there instead.

As with the other windows, the plantation shutters were tilted open allowing a clear view. This presented a severe problem for al-Himyari, he would be in clear sight if the Agent looked through those windows. He quickly dove to the floor near the table pushed against the back of the large sofa. He laid there still watching the light shine from the other angles. He stayed there until he was sure the agent had left.

Al-Himyari carefully searched the home, finding Cameron's gun safe in the master bedroom closet but it was of no concern. Cameron would not be given the opportunity to access it. He recognized the daughter's room and a guest room, each with their own bathroom. Al-Himyari thought the best option was to hide in the guest room and wait for the Camerons to come home. *First the girl, then him*, he considered as he sat in the dark room on the floor.

He placed his small backpack in his lap and removed its items. A roll of duct tape, rags, bottle of chloroform, and a GoPro camera for his production and his faithful companion, the black bladed Kizlyar knife. *Once the recording is posted, he will be a hero to millions.* He thought.

CHAPTER 32

Washington, DC

Cole was being pulled in multiple directions as everyone wanted answers. Finally, the Director sequestered Cole in a small room that the CIA brass took over. Charlie, McCune's assistant, was there but heading to the hospital to check on McCune. He had heard that she was in stable condition. Capps also came by to see how he could assist and brought Cole a clean shirt to wear as the police bagged the other. Cole was glad to see a friend.

"How's Jess doing?" Capps asked.

"She's holding up better than expected."

"She's stronger than you think, I'm telling you she's got some fight in her," Darryl said referring to the week he had spent training with her.

"Yeah, I think you've got a new buddy there."

Capps offered to stay and take Cole home when they were finished.

At the Warf District, the FBI suburban with Agents Kincaid and Yarbrough sat outside Hannah's condo. Inside, Hannah quickly tossed a change of clothes and her travel essentials into a small bag. She was unsure how long Cole would be, but thought she might surprise him in the dress. She used her thumbprint to open her gun safe and pulled out her compact Glock 23, holster and two extra mags and zipped them in the outside compartment of her bag.

By the time she got back to the suburban, Brittany was asleep leaning against her taller friend, Jess. Hannah tried to squeeze in without waking her, but she stirred when the door closed.

"That was quick," Jess said.

"I thought I would just change at your Dad's. You think that's OK?"

"I think whatever you do is going to be fine with my Dad," Jessica said with a tired yawn.

Hannah caught Yarbrough's look in the mirror, and she wanted to be careful with her words, but she wasn't sure how to take what Jess was saying.

"Jess, are you alright?" she asked anyway.

"Oh, I mean, I've never seen my dad so happy," Jess said realizing she may have been misunderstood.

They sat quietly as the SUV made its way to the Cameron house. When they were near the house, Yarbrough flicked his lights to signal to the other car out front that their relief had arrived. The vehicle pulled off as the SUV turned into the sloped driveway. Both agents exited and opened the doors for the women.

From the window of the upstairs guest bedroom facing the front of the house, al-Himyari watched the two agents and gasped when he saw two additional women accompanying the Cameron girl. He had planned for Cameron and his daughter, but it hadn't occurred to him that the guest room may be used. He had closed the door to the room but remembered that it had been opened when he entered.

He ran and opened the door and grabbed his bag as he heard the alarm beep signal entry into the home. Their voices carried over the hardwood floors as he eased his way to the walk-in closet next to the bathroom to hide.

"Ma'am let us clear the house first," Yarbrough said.

The girls shuffled around the dining area and Cameron's study that sat to the front of the house. They each were holding their shoes in their hands giving their feet much-needed relief. Yarbrough walked upstairs to clear the second floor while Kincaid and Hannah stayed on the main floor.

Kincaid and Hannah opened every door and examined

every entry and went out to the garage and checked out the back of the house. Yarbrough was tired of the night shift and knew this assignment was scheduled to end at 06:00. He was counting down the minutes. He did a quick peek into each room.

Abu stood in the guest bedroom closet, his knife in hand ready for the agent to open the closet door. The light protruded from the gap at the door. He heard the steps on the hardwood floor as the agent walked to the bathroom. He flicked on another light.

Then Abu heard the sound of the man pissing in the toilet. He thought perhaps he should take advantage of the opportunity. Instead, he stayed ready.

"You good up there," yelled Kincaid up the stairs.

Yarbrough flushed the toilet and yelled, "We're all good!"

Al-Himyari saw his good fortune as a sign that Allah would be with him tonight as he carried out his will.

As the agents left the house, Kincaid gave Jess a smile.

"Goodnight," Jess said, smiling back and locked the front door.

All three headed upstairs. Hannah was having second thoughts about her special dress for Cole. She wondered if she had taken too much liberty in the situation. She had been to Cole's house a couple of times, but she had never gone upstairs.

She saw Jess and Brittany head into Jess' room as she stood in the doorway to the guest room.

"Jess is it OK if I use the guest room?"

"What? No, I think Brittany may go in there later," she said enjoying the torture she was putting Hannah through.

Hannah stood there for a second, truly conflicted, she wanted to be respectful and was also struggling with interpreting Jess' motives. Jess decided to let her off the hook, walked over and took her bag.

"This way Agent Jacobs," leading her to the double doors of the master bedroom.

Jess tossed the bag on a chaise that sat near the window.

She saw Hannah looking around at the room.

"Don't worry, he changed everything."

"You mean the sheets?" Hannah asked.

Jess laughed. "No, I mean the décor, well everything really, a few months back once when the divorce was done."

"Oh."

"Meet you downstairs in ten? I'm going to see if I can't revive Brittany so we can watch a movie and wait for Dad."

Definitely changing now. So much for the dress, Hannah thought.

"Sure, see you in a few… Oh, where's your Dad's phone charger? I'm almost dead, and I want to charge up in case he tries to reach us."

"I think he's got one by the nightstand and there's one down in the kitchen."

Hannah plugged the phone in, and Jess closed the door to give Hannah privacy. Hannah shot a text to Cole, *Miss you!* "Oh my gosh, hanging around these girls has me acting like a school kid," she said to herself. Then she smiled as her phone vibrated with the return message, *Miss you more!*

Then a second message, *hope to be able to leave in a few minutes. I'm getting a ride home with Capps. Will get my car tomorrow.*

A few minutes later Hannah was downstairs and saw Jess alone on the couch working on her phone.

"There's wine in the fridge, I'm assuming Dad bought it for you, because he doesn't drink very much, but when he does it's usually light beer."

"Yeah, I noticed that. I think I'm OK though, thank you." She joined Jess on the couch and hoped she could stay up and awake for Cole.

Soon Jess laid her phone down, and they sat there in quietness.

"Oh, your Dad texted and said that he hoped to be home soon," Hannah said trying to get a conversation started.

"Really? How long do you think? Wait, did you hear that?

"Hear what?"

"I thought I heard something, anyway it's probably Brittany. So how long?"

Hannah laughed, "I don't know. I'm learning your Dad isn't the best with details."

There was another wave of quietness, Jess rechecked her phone then put it back down. Hannah yawned and noticed Jess looking at her.

"Jess is everything alright. I mean you've been through a lot."

"You know, I have my flight home tomorrow afternoon, but with everything going on I feel like maybe I should stay."

Hannah thought Jess may be feeling protective of her father, but said, "I'm sure your Dad would love it if you stayed longer." Jess remained quiet, so Hannah continued, "I see how he is with you, and it reminds me of my father, and that really tells me the kind of man he is."

"Is that why you like him?"

"Oh Jess, I like your father for many reasons."

"Do you love him?"

"Jess!"

"I mean, if he is in love with you, how do I know you will love him back?"

Hannah thought. *I should have grabbed a whole bottle of wine.*

"Well…"

"I mean how do I know that you won't hurt him? He's like what ten years older than you, and you are this amazingly beautiful woman."

"Thanks, but…"

"Not that my Dad is bad looking or anything, but you could probably have any guy you want. Why do you want my Dad?"

"Jess, Jess." Hannah held up her hands. "Where's is this coming from?"

Jess' head dropped, "Why did those guys say what they said about you in the bathroom?"

Hannah took a deep breath.

"Guys say stupid shit like that all the time. Yes, I've made some bad choices with guys before, and I got married a few years ago. It only lasted for a brief six months. Biggest mistake of my life. Wish I would have listened to my Dad. Anyway, when it ended, he posted some revealing photos and spread hellacious rumors to protect his delicate ego."

"Are you serious?"

"Girl, unfortunately, yes. Anyway, he is a close friend with a congressman who was in attendance at the event. It was his crew that egged on your Dad. So, I feel horrible, because I feel like it was my fault. And no, I am not a walking 'petri dish,' thank you."

"I'm sorry. Those guys were jerks! I'm so sorry. I know I can be up and down. I was just starting to learn to be the daughter of a single Dad, and now you're here."

"Look, I know things have moved fast…"

"No, no, you're here, and it's a good thing. It's a great thing for my Dad. I've not seen him this happy since I was a little kid. I just need to be open." She wiped a tear away.

"Well, you're doing a hell of a job at it, if you ask me. I know you make your Dad very proud and I promise you I'll do my best to take good care of him."

"Shh! Did you hear that?" Jess asked again.

Hannah shook her head, no.

"I'm going to go check on Brittany," Jess got up and wiped her eyes again. Hannah stood and gave her a hug. She sat back down and blew out her cheeks as Jess went upstairs. *Maybe Cole was right, this could be complicated,* she thought.

Jess opened the door to her bedroom and froze seeing Brittany lying unconscious on the bed tied and gagged with duct tape. She began to scream but was pulled from behind by a hand with a cloth covering her mouth.

She instinctively reacted with a sharp elbow in the ribs of her assailant grabbing the hand away from her face. But the chloroform was already working. She felt light-headed as she attempted the second move, a hard knee to the groin. She grew dizzy and unsure of how hard she had connected on the hit. She fell out of the doorway screaming.

"Hannah! Hannah!" She struggled toward the stairway.

Downstairs Hannah heard a faint scream, then a couple of

thumping sounds, she jumped through the barrel archway leading to the foyer where the stairs were. She heard Jess' screams, as she reached the bottom of the stairs, she looked up to see Abu al-Himyari holding Jessica by her long blond hair with Hannah's Glock 23 pointed to her head.

"Stay there!" he screamed at her.

She froze, she knew the score. Jess would die if she made a move. She put her hands up and prayed that Cole and Capps would arrive.

Soon, al-Himyari had both women gagged and duct taped to the chairs at the kitchen table. Blood ran down Jess' head from where Abu had smashed it against the banister during her attempt to escape.

Hannah's face was still red from the hard slap of al-Himyari. Before he had gagged her, she attempted to reason with Abu, so he slapped her. Then she began to tell him what would happen if he hurt Jessica. He punched her in the stomach. Then used the chloroform to put her out.

Jessica screamed through the gag telling him to leave her alone. Al-Himyari had enough from the disrespectful woman, so he took his knife and pushed it into her waist. She screamed through the gag in horror, tears of pain streamed down her face. He drove in about an inch and pulled it out. Her white tee shirt now had blood soaking through.

"Keep screaming little girl, and I will do this all over your body until no one can recognize you,"

The fighter in her would not sit for it. She screamed again through the gag. Abu recognized the muffled 'fuck you' being repeated so put a second cut into her left side. There were more horrific screams, crying, and tears. Another wound to her back, she cried out in pain and shook her head violently trying to will herself out of the chair. Then another stab. Abu was careful with the cuts, he wanted her alive, but she had been so disrespectful. Now he was concerned she may bleed to death before Cole arrived. *At least I have the other one*, he thought.

Then a calmness came over Jess. She resigned herself to

the fate that awaited her. Blood dripped on her bare legs that were taped to the chair. She slowed her breathing, closed her eyes and remembered her Dad putting his arm around her at the Lincoln Memorial. She felt herself drifting away and forced one last thought, she visualized her father killing the evil man.

Capps drove his car up next to the FBI car, and Cole waved at the two agents to let him know he was home. Capps pulled up the driveway.

"Tell little girly, I'll see her next time she's in town, and she better be ready to kick some ass."

"Will do," the weary Cole said.

"Call me if you need me."

Cole was checking his phone for text and messages and shot a quick thanks to Capps, as he opened the front door. It was dark except for a light coming through the barrel archway to the kitchen and living area. He thought perhaps they had all called it a night and were asleep upstairs. He took his Jacket off and folded it over his right arm with his phone still in his hand as he walked toward the kitchen.

He entered the room and nearly collapsed. Directly in front of him, Hannah and Jess were strapped to the kitchen chairs pulled close to the kitchen island. Jess appeared unconscious, and Abu al-Himyari stood behind Hannah with a knife in his left hand resting on her throat and the Glock 23 in his right hand. Hannah's face was red, but she seemed to be regaining consciousness.

Tears ran down his face, and he gasped for air as he saw Jess with a blood-soaked shirt and blood dripping down her legs. He was uncertain if she was alive or dead.

"Put your jacket down," Abu said pointing to the chair he had positioned for the camera angle.

Cole pressed keys on his phone under his coat. He hoped to God his attempt to redial Capps was successful. He laid the coat down on the table against the back of the couch keeping the phone between the fold of the jacket.

"Now put your gun on the table as well." Cole wished he

had kept his jacket on. He needed to change it up on Abu.

"I don't think so," Cole said with all the calmness he could muster.

"I don't think I want to be the star in your sick little fantasy flick where you kill Americans for a PR reel."

Cole was calculating the odds of successfully nailing a headshot without casualty to Hannah. The odds weren't strong enough for him. All of the training drills he had worked on for holster drawing had been with hip or thigh holsters. He had never imagined needing to quick draw from the shoulder holster he seldom wore.

Al-Himyari began a wild rant about American policy and the countless deaths through drone strikes and military operations. *Good, keep talking asshole*, Cole thought. Then speaking directly to his camera, he made accusations against Cole, citing the specific operations he had helped plan. *Where did he get this intel?* He hoped to God Capps was on his way.

A few blocks away Darryl Capps' car audio system showed an incoming call from Cole Cameron. He pushed the accept call button.

"I said to call if you need anything, but I really didn't mean it," Capps said jostling with his friend.

Capps heard muffled sounds and yelled, "Cole! Cole! You old fart, you butt dialed me!"

He was about to end the call when he heard Cole's voice, *'sick little fantasy flick where you kill Americans for a PR reel.'* Capps whipped a hundred and eighty-degree turn at the next intersection and floored the accelerator.

"Keep him talking." He said hoping his friend could hear him.

"Where's the other one?"

"Oh, she's upstairs. She was the easy one. Unlike these two that do not know their place."

"What did you do to my daughter?" Cole asked and saw Hannah coming to her senses.

"She was too disrespectful. She must take after you. An arrogant American."

"If anyone here dies…"

"Well," Abu said nodding toward Jessica, "Maybe she's already dead, I'm not sure. Shall I make sure for you."

Capps was still two blocks away and slammed his fist against the steering wheel when he heard al-Himyari talk about Jess.

"You fight, little girly! You fight!" His eyes teared up.

As Hannah became more aware, she was relieved to see that Cole had not relinquished his weapon, but saw that it was still holstered and suspected that cold blade against her neck kept Cole from drawing. She looked through the corner of her eyes and saw all of the blood on Jess, and tears began to flow. She prayed she was still alive but knew they did not have much time.

Mr. Strawman, the calico cat that lived next door to the Cameron's, was out on his nightly prowl. He loved the straw area over near the Cameron patio. He found it very interesting that a light would shine just for him as he took care of his business at his neighbor's place. Mr. Strawman swayed his way up from the woods to his favorite spot and Voilà!

Al-Himyari was growing weary of the debate and decided it was time to end the matter. He had wanted more theatrics, but the cast was just not cooperating. He was set to run his knife across the throat of Hannah, and the bright LED motion light lit up the outside. He turned to look out the patio door, and one second later the .40 caliber slug from Cole's Glock was exploding in his skull.

CHAPTER 33

McLean Virginia

The bright light from the June morning sun fought to break through the plantation shutters in Cole's bedroom. It peaked through the cracks and boldly summoned him from his rest. His mind wrestled with the unwelcome call from nature.

There was indeed much to do even though it was a Saturday. He knew he had to tackle some chores before the summer heat and humidity made it unbearable. Just one glance at the lovely figure of Hannah next to him was all he needed to procrastinate climbing out of the sheets.

She gently moved, and briefly caressed his leg with her foot. He ran his fingers through her hair and softly across her shoulder as he gazed at her curved body. She laid there in effortless beauty with her back to him, facing the window. She moaned, "Good morning," to which Cole responded with a kiss upon her bare back.

He looked upon her in amazement. Amazed at her beauty. Amazed at how badly he had fallen for her. Amazed that after all of the challenges they faced and all of the losses they experienced, there she was, lying in his bed.

He rehearsed their love-making over and over in his head and found himself aroused by the thoughts. He moved his body closer to hers, pushing his groin against her as if to telegraph his intentions. She pushed back against him, teasing him with her movements as she took his hand from her hips and brought it to her breast. He whispered something naughty in her ear, and she laughed. Soon their bodies were again moving as one.

Later, they each looked as if they had just finished a grueling workout with sweat now dripping off Cole. They gasped for air to replenish their oxygen levels.

"Oh my God!" Cole shouted, falling backward on the bed. His lover repositioned herself to see his face and offered him an equally gratified look.

"How old did you say you were?" she jokingly asked him.

"Still young enough!" he replied as his breathing stabilized. "We've got to crank up that air conditioner!"

Cole stepped out of bed and threw on some shorts.

"Can I bring you some coffee?"

She pulled at the sheets, moving to sit up in the bed.

"Oh yes! Please! You are amazing!"

"Be right back," Cole said heading out the door to the stairway.

"Take your time, Cole," Hannah shouted from the bedroom, as she headed to the bathroom.

"I'm just going to jump in the shower really quick while you get that ready."

Cole searched through the coffee flavors he had bought along with the one cup dispenser machine. He did not drink coffee but had purchased the gadget in an attempt to be hospitable to his guest. Cole hoped it would get frequent use. He found Hannah's favorite and popped it in.

As he waited for the fresh brew, he stared across to the kitchen island where two months earlier he had come home to find Hannah and his daughter tied to chairs. He tried to push away the images of his Jess' blood-soaked shirt and blood dried hair from his mind, but they reappeared. *The bastard got off too easy*, he thought to himself remembering how he had quickly drawn and shot Abu al-Himyari dead.

Soon her cup was poured, he fixed it the way she liked and carried it upstairs to the bedroom and placed it on the end table.

"How about some breakfast?" He stepped into the large

bathroom and handed her a towel as she stepped out of the shower.

"Do we have time?" she asked. "I mean we have a lot to do." Hannah knew they had several chores to complete before the afternoon BBQ they were hosting at the house.

"I think we can squeeze it in. I don't know about you, but I worked up an appetite."

Cole couldn't help himself. He had fallen for her so hard, in spite of the chaos, he could not imagine a world without her. He also knew his infatuation was apparent, regardless of how cool he tried to play it.

She pulled her sundress over her head and took the cup of coffee and began sipping while lifting up her eyes to look at Cole. Her eyes said so much to him. It was a deep and intimate communication. No games, no pretense, just pure openness to her soul, he loved that connection with her.

He leaned over and kissed her.

The doorbell rang.

"Shit," Hannah said, as the moment was spoiled.

There was so much she wanted to tell him, and so much she wanted to experience with him. He was the one that her Dad had hoped for her to find. He was the one that she could love without reservation. It took everything within her to pace herself in the relationship, desperately not wanting to spoil the magic they had together.

Cole threw on his tee shirt and turned away, but Hannah grabbed his hand. She pulled him to herself and kissed him. When they released Cole looked at her in awe of how, from all of the death and suffering, true love had sprung forth in his life.

Her touch, her kiss, and her eyes said to him *'I love you'* and he could not contain it any longer.

"I love you, Hannah."

The doorbell rang a second time.

"I love you, Cole."

"I'm coming right back," he said with a big grin on his face as he headed out of the room.

Hannah sat down at the chaise by the window and covered her own big grin as she soaked in the moment of joy. She heard him taking the hardwood steps downstairs, and a tear of joy slowly rolled down her cheek as she imagined their happiness together.

Cole had grabbed his phone and started scrolling through the encrypted text message from Nancy McCune as he approached the door. Multitasking as he usually did, ready to respond to the message with one hand and shoo off the solicitors with the other. Again, the doorbell rang.

"Cole, are you getting that?" Hannah called from the upstairs banister.

The encrypted text message read *we found Grant Ramsey. Sending a team. Will keep you posted.* Cole knew it was only a matter of time before the Agency would catch up with Ramsey. He still had the key Grant had given him, never learning its purpose.

He looked through the glass side windows next to the large front door and saw the backside of a tall blond woman. He opened the door, and the woman spun around and lunged toward Cole.

Jess gave her Dad a big hug and kiss, and Cole nearly fell over.

"Surprise!" Jess yelled.

"Did you know about this?" Cole yelled to Hannah now at the bottom of the stairs.

She nodded, yes, and put down the phone she had used to record the greeting.

"Jess, I thought you weren't coming until next week for Father's Day?" Cole questioned hugging his girl again.

"Let me get your bags."

"I caught the redeye last night when Hannah told me about the BBQ you are having here today," Jess said. "And I invited Brittany over."

"Yeah, no problem, that's awesome." Cole was happy that Brittany had little memory of the night's events as she had been put out with chloroform quickly.

"And I invited David as well," Jess said waiting for the reaction.

"Kincaid?"

"Yes, Dad, Agent Kincaid."

"He's a hell of a man, he's welcomed here anytime," Cole said with a wink remembering the agent's help that fateful night at their home. He had applied bandages to her wounds and carried her in his arms to the arriving ambulance.

"Come on we're making breakfast," Hannah said taking Jess's hand.

Cole watched them walk through the barrel archway into the living and kitchen area and thought about how fortunate he was. He had nearly lost them both. He committed to himself to do everything in his power to keep them safe.

The events they had experienced altered each of their lives and in some way brought all of them so much closer. Cole was initially worried that Jess would be so emotionally wounded from her experience that she would live her life in fear. Instead, his daughter emerged with a warrior mentality and dedicated herself to fighting injustice.

She sought advice from Hannah about pursuing a law enforcement career, and specifically the requirements for the FBI academy. As a result, she changed her major at UCLA to criminology and lined up her course track for the next fall. Cole stood there proud, *damn proud.*

"Let me guess scrambled eggs." Jess teased.

✳✳✳

Private Island resort in the Caribbean

It had been several weeks since he had been forced to tie up loose ends, now Grant Ramsey sipped on a tropical drink as he stretched out in his lounge chair on a white sandy beach of the private island resort in the Caribbean. He had completed his part of the obligation for the Bear, Gavriil Medvedm. He and Katrina were now free of the glutton's grasp and enjoying their well-deserved early retirement.

Ramsey had walked away with roughly five million dollars' worth of untraceable bearer bonds. A 'just reward' for his sacrifices through the years, he reconciled. The new cryptocurrency for the DC hotel job was icing on the cake. It was a quick and dirty job. He thought carefully about ending Nancy McCune's life when he had the opportunity but thought that by sparing her, he could keep his double agent game in play, buying himself much needed time.

What had started as a trap to expose a CIA mole had backfired on the Agency. Once Katrina Nikolin had sniffed around Grant Ramsey, the Agency developed a plan for him to play along, even terminating his employment as part of his cover. He was to be a double agent, give to the Russians what the Agency wanted him to offer, and in return, help the Agency build the file on the Russian network of Gavriil Medvedm.

Grant Ramsey, however, did not expect to fall for Katrina or receive such a handsome reward in payment. In the end, it was the money that was most rewarding. The infatuation of Katrina had served to fuel the fire, but he would be a fool to think that would last forever. But the money, well, that would buy everything he really needed, his boat, provisions, privacy and of course women.

"This is what I'm talking about," he muttered to himself as he watched a local dark-haired beauty in a bikini stroll by. His stare was interrupted as the brunette lying next to him cleared her throat and mildly chastised him.

"Now, now, lover boy. Don't bite off more than you can chew!"

Katrina Nikolin was the same woman Cole Cameron had seen on the day he met Grant at the coffee shop and failed to recognize her at the Owl's Club bar in Tucson. She had adeptly tapped into Grant Ramsey's vulnerabilities and satisfied his cravings, all of them.

"Sir, your drink," the server placed the next round for Grant on the table next to the lounge chair.

"Ma'am, here is yours as well."

"Thank you, my good sir," Grant Ramsey responded with a smile. Life was good now. In his mind, he had paid his dues and was finally getting his share of the booty. Sure, there were causalities along the way, but that goes with any war. Cole Cameron was just another causality, he had to be pulled into the game for Hasni's revenge.

"The poor bastard," Grant Ramsey said audible with a sad grin, as he thought about Cameron and his daughter Jess.

"What was that dear?" Katrina looked over to her lover. "I know...you're thinking about your friend at the CIA. You underestimated him, didn't you? It's a shame that our friends from Yemen weren't able to satisfy their blood thirst. We'd worked so hard to give them that opportunity."

Grant was growing uncomfortable with the conversation. "I still think it was unnecessary to go after the man's daughter that way."

"Hmm..." the brunette mused playfully, "I'm not sure I like this soft side, Mr. Adams," using his new alias.

"We Russian women like our men to be strong." She teased him as she rolled her finger around the rim of her glass and took another sip.

Grant Ramsey took another sip of his drink that was a unique blend of tropical fruits, alcohol, and a pinch of Batrachotoxin, compliments of the Bear.

Gavriil Medvedm watched through binoculars from the balcony of the couples' suite at the resort. The events from the DC hotel had served to accelerate Medvedm's bold agenda. Not since the Cuba crisis had tensions been so high between the two countries. The murder of the deputy director of SVR for North America in a Washington DC hotel was like 'the shot heard round the world.' The political ramifications could not be understated.

Medvedm knew that his superior had a back-channel relationship with Nancy McCune. A relationship that had been established when she served in the EU office. The Deputy Director had sought to use McCune and the CIA to neutralize his rival, Medvedm. But many within the deputy's own office were aligned with the Bear's bold goals. Now the Bear kept the deputy's eye in a jar of solution as a souvenir and a reminder to others.

Medvedm had effectively eliminated his roadblocks in the SVR and created the perfect environment to fan the flames of his inspired vision. The clamor for aggressive action intensified. The Kremlin was listening to his advice now.

Ramsey served his purpose, but with McCune still alive he was no longer useful.

"You foolish cowboy, the butterfly, and the bonds belong to me," he mumbled, as he waited for the inevitable.

Then, there it was. Grant Ramsey grabbed his throat. He looked desperately toward Katrina, and his eyes revealed the panic as he saw her casually gathering her things to leave. As his chest tightened, he reached for his lover but only managed to pull at the Russian spy's sarong as she wrapped herself. She gave a gentle tug to release his grip. His head slumped forward. He was finished.

✳✳✳

McLean Virginia

Cole Cameron stood at the grill on his patio and flipped chicken breasts and burgers with one hand and nursed his light beer with the other. To his left he saw Mr. Strawman the cat, coming out of the woods and scooting around the edge of his property before heading to his own house. *Damn cat!* He muttered to himself.

Cole took a sip and reflected on the fact that one of the upsides to the event at his home was that the escrow fell through. As it turns out, shooting and killing a terrorist in your home while it is in escrow is frowned upon. The buyers quickly pulled out of the deal, and the events had frightened off other prospects. Cole extended his original offer to his ex to buy out her half at the initial appraised market value, and she jumped at it. He smiled. He loved this house.

The outdoor speakers carried the sounds of a playlist that Jess had put together for the BBQ. The folks gathered were enjoying a relaxing afternoon. The patio misters kept the area cool and large buckets kept the beer ice cold. Cole saw Darryl Capps ramming his big hand into the ice, finally fishing out his choice.

Brittany and Jess were chatting with David Kincaid and a friend that he brought. The rookie agent looked toward Cole. There was a part of Cole that wanted to shoot over a stern look to remind the young man that Jess' father was watching him, but instead, he raised his beer bottle and offered a smile.

Amy Wiggins and her boyfriend Richard *or is it Robert* were seated with Bridgette Robinson, Sara Wang and Steve Sinha. Cole had invited his team leads to build rapport. And to his surprise, Raymond Hernandez and his wife had also joined the party.

Hannah was standing and talking with a couple of her friends as Capps came to give Cole cooking instructions.

"Man, you are overdoing 'em burgers," he chided.

"Back off big man!" Cole said. "Two more minutes."

"I don't want no hockey puck burger."

"There's more raw ground beef in the fridge, why don't you just go grab that and shove it in your mouth," Cole laughed.

After everyone had eaten, they all gathered around in chairs talking as music softly played in the background. Kincaid's friend asked the team what they did at the CIA. Sinha said, "We just look at data and write reports all in a place that looks like the bat cave."

"I am Batman!" Cole deadpanned.

"Can you believe they're given his boney ass another award and more time off?" Capps hollered out.

"Two actually," Cole corrected, "One for the Hilton, and one for here. Big ceremony. Monday after Father's Day. You're all invited. I had them wait until Jess would be here."

He was set to receive another award for killing al-Himyari and saving the others in the home as well as the rushing to save McCune at the Gala. He and Hannah were both getting more attention than they cared for. Hannah had received the FBI Medal for Meritorious Achievement for saving her fellow agent's life in the New York bombing, and Cole was becoming the poster child for the CIA since the events had garnered so much media attention. He knew it was all a PR move, but he would leverage it to get things done.

"Bullshit! Your boney ass is getting two?" Capps fired back.

"I wouldn't call his ass boney," Hannah laughed.

"Are you saying my Dad has a big ass?" Jess jumped in the mix.

"No!" Hannah laughed.

"I'm just saying I like his ass. It's a very nice ass."

"Hey, would everybody please stop talking about my ass!" Cole yelled.

Raymond Hernandez caught everyone off guard when he jumped into the fray.

"No wait, turn around, let me see that thing. Yep, there's plenty of room for medals back there!"

Everyone was rolling in laughter except Cole.

After a few minutes, Amy asked Cole and Hannah what their plans were for the time off. They looked at each with a grin.

"Well, Jess is here for a week, so I want to spend as much time with her as she and Brittany will let me and then Hannah and I are taking a little road trip to Tennessee to see her parents."

"Oh shit." Hannah was surprised and considered the consequences. Cole locked eyes with her to let it sink in.

"Mr. C! Mr. C!" Brittany yelled as the volume of music increased.

"It's our song!" she said clapping her hands.

"Come on," she said grabbing him by the hand along with Jess.

The Crowded House chorus lyrics to *'Don't Dream It's Over'* blared yet again, and they danced, sang and laughed.

Soon, everyone was joining in. Kincaid cut in, taking Jess' hand. Hannah slid over to her man and danced with him. True to form, Cole made a few of his spaz moves drawing laughter from all. He didn't mind. He was a happy man.

The next song shuffled in the playlist and soon the galloping rhythm of *'Between the Raindrops'* by the alternative band Lifehouse and British singer, Natasha Bedingfield, reverberated across the flagstone patio area. Hannah stood enjoying their moment holding Cole's hands

"So, you want to meet my parents?" she said.

"Hannah, I'd love to meet your parents."

She paused, looking into his eyes, then said with a tear falling, "Cole Cameron…"

With the wink of an eye, he spun her around and sang aloud the chorus of the song.

ABOUT THE AUTHOR

Camden Mays is the pen name for the author who lives in Atlanta, Georgia with his wife, Debbie.

Facebook: https://www.facebook.com/camden.mays.author

Made in the USA
Las Vegas, NV
08 June 2021

24419016R00187